JACI BURTON

Love After All

A HOPE NOVEL

JOVE

$7.99 U.S.
$9.99 CAN

ISBN 978-0-515-15563-1

5 0 7 9 9

continued . . .

Hope Flames

"Jaci Burton's books are always sexy, romantic, and charming! A hot hero, a lovable heroine, and an adorable dog—prepare to fall in love with Jaci Burton's amazing new small-town romance series."　　　—Jill Shalvis, *New York Times* bestselling author

"A heartwarming second-chance-at-love contemporary romance enhanced by engaging characters and Jaci Burton's signature dry wit."　　　　　—*USA Today*

"If you're looking for a sweet, hot, small-town romance, *Hope Flames* fits the bill perfectly."　　　　　—*Dear Author*

Straddling the Line

"A sizzling erotic romance with heart."　　—*Publishers Weekly*

"Jaci Burton can write a pants-on-fire sex scene better than anyone I've read in a while."　　　—*Romance at Random*

"Burton's writing is seemingly effortless and just flows beautifully. Her storytelling is effective and gets everything across to the reader. *Straddling the Line* is sexy, heartwarming, and sweet."　　　　　—*Fic Talk*

Melting the Ice

"Fast-paced, with intense sex scenes and an intriguing jumble of the sports and fashion worlds, this steamy novel will satisfy those who like a little heat in their love stories."　　　　　—*Kirkus Reviews*

"*Melting the Ice* is a hot frenemies-to-lovers romance that will make readers cheer. Do not miss out on this one."　　　　　—*Romance Novel News*

One Sweet Ride

"Fun and sexy." —*Fiction Vixen*

"Refreshing." —HeroesandHeartbreakers.com

"Hot sensuality and [a] riveting plot."
—*Romance Reviews Today*

Playing to Win

"Burton knocks it out of the park with the latest installment of her super steamy Play-by-Play series . . . Readers will not be able to race through this book fast enough."
—*RT Book Reviews*

"This series [is] high on my must-read list." —*Fresh Fiction*

"The perfect combination of heat and romance that makes this series a must-read." —HeroesandHeartbreakers.com

Taking a Shot

"Plenty of romance, sexy men, hot steamy loving, and humor."
—*Smexy Books*

"Hot enough to melt the ice off the hockey rink."
—*Romance Novel News*

"A very spicy read. Jenna and Ty [have] great chemistry."
—*Book Binge*

continued . . .

Changing the Game

"An extraordinary novel—a definite home run!"
—*Joyfully Reviewed*

"A must-read."
—*Fresh Fiction*

The Perfect Play

"Holy smokes! I am pretty sure I saw steam rising from every page."
—*Fresh Fiction*

"This book delivers."
—*Dear Author*

"A beautiful romance that . . . leaves us begging for more."
—*Joyfully Reviewed*

"Hot, hot, hot! Romance at its best! Highly recommended! Very steamy."
—*Coffee Table Reviews*

"The romance sparkles as the sex sizzles."
—*RT Book Reviews*

Love After All

JACI BURTON

WITHDRAWN

JOVE BOOKS, NEW YORK

THE BERKLEY PUBLISHING GROUP
Published by the Penguin Group
Penguin Group (USA) LLC
375 Hudson Street, New York, New York 10014

USA • Canada • UK • Ireland • Australia • New Zealand • India • South Africa • China

penguin.com

A Penguin Random House Company

LOVE AFTER ALL

A Jove Book / published by arrangement with the author

Jove Books are published by The Berkley Publishing Group.
JOVE® is a registered trademark of Penguin Group (USA) LLC.
The "J" design is a trademark of Penguin Group (USA) LLC.

For information, address: The Berkley Publishing Group,
a division of Penguin Group (USA) LLC,
375 Hudson Street, New York, New York 10014.

ISBN: 978-0-515-15563-1

PUBLISHING HISTORY
Jove mass-market edition / April 2015

PRINTED IN THE UNITED STATES OF AMERICA

10 9 8 7 6 5 4 3 2 1

Cover photography: Man © Claudio Marinesco;
Pub © Bikeworldtravel / Shutterstock; "Kyle" © Judy Lagerman.
Cover design by Rita Frangie.
Text design by Kelly Lipovich.

Acknowledgments

Special thanks to my awesome friend, Shannon Stacey, ATV rider extraordinaire, for her knowledge and assistance in crafting the ATV scene. I couldn't do it without you, Shan.

Chapter 1

CHELSEA GARDNER SAT at the No Hope at All bar, waiting for her friends.

While she waited, she got out her notebook and doodled.

Okay, maybe she wasn't doodling. She was on a mission.

The ten-point list made perfect sense to her. She'd fine-tuned it, but really, she'd had this list in her head for a while now, and decided it was time to memorialize it, get it down on paper. Maybe even laminate it.

Chelsea was thirty-two years old, and the one thing she knew and knew well was men. She had years of dating history, and she could weed out a decent man from a loser in the first fifteen minutes of a date.

She should write a book about it. She'd probably make millions.

Okay, in reality, maybe not. But she had a lot of experience in dating. She could offer up some valuable advice. At least advice on how to date the wrong man. Had she ever dated a lot of the wrong men. She was an expert on that.

Hence the list.

Her list would ensure she found the right man—finally. She

was tired of going out on useless dates. From now on, she was going to ask the correct questions so she wouldn't waste any more time on the wrong man. If a prospective date didn't meet the criteria on her list, then he wasn't the perfect man for her.

Her list wasn't going to focus on personality traits—she already knew in her head the type of guy she wanted—warm, caring, compassionate, with a sense of humor. If he didn't possess those basics, he'd be out of the running before they even got started. And those she could suss out right away without a list. Nor did she have a preference for looks. No, this list was compatibility-based. That's where she'd run into roadblocks in the past and where she was going to focus her efforts on in the future.

She scanned her list, nodding as she ticked off the attributes in her head.

1. Never married. Guys with exes carry a lot of baggage and woes.
2. Has to be a suit and tie kind of guy, because it means he cares about his appearance.
3. Has to work a 9-to-5 job, so he'll be available for her.
4. No crazy ex-girlfriends. This one needs no explanation.
5. Likes fine dining and good wine. No more burger joints! Some guy out there must like something other than hamburgers, right?
6. Hates sports. Everything about sports. What is it with men and sports, anyway?
7. Must want at least two kids. A man who doesn't want children is a deal breaker.
8. Must love animals—preferably big dogs, not those yippy little dogs.
9. Doesn't spend all his time at the bar with his friends. If he's always hanging out at the bar with his friends, then he isn't with her.
10. Idea of a perfect vacation getaway is somewhere warm and tropical. With room service.

She studied the list, tapping the pencil on the bar top.

"You look deep in thought."

Her head shot up as Sebastian "Bash" Palmer, the owner of the bar, stood in front of her.

Talk about the wrong guy. Bash was the epitome of wrong, on so many levels.

"I'm . . . working on something."

He cocked a dark brow. "Yeah? I noticed you were intently focused on writing. So . . . grocery list?"

"Funny. And no."

He leaned over, trying to sneak a peek. "The perfect—"

She shut the notebook. "None of your business."

He laid the rag on the bar. "Hmm. The perfect something. The perfect steak. That was it, wasn't it? You've got some secret recipe for the perfect steak. That's the way to a man's heart, you know."

"You think I'd try to capture a man by cooking? Well, you're wrong."

He laid his palms on the edge of the bar. "So, it does have something to do with a guy, doesn't it?"

She refused to take the bait. "I didn't say that."

A couple guys came into the bar and took a seat.

"We're not done talking about this," he said, his stormy gray eyes making contact with hers before he walked away.

Oh, they were so done talking about it.

Typical Bash, always up in her business.

And he was definitely the wrong type of man for her.

While Bash attended to his customers, she opened the notebook and checked her list.

Yes, Bash was the perfect example of the wrong type of guy. She mentally ticked off all the items on her list that he *didn't* fit.

He was divorced. He was a jeans and T-shirt kind of guy. And while he might look super hot in said jeans and T-shirt, it still counted against him.

She wasn't sure he even owned a suit. As owner of the No Hope at All bar, he worked terrible hours. As a teacher, she

worked during the day, and he worked afternoons and eve-
nings. They'd never see each other.

She had no idea who he was dating, but he was always going
out with some woman or another, so he likely had some crazy
ex-girlfriend somewhere in his past. She knew he was a beer and
hard liquor guy, and his idea of fine dining was a burger and
onion rings from Bert's. He wouldn't know fine dining if he fell
into it. She had no idea how he felt about kids, but the guy practically lived at the bar, and he hadn't had a serious relationship
since his divorce, so it wasn't like he was in any hurry to have
children. Plus, he didn't have any animals.

Then again, she didn't have pets, either. But that wasn't her
fault. Her apartment didn't allow them. She just wanted to make
sure whatever guy she ended up with loved them. She wanted a
dog. Or a cat. Her best friend Emma had two dogs, Daisy and
Annie, and her other best friend Jane had a dog. Logan and Des
had several dogs on their ranch.

She'd always wanted pets, and she hadn't had one since
her childhood dog, Scotty. She'd missed having a dog to
cuddle with.

She shook her head. Back to her list. She scrolled down
the list and stopped at the next item.

Oh, right. Not hanging out at the bar with the guys all
night. That answer was self-explanatory, since that was pretty
much all Bash did. All the time.

She knew he loved sports because there were several TVs
set up at the bar, and Bash was always cheering for some team
or another. The man was sports-crazy.

And she had no idea what his idea of a perfect vacation would
be, but she highly doubted it involved room service. Bash had
an ATV and she knew he was an outdoorsy kind of guy.

Whereas Chelsea was allergic to everything outdoorsy.
Anything involving the outdoors typically meant you couldn't
wear high heels, and Chelsea lived for her heels.

See? They were not compatible in the least. Bash had failed
everything on her list.

She closed her notebook and tucked it back into her purse.

Why was she even comparing Bash to her list, anyway? It

wasn't like he was remotely in the running. Even if there had been that night she and the girls had come here during the holidays. And maybe she had been a little on the inebriated side, and maybe Bash had whispered something in her ear that even several months later still made her blush hot, and still kept her up at night thinking about—

"The perfect drink."

She pulled herself out of that very erotic daydream and met Bash's teasing gaze. "What?"

"You were going to give me ideas for the perfect drink. That's what you were writing in your secret notebook, right? I know you like to challenge me."

She sighed. "Believe it or not, Bash, not everything is about you."

He feigned a shocked look. "It's not?"

She rolled her eyes.

"What are we talking about?"

Her best friends, Emma and Jane, grabbed seats on either side of her.

"Chelsea's hitting on me," Bash said.

"She is?" Emma grinned at her.

"I am not hitting on Bash. He's being ridiculous."

"She's writing love notes to me in her notebook and won't let me see them."

She shot him a glare. "Are you twelve? Stop it."

Jane looked over at her. "You're writing love notes? To Bash? This is the most interesting thing that's happened all day. Please continue."

She was going to throw her drink at Bash. "No. I am not writing love notes to Bash."

"Then who are you writing them to?" Emma asked.

Chelsea wanted to scream. "No one. No love notes."

"She doesn't want you to see them, because they're for me," Bash said.

Emma looked at Bash, then at Chelsea, a questioning look in her eyes.

"He's full of it," Chelsea said. "And he's just giving me a hard time, because that's what he does."

Bash slanted her that look again, the one he'd given her that night a few months back. Smoldering. Filled with promise. The kind of look that made her squirm on her barstool.

"I have never given you a hard time, Chelsea." And as if he hadn't just infuriated her, he calmly asked, "What would you ladies like to drink'?"

Jane and Emma both ordered sodas, so Bash poured their sodas, then went off to tend to his other customers.

"He drives me crazy," Chelsea said.

Jane cocked her head to the side, studying Bash's retreating form. "Oh, I don't know, Chelse. He's funny. And so hot."

"He is not." Chelsea refused to acknowledge the way Bash's black T-shirt fit so snugly across his incredible chest, or the bulge of his biceps beneath the hem of the shirt. Or his flat abs, or his incredible ass.

Not that she'd noticed. At. All.

"This is true," Emma said. "Why haven't you ever dated him?"

"Bash?" Chelsea slid a look down the bar at him, then at Emma. "Totally not my type."

Emma laughed. "I think Bash is every woman's type. Tall, great muscles, killer smile—and those eyes."

"Phenomenal butt, those tattoos, a goatee. We have discussed your standards being impossibly high, haven't we, Chelsea?"

Chelsea shifted her attention to Jane. "Like I said. He's not my type. I'll just leave it at that."

"And what exactly is your type, Chelsea?" Jane asked. "Are you holding out for royalty or something?"

She lifted her chin. "No. I've actually made a list."

Emma's brows arched. "A list? What kind of list?"

"A list of the qualities I'd like my perfect man to have."

Jane laid her hand on Chelsea's arm. "Honey. You do realize the perfect man doesn't exist."

Chelsea took another look in Bash's direction, then turned her back to him. "Yes, he does. The perfect man does exist. And trust me, it isn't Bash."

Chapter 2

BASH BUSIED HIMSELF with his customers. On a Friday night, the No Hope at All bar would be filling up as people got off work and came in for drinks and to play pool or watch sports on several of the televisions scattered around.

While he drew a few tap beers for some of his regulars, he kept an eye on Chelsea, who was waving her hands as she animatedly explained something to Jane and Emma.

He shook his head.

That woman was a piece of work. A hot, sexy, redheaded piece of work.

He knew he had to steer clear of women like Chelsea. She was not the type of woman for him.

No woman was. Easy, no-strings relationships were perfect. They'd satisfied him for years, and he saw no reason they couldn't continue to keep him . . .

Maybe *happy* wasn't the right word. He hadn't been happy since the day he'd gotten married. Even that happiness had been short-lived.

Content. That worked. Nothing wrong with content.

He shifted his attention as Luke McCormack came in. Luke

wore a T-shirt and jeans instead of his Hope police officer uniform, so he must be off duty. Bash grabbed a bottle of Luke's favorite beer from the cooler and popped the top off, sliding it across the bar while Emma, Luke's wife, came over and gave him a kiss. Then Jane and Chelsea moved over as well.

"Just get off work?" he asked Luke.

"Yeah."

"Thanks for showing up, man. You know I hate these lonely Friday afternoons."

Luke took a long pull of his beer, then set it down and looked around. "You're never lonely, Bash. Besides, the place is picking up. You've always got a crowd in here."

"Business is looking great."

Luke nodded. "You should consider offering food."

Bash leaned against the bar and nodded. "Funny you should mention that. I'm thinking of expanding the back of the bar on the east side and adding a kitchen."

"How hard would that be?" Chelsea asked. "Because if you serve food, you could really draw in a lot more people."

He cocked a brow. "I bring in a good-sized crowd already, and I don't want to offer a big menu. Just bar-type food."

Chelsea wrinkled her nose. "You mean like burgers or wings and stuff."

He grinned. "Something like that. I've had the plans drawn up for a while. I just need to pull the trigger on it, get the permits, and start the project."

"Great idea, Bash," Luke said.

Chelsea sighed and sipped her soda. "What Hope really needs is a place that offers fine dining."

Bash shook his head. "You can go into Tulsa for that. We're too small a town for a fine-dining restaurant. It wouldn't get the draw. Folks here like their small-town restaurants, bars, and easy comfort food."

"I agree," Jane said. "Tulsa's just a short drive, and there are lots of restaurants to eat at there."

Chelsea played with her straw. "I suppose."

"You could always move to Tulsa," Bash said. "Then you'd be near all that fine dining and culture."

She cocked a brow. "Trying to get rid of me, Bash?"

"Nope. I like you just fine right where you're sitting."

She gave him a confused look, and he smiled at her.

He loved teasing her, maybe because she made it so easy. He was about to say something, but then there was a commotion at the front door. A woman had walked in with a dog, drawing everyone's attention.

Oh, shit. Gerri.

"Aww, who's the cute brunette with the Chihuahua?" Emma asked.

"I'll be right back," Bash said.

He moved around the bar and caught Gerri by the arm as she stalked her way in. He could tell by the look on her face that she was ready to do battle.

He pulled her to the side of the room.

"Hey, Gerri. What brings you here?"

She handed Lulu to him. "Here. You take her."

He barely had time to catch the poor dog before it went tumbling to the floor.

"Hang on. What am I supposed to do with your dog?"

Gerri wagged her finger at him. "No. Now she's *your* dog. I only got her to impress you, which apparently was an epic fail, since you broke up with me."

The poor dog trembled against his chest. He wrapped both arms around her to comfort her. The dog, that is. Not the obviously batshit-crazy woman currently glaring at him.

"Wait. You bought this dog to impress a guy? What the hell, Gerri. I never asked you to get a dog. I thought you wanted this dog."

She shrugged and affected a pout, her full lips glossed to the max.

"She pees. Like . . . everywhere. And barks at everything. And shakes. She's a pain and I can't deal. I travel all the time, and do you have any idea what it costs to board that thing?"

Yeah, he knew. Apparently, though, Gerri hadn't done her homework. "You can't just give her away like some purse you decided you didn't like."

She gave him a bitchy smile. "Sure I can. She's all yours

now. I'm done with her as quickly as you were done with me. See you, Bash."

Before he had a chance to object, Gerri pivoted and was out the door, leaving him holding a very scared little dog.

Jesus. That had been fast. Kind of like his relationship with Gerri had been.

The dog lifted her soulful, dark eyes up to his. He swept his hand over Lulu's back. "Trust me. You're better off without her, honey."

When he turned around, the entire bar was staring at him. Great.

He went back around the bar, still holding Lulu in his arms.

"Who was that?" Chelsea asked.

"That was Gerri. We . . . uh . . . sort of dated for about a month. She was a little high-strung at times, so I broke it off."

"And who is this?" Emma asked, reaching across the bar to take Lulu from Bash.

"That's Lulu. Gerri told me she'd always wanted to adopt a shelter dog, so I went with her one day. Lulu's a year old. Cute little thing, and Gerri just gushed about her, saying she was the perfect dog for her."

Emma looked up at him. "And now?"

"She just told me she only got the dog to impress me. And that Lulu pees everywhere and barks a lot. And since I stopped seeing Gerri, she apparently has no use for the dog anymore."

Chelsea's expression changed from curiosity to anger.

"What? She used a dog to score points with a guy? What a bitch." Chelsea gently ran her fingers over Lulu's back, then took her from Emma. "Come here, sweetheart. Was that horrible woman mean to you?"

"She seemed a little immature, and maybe a bit . . . young for you, Bash?" Jane said, clearing her throat.

Bash shrugged. "We got along fine for a while, until I realized she had a habit of pouting when she didn't get her way, and yelling at me whenever I had to cancel a date. So yeah. Maybe you're right, Jane. She was too young for me. Clearly she has issues."

Emma looked angry, too. "Clearly. So what are you going to do with Lulu?"

He looked over at the dog, who was happily curled up against Chelsea. "I have no idea."

"You're keeping her, right?" Chelsea asked, cuddling Lulu close. "I mean, you can't just abandon her."

Bash stared at Chelsea. "What am *I* going to do with her?"

"Raise her. Love her. Be patient with her. Everything you're supposed to do, Bash."

All eyes landed on him, and rather expectantly, too. Even Luke, who just shrugged in sympathy.

Chelsea handed Lulu back to him. "She's yours now. Be good to her."

Shit.

He glanced down at Lulu, who raised her head and looked up at him as if to say they'd both been hosed by Gerri, so they were going to have to deal with it together.

"Okay, Lou. I guess it's you and me against the world now, girl."

Chapter 3

———

BASH LEFT LOU—because no way in hell was a man like him having a dog named Lulu—in the care of one of the waitresses, who he promised to pay extra tonight while he made a mad dash to the pet store for food, bowls, a collar, a leash, toys, treats, a crate, and a dog bed. An extremely long damn list provided to him very sweetly by Emma.

Lou wasn't all that thrilled with the crate, but she finally settled in at his feet while he managed to get his job done.

At least Chelsea, Emma, and Jane took off to go to the movies or a girls' night out or something, leaving him in peace about the dog once he promised them he intended to keep and care for her. Luke lingered for a while, but then he had to go home to check on his and Emma's dogs.

Chelsea seemed relieved when he told her he was keeping Lou. Not that her opinion mattered. He just wasn't the type of guy to abandon a dog. And okay, maybe Chelsea's opinion mattered a little. All of their opinions mattered. Emma told him to bring Lou in to the vet clinic on Monday and she'd look her over.

So after the bar closed, he loaded Lou and all her new belongings into his truck and drove home.

He was bone-weary, and he still had the busiest night of the week at the bar tomorrow night.

He pulled up in the driveway and got out, then pulled Lou's crate out, taking it into the house. He set it down on the floor in his living room.

"Be right back. Chill here for a few seconds, okay?"

Lou lay there staring up at him. He dashed outside and grabbed the bag of supplies and food, then came back in.

No barking. Nothing.

Yeah, Lou just hadn't liked Gerri, no doubt because Gerri was high-strung and nervous all the time. Dogs could read that kind of tension, and they reacted to it.

He let Lou out of her cage, connected the leash to her collar and took her outside, where she did her business in a hurry. He walked her around a bit to let her stretch her legs some, then they came back in.

He disconnected the leash to give Lou an opportunity to wander around.

Instead, she sat on his foot, shaking.

Bash shook his head. "My guess is she didn't exactly give you the run of her place, did she, pal?" he asked, then figured if Lou wasn't going to go exploring on her own, he'd help her out. He turned the light on in the living room, then took off toward the kitchen, taking it slow.

As he suspected, Lou followed along, keeping her body right next to his feet as they moved past the living room into his kitchen, where he hit the light switch and opened the fridge, pouring himself a glass of water.

He'd brought the bag of supplies, so he got out Lou's bowl, put water in it, and set it down against the wall in the kitchen. Lou went over and sniffed it, then lapped up a couple sips. He leaned against the counter and waited a bit, hoping Lou would explore on her own.

She didn't, moving back over to his feet after she'd taken a drink.

"Okay, pal, let's go see the rest of the house."

He walked her through every room, including the bathroom, and ended up out in the backyard, where she peed—again.

"For a tiny dog, you have a great bladder. Let's see if you can hold it all night, okay?"

He let her back inside and found his water. He sat on the sofa, kicked off his shoes, and laid down, and turned on the TV. He'd already had his fill of sports from the bar, so he decided on an old action movie and settled in.

It didn't take more than five minutes to hear the whimper from the floor. He tried ignoring it, but apparently Lou was an expert whimperer.

He took a peek over the edge of the sofa to find her sitting on his shoe, looking up at him with her sad, dark eyes.

"No sofa for you. Go lay down in your crate."

He resumed watching the movie. For another five minutes, anyway, until the whimpering started up again.

"Christ." With one hand, he scooped the dog up and laid her on his stomach, where she turned around in a circle three times, laid down, and promptly went to sleep.

"Fine. But don't get used to this."

Bash was asleep a few minutes later.

Chapter 4

CHELSEA PULLED UP in front of Bash's house and turned off the engine, then wondered what in the world she came there for.

To check on the dog, of course. She'd seen the indecision on Bash's face last night. He didn't want that dog, and he'd ended up stuck with her. And then she, Jane, and Emma had had to leave, so she hadn't had an opportunity to follow up and make sure the poor little thing would be well taken care of.

Not that it was any of her business, really, but she couldn't help herself. One look at the sweet little pup's face and she'd fallen madly in love. She'd thought about her all night, worrying about her, and she just wouldn't be able to run her errands today until she was sure the dog was well settled.

She went up to the front door and rang the doorbell, smiling when she heard the sharp little bark. She waited, but didn't get an answer, so she rang the bell a second time. And again, another bark. After a minute, the door opened and Bash leaned against the doorway, wearing his boxers, a sleeveless tank, and nothing else.

Chelsea held her breath. Oh, did Bash have a body. She

normally saw him in jeans and a T-shirt, so this was the most skin she'd ever seen exposed on him. He was tall and lean, but well-muscled, with great legs, amazing shoulders, and those arms . . .

"Chelsea. What do you want?"

She finally exhaled and looked down at his bare feet, where the adorable dog sat perched next to him.

"I wanted to check on Lulu."

"*Lou* is fine, as you can see. And it's eight goddamn thirty in the morning."

"I know what time it is, Bash. Shouldn't you be up by now?"

"I don't close the bar until two. By the time I clean up and get home, it's after three."

She'd sort of forgotten about his crazy hours. "Oh, right. Sorry."

The dog wriggled against his foot. "Shit. Hang on a second while I put some pants on. Or just . . . never mind. Come in since you're already here."

He walked away, and Lulu—or Lou—followed him. Since he'd left the door open, she went inside, closing the front door behind her.

She'd been to Bash's house before when he had a party one night a few years back. She remembered she'd brought a date.

That had been a disaster. The guy had gotten so drunk in the first hour that Luke had driven him home and Chelsea had ended up begging a ride home from Megan Lee that night. She'd been so embarrassed she'd hidden out in a corner with her friends.

Bash had been dating some hot blonde at the time who'd hung on him all night long.

So not a surprise, since Bash was always dating some hot woman. There were so many women in and out of his life on a regular basis, no one could ever keep track of their names.

But none of them had ever dumped a dog on him.

He came out of what she assumed was his bedroom. This time, he had on pants and a T-shirt. "Come on," he said to her. "I need to take Lou out back."

The dog stayed right next to his feet as he walked from the hallway toward the back door. When he opened the door and stepped outside, Lou went with him.

Obviously, the two of them had already formed an attachment. Chelsea supposed that was a good thing.

While Lou ran outside to do her business, Chelsea took a seat on one of the chairs on the patio.

"You look terrible," she said to him.

He ran his fingers through his hair. "Let's see how you look on four and a half hours' sleep."

"Sorry. Again. I wasn't thinking about the hours you keep." She was an early riser and tried to maximize her weekend time. Which made her very happy that she'd added the "nine-to-five job" on her perfect-man list. A man like Bash, with the hours he worked, would never do.

Though watching Lou, who pranced her way back to Bash and happily sat while he scratched her ears, made her wonder about revising the small-dog thing on her list. She didn't seem yippy at all. In fact, she was awfully cute and had only barked when she rang the doorbell.

"So you're keeping her?"

Bash yawned. "What?"

"Lou. You're keeping her?"

He shrugged. "For now, I guess."

"What does that mean?"

"It means that as of today, I have a roommate." He pushed off the railing he'd been crouching against and stood. "I need coffee."

He walked to the back door and went inside, Lou following him. And, of course, he'd left Chelsea, which she supposed meant that was an invitation for her to follow as well.

He was such a terrible host. She sighed and went inside, again shutting the door behind her.

"You want coffee?" he asked.

She shook her head. "I've already had a couple of cups. But thanks."

He ignored her while he dragged out a sauté pan and started pulling things from his refrigerator, so she decided to ignore him as well. She sat on the floor in between his kitchen and dining room, trying to coax Lou to come to her.

At first, the dog wouldn't leave Bash's feet. But eventually, she came over and crawled onto Chelsea's lap.

She was so tiny, and kind of adorable.

"Do you have the capability to care for a dog?" she asked.

Bash turned away from the stove to shoot her a look. "She survived the night, didn't she?"

"It requires a commitment of more than one night, Bash. She isn't one of the women who slide in and out of your life."

He waved the spatula at her. "Funny. And yes, I'm aware of what it takes to care for a dog. I had several when I was a kid."

She looked around at his spacious house. The kitchen was open and led into a dining and living area that afforded awesome entertainment space. The kitchen was tiled and the other rooms had wood floors. Much better than carpet, especially with a dog.

"You've had this house for how long now?"

"About four years, I guess."

"So how come you never got a dog before?"

He shrugged. "Never got around to it, I guess. Plus I work odd hours."

"Aha. So what are you going to do with Lou while you're working?"

He got two plates out and set them on the kitchen island, then laid bacon on the plates, as well as the eggs he'd made. "Come on and sit."

She'd had no idea he'd cooked breakfast for her as well as himself. "I didn't expect you to cook for me."

He frowned. "You're here. Why wouldn't I cook for you?"

First he ignored her, then he fixed her breakfast. She could not fathom Bash at all. She stood, placing Lou on the floor. "What if I'd already had breakfast?"

He smiled at her. "Then I'd have eaten your portion."

He poured out food for Lou, who dashed over to her bowl and started chowing down. Chelsea took a seat at the breakfast bar and Bash got out some orange juice, hovering over her glass, giving her a questioning look.

"So have you eaten yet?"

"Well . . . no."

He poured juice into her glass. "Okay, then. Let's eat. I'm hungry."

She dug into the food, which was surprisingly good. Maybe she should have added "a man who can cook" to her list. It wasn't too late to revise it, or add items. It was, after all, her list. She could do anything she wanted to it.

"Maybe you could become the cook at the bar," she said. "What did you do to these eggs?"

"It's a secret recipe. I can't divulge the ingredients."

She shot him a look. "Seriously."

"I am serious. Besides, if they're that good, I might consider using the recipe for the bar."

"You'll serve eggs at the bar?"

He shrugged. "I don't know. Maybe I'll do an 'after midnight' menu, with breakfast choices."

"It's not a terrible idea."

His lips curved. "Thanks for the vote of confidence. Anyway, I have to give the customers something to eat besides burgers."

"Well, thank God for that." She studied him as she ate. "You're serious about expanding the bar."

He leaned a hip against the counter, his plate in his hands as he scooped the last of the eggs onto his fork. After he took the bite, he swallowed and nodded. "Yeah. It's something I've been working on for a while. I needed to save the capital first, and work out a design scheme that made sense, but I think I'm ready. I've already got the permit work started and a contractor picked out. Once that's all in place, it shouldn't take more than three to four months to get the project finished."

"Do you know who you'll hire to cook for you?"

"Jason Longmire. He works at Tadashi's in Oklahoma City as a chef right now, but he was raised in Hope. We went to school together. Do you know him?"

She shook her head. "The name doesn't ring a bell. I know the restaurant, though. It's a good one. Why would he want to leave there and work at your bar? No insult intended."

Bash finished off his juice and set the glass on the counter. "None taken. His mom is selling her house and wants to move in with her daughter—his sister—in Tennessee. Jason wants to buy the house and live here."

"He could probably get a job as a chef in one of the Tulsa restaurants."

Bash laid his hands on the island. "Are you trying to find my chef another job?"

She tore off a piece of bacon and slid it into her mouth, chewing thoughtfully before answering. "No. Just playing devil's advocate. I mean, the bar is basically a bar, not a restaurant."

"Not yet."

She studied him, trying to figure out his angle. Then it hit her. "You're thinking of expanding into the restaurant business and you need a really good chef to help you."

"Maybe." His lips curved.

She had no idea he had such grandiose plans. "How long have you had this idea?"

"Awhile. You finished with this?" He motioned to her now-empty plate.

"Yes, but why don't you let me do the dishes?"

"Nah. I've got this." He pulled her plate across the island and went to the sink.

Refusing to just sit there after he'd fed her, she slid off the barstool and went into the kitchen, taking a peek at Lou, who'd finished her food and was taking a snooze next to her food bowl.

"Seriously, Bash. I didn't pop over for you to feed me breakfast and then clean up after me." She hip-checked him and shoved him out of the way of the sink.

"Fine. I'm going to go grab a quick shower while you do that."

"Okay."

She looked down at the dog, who raised her head when Bash left the room. Lou tracked his movements, then looked up at Chelsea. Obviously happy to have someone in the kitchen with her, she went back to sleep.

"You sure are cute," Chelsea said, going back to the dishes.

"You know, I always thought I wanted a big dog, like a Labrador or a golden retriever. Maybe even a Great Dane, though those dogs are pretty big. I'd need a huge house for a dog that size. Anyway, I never wanted a little dog. I thought they'd be too noisy and high-strung. But you? You seem kind of mellow, Lou."

After loading the dishes in the dishwasher and laying the clean pans in the dish rack to dry, she bent down to swipe her hands over the sleeping dog. "And you sure have taken to Bash in a hurry, haven't you? That says a lot about the guy, doesn't it?"

The dog slumbered peacefully. God, she was cute.

"Though he still has a lot of marks against him on my list. Not that I'd consider him, anyway."

"What list, Chelsea?"

Her head shot up and she saw Bash leaning against the doorway in the hall. He was wearing jeans and a T-shirt, with his hair still damp from his shower.

And he'd obviously heard her talking to the dog about her list.

Dammit.

Chapter 5

CHELSEA STRAIGHTENED. "SO, thanks for breakfast. I should be going now."

He walked into the kitchen and grasped her wrist, his fingers on one very fast racing pulse.

"What list, Chelsea?"

There was something about her that got to him in the most basic of ways. He dated a lot of women, and typically not for long. He'd known Chelsea for a lot of years, but she wasn't the type of woman he went out with. First, he figured she was high maintenance, with her fancy clothes and her high-heeled shoes and her ideas about men. They just didn't mesh.

But there was chemistry between them—something he'd definitely been noticing a lot more in the past several months. And the way her pulse ticked up and her eyes dilated, and the way she licked her lips whenever he got close?

Yeah, she noticed it, too.

Plus, she had a fiery personality, and he knew damn well that would translate to a spitfire in bed. He couldn't deny he wouldn't mind experiencing a little of the wildcat Chelsea in bed.

But he'd garnered enough from the conversations she'd had with her friends at the bar to know she was looking for a relationship. And that was the one thing he wasn't at all interested in. He didn't mind dating the same woman for a while, but he always made it clear he wasn't into anything permanent. Being married once had taught him an awful lot about what not to do. He wasn't ready for another round of bruised emotions and battered hearts. He was better off keeping things light and simple between him and women.

But Chelsea? He couldn't seem to stop himself from teasing her. After all, they weren't dating. They were just friends, and had been for a long time.

So when she didn't answer his question, he had to press the issue.

"You were talking to my dog about your list. And the fact that I don't meet the criteria."

"I said no such thing. You misheard me. I was talking about my grocery list."

Now he was really curious, because she sure as hell hadn't been talking about him and food in the same sentence. "I don't think so. You said I still have marks against me on your list, and you wouldn't consider me anyway. So what list is this? The one you were making at the bar yesterday?"

She looked down at where he had hold of her wrist. He let her go, and she went into the living room to grab her purse.

He followed.

"If you don't tell me, I'll just start making things up. Like maybe you're making up a list of men you'd like to help you make a baby."

She stopped and turned to him, her eyes wide. "I do not need any man to help me make a baby."

He scratched the side of his nose and slanted a grin at her. "Well, yeah, you kind of do."

In answer, she rolled her eyes at him. "You know what I mean. I'm not trying to have a baby right now, Bash."

"Then why don't I qualify for your list?"

She huffed in a breath of frustration. "None of your business."

"It is my business if my name is on it."

"That's just it. Your name is not on it. It could never be on it."

He stepped in closer. "Yeah? And why's that?"

"I'd prefer not to say."

"So back to my idea about you finding a man to make a baby with . . . "

She gave him an exasperated look. "Bash."

"I'm only trying to help, Chelsea. Not that I'm going to give you a baby, but I know a lot of guys . . ."

He liked seeing that fire in her eyes, the one that turned her emerald green eyes dark.

"This is ridiculous. But fine. You're not on the list because you're not my idea of the perfect man."

His brows rose. "You made a list of the perfect man? You know the perfect guy doesn't exist, right?"

"Of course he does."

"You've met him." He didn't like the way his gut tightened at the thought.

"Not yet. And that's the problem. But I know what I want, and I'll know who he is when I do."

"Really." He sat on the edge of the sofa. "Show me your list."

"I don't think so." She wrapped her arm tighter around her bag, as if he were going to wrench it away from her. Obviously, whatever was on Chelsea's list was important to her. That made him eager to see it.

"No, really. Maybe I can help. Show me your list."

She hesitated, but finally dug into her purse and pulled out her notebook, flipping the pages, then gave him a hard stare. "You cannot laugh."

"I promise I won't laugh."

She thrust the notebook at him.

He scanned the list, the corners of his mouth ticking up. "Bash."

He held up his hand. "I'm not laughing. But yeah, I can see why I'm not the man for you." He handed the notebook back to her and met her gaze. "I'm divorced, I work at night,

I love sports, and you've already met one of my crazy ex-girlfriends. Though she's not my fault. She was normal when I met her."

Chelsea arched a brow.

"Hey, I don't set out to date crazy women. I like them unemotional and uncomplicated."

That won him an even harder stare.

"Maybe I'm not making myself clear enough."

"Obviously not."

He figured the best way out of that one was to leave the crazy-ex-girlfriend topic alone. "As far as the rest of your list, I'm a beer-and-burgers kind of guy. I spend all my time at a bar, I'm definitely not a suit guy, and my perfect weekend getaway is camping. And while I like kids, I'm not ready to have any yet. Plus, I apparently just adopted one of those yippy little dogs."

She crossed her arms and nodded. "Exactly my point. We have nothing in common. Nothing at all."

He stood and approached her. "You're right. Nothing in common."

They were standing only inches apart, and damn, she smelled good. Like a cinnamon roll and fiery brandy or something. Hot and spicy—and he suddenly wanted a taste of her. If he was being honest with himself, and he always tried to be, he'd wanted a taste of Chelsea for a long time now.

She tugged on her lower lip with her teeth, and he felt the tight pull in his groin, the fierce rush of desire that had nothing to do with a list and everything to do with basic chemistry.

"So . . . I should go," she said, her eyes a crazy mix of blue and green and fixated on his.

Bash moved forward, but Chelsea didn't step back. And when he picked up her hand and entwined his fingers with hers, that tiny little voice inside her head said, *Run like hell*. Only she didn't run like hell.

"You know, Chelsea, sometimes you just have to go with your gut. And sometimes what's between a man and woman has nothing to do with a list, or what's in your head." He picked up her hand and laid it on his chest. "It's what's right here. It's that feeling of chemistry, that sensation of 'Wow, if I don't kiss this person right now, I Might. Just. Explode.'"

Chelsea was certain she'd forgotten how to breathe. Her palm against Bash's chest was damp, as were other, more vital, throbbing parts of her.

She was out of her mind for even entertaining the idea of kissing him, but here she was, moving in closer to the temptation. Clearly she was having an out-of-body experience. Her normally logical self had fled, and had left in its wake this needy, lustful being whose only thought was naked desire.

Maybe it was the way Bash looked at her. Could she ever recall a man devouring her with his eyes like this before? Not in recent memory. Or the way he held her hand—so light and easy. But his thumb swept across her skin, sending skittering zings of sensation through every part of her—all the good parts that stood up and took notice.

Sure, it had been a long time since she'd had sex—way too long, because after all, she was really picky. But it wasn't like she didn't know how to take care of those kinds of needs on her own.

Still, that wasn't at all the same as having a man touch you and take care of those needs for you.

Merely imagining all the ways Bash could take care of her needs had her going up in flames. She had a habit of watching him whenever she stopped in at the bar. He had great hands, always so sure and confident. What would those hands feel like gliding across her body?

Suddenly, that low throb turned into a constant thrum that beat incessantly throughout her. And that lustful being grew more demanding.

So when he lifted his hand to her jaw, then slid his palm around the nape of her neck and aligned that rock-hard body of his against hers, any thoughts of running like hell were gone, baby, gone.

"So what do you think, Chelsea?" he asked. "I'm not list material, but let's just try this out and see how it goes, okay?"

She only had a split second to give him a short nod before his lips descended on hers.

It was magic. An explosion that threatened to make her implode from the inside out. She grasped hold of Bash's shirt with both hands and held on for dear life as his mouth moved over hers. She vaguely registered her breaths going shallow, the hard pump of her heartbeat, and the trembling in her legs, but those were minor things, because honest to God, she was drowning in the sensation of a hard-bodied man doing delicious things to her mouth.

She hadn't had much luck in the dating department lately, and she couldn't even remember the last decent kiss she'd gotten.

This wasn't dating. And what Bash gave her wasn't a decent kiss at all. It was hot and wicked. It was fireworks. The kind of kiss a woman could feel all the way down to her toes, and in every follicle of her hair. In every cell, and in all the good female parts of her as well.

Bash knew how to kiss. It went beyond every fantasy she'd ever had. It was firecracker-worthy, and she couldn't help but clutch his shirt and lean in for more. And when his tongue slid inside her mouth to deepen the kiss, she could feel herself falling deeper and deeper into the web of desire he weaved around her. Every part of her felt oh so good, oh so needy, and she wanted to rub against him and beg him to touch her.

It would be so, so easy to fall into bed with him, to let him tease her and taste her and touch her and see where this led.

Unfortunately, she still retained some of her common sense. She knew exactly where it would lead with someone like Bash.

Nowhere.

That's when the warning bells started to clang.

Not the right man for you, Chelsea.

She smoothed her hands flat on his chest, and with deep, deep regret, she pulled away.

He still sat on the arm of the sofa, giving her that smoldering look of intense desire. It had taken everything in her to stop that kiss, and if she really wanted to, she could fling herself against him, topple them both over, cover his body with her own.

She could already envision the tangle of arms and legs,

the way their bodies would entwine on the sofa. And as she shifted her gaze from the sofa onto Bash, she was crushed under the heated weight of the look he gave her.

This is not helping, Chelsea. Snap out of it.

She blinked, drew in a deep breath, and grabbed her purse from the floor. "I should go."

He still hadn't moved from his perch on the sofa. He inhaled on a deep breath, then nodded.

"If you say so. But you know, I could help you with your list."

She stilled. "What?"

"Your list." He motioned with his head toward her purse, where she kept her notebook. "You're looking for that perfect guy, right?"

"Well, yes."

"I can help you find him. I know a lot of guys."

He'd just kissed the living hell out of her. And now he wanted to find her the love of her life?

She did not understand men. At all.

"I don't think you'll find me the perfect man at your bar, Bash."

"I didn't say they were all at the bar."

Now she was curious. "Really. You know guys who wear suits."

He nodded, then pushed off the sofa. "And who work nine-to-five jobs. Though I think your whole idea of making a list is a little stupid."

She blinked, the wash of his words more than a little chilling, effectively banishing the heat from their kiss. "Really."

"Yeah. Which is why I'm going to help you."

"That doesn't even make sense."

He laid his hands on her upper arms. "I don't fit your list parameters at all, but you can't deny that kiss we just shared was smokin' hot."

She would very much like to deny it at the moment, especially since she felt the heat of his hands through her long-sleeved shirt. "That's just chemistry, and chemistry can burn out in a matter of weeks."

His lips tilted upward. "Wanna give it a try and see how fast we burn out, Chelse?"

It might be an interesting experiment. And she'd definitely enjoy some awesome sex with Bash, no doubt. But he wasn't relationship material, and she was bound and determined to have a bona fide relationship with the "right" guy—not the wrong one.

But he'd so easily made the transition from hot kiss to finding her another guy. A man who was interested in her would never do that. If he could turn it off that easily, so could she, right? "No, thanks. But you're right about one thing—the kiss was amazing."

"Glad I wasn't the only one who thought so." He dropped his hands, and she immediately felt the chill. "So what do you think? How about I go through your list and play matchmaker for you?"

"I'll have to give that some thought."

"You do that." He opened the front door. "In the meantime, I'll be on the lookout for that perfect guy for you."

She couldn't tell if he was teasing her, or serious about this. "See you later, Bash."

"Bye, Chelsea."

As she walked out to her car, she pondered a lot of things, not the least of which was that kiss. And as hard as she tried to shove it out of her mind, her lips still tingled.

Bash was trouble, and she wasn't sure she could actually trust him to find the right man for her. If she couldn't find the right guy, what made him so sure he could?

She was still convinced she was on the right track with the list.

The right man was out there—she just had to find him.

BASH SPENT THE day cleaning his house and playing with Lou, getting her accustomed to her new surroundings.

He also spent a lot more time than necessary replaying that kiss he'd had with Chelsea.

What had he been thinking, pulling her into his arms and

laying a hot one on her? She was dangerous territory, and he knew better than to wade into waters like that.

But she'd been there, and tempting him, and for some reason he hadn't been able to resist. Maybe it was reading her list and seeing nearly every damn thing represented on it—not be him. It had hit a nerve inside him.

Suit and tie. Nine-to-five job. Fine dining and wine. Never been married. What the fuck? It wasn't like there was anything wrong with him. He was a damn fine catch.

Not that he was looking to be caught, because he wasn't. But if he was, he'd be perfect for someone like Chelsea.

Okay, maybe not Chelsea, because she wasn't exactly a ten on the perfect meter herself. She bought too many expensive shoes, she was too picky, too opinionated, too high-maintenance, and she . . .

Well, shit. He dragged his fingers through his hair and decided he was going to spend the remainder of the day *not* thinking about Chelsea. About how full her lips were or about how sweet she'd tasted when he kissed her, or how curvy her body was and how good it had felt to feel it aligned with his.

Hell.

He needed to go take his frustrations out by cleaning his dirty shower. Or maybe just take a goddamned cold one.

Chapter 6

"NO, JACOB, HERE'S where you went wrong in your calculations."

Chelsea sat with one of her algebra students. "Follow your order of operations. Inner brackets first, then power, then multiplication. You just mixed them up."

Jacob was one of her brightest students. He nodded as he followed along.

"Why don't you rework the problem here for me, and if you get it right, I'll give you credit for it?"

She'd asked Jacob to stay after class. She knew he had a heavy workload of honors classes and that his parents put a lot of pressure on him to succeed. She wanted to help.

She waited while he reworked the problem, and noted he'd done it successfully.

"That's correct."

Jacob frowned. "I can't believe I screwed that up. It's an easy one."

"Don't worry about it. Next time, just take your time and don't try to work so fast. You know you can do it, and you have plenty of time to get through the test. Sometimes you try to zip through too quickly and make simple mistakes. The smarts are there, kid."

She regraded his paper, and now she could give him a perfect score.

"Thanks, Ms. Gardner."

"You're welcome. And Jacob? Try to have a little fun and don't make it all about schoolwork, okay?"

He gave her a shy smile. "I'll try."

He left her classroom and shut the door. Sometimes she worried more about the overachievers like Jacob than she did about some of the underachievers. Kids like him worked so hard to be perfect. And there was no such thing.

Except the perfect man for her, of course.

Now all she had to do was find the right man who fit those parameters. Not an easy task, as she tended to go out on a lot of first dates, very few second, and hardly any third.

Her friends said she was picky. There was nothing wrong with being choosy about men. And there was no point in wasting her time on the wrong man.

She'd dated a lot of wrong men. She was in the market for the right man, and sooner or later the right one would come along.

When the bell rang, she pushed that thought aside and prepped for the next class of students, who piled in for another math class.

Teaching high school math was her passion and focus and had been for the past ten years.

Now she was ready for a new passion, a new focus—finding the right man.

After classes ended for the day, she packed up the homework to be graded for the night and drove to her apartment.

It had been a grueling week, and she was happy to go home.

She was always happy to go home. She liked her place. It was a small one-bedroom located near downtown Hope. She'd had it for several years now. It was close to the high school, and to the newly renovated town square and park. It suited her purposes as far as convenience. It was within walking distance to shops and restaurants, and she liked to get out and walk a lot, so for her, it was perfect.

Perfect. There was a word she'd been using a lot lately. Perfect job, perfect apartment. Now all she needed was the perfect man, and her life would be . . .

She smiled at the thought—perfect.

She laid her things down on the kitchen table, then went to the refrigerator to pour herself a glass of iced tea. She started grading papers, her mind lost in math and calculations.

Until her phone buzzed. She laid the glass down and picked up the phone, checking the display.

Bash. She frowned, then clicked.

"Hi, Bash."

"I found a guy for you."

That was unexpected. "Excuse me?"

"Your list. A man who ticks off all your idiosyncrasies."

"They are not idiosyncrasies. They're guidelines."

"Whatever. I found the guy. His name is Kristofer Steele. Kris. He's an attorney, a partner with a firm in Tulsa."

Okay, so this Kris guy sounded decent enough. "How do you know him?"

"He's my attorney. Plus, I've known him since college. He's a great guy, Chelsea. I trust him, or I would never set you up with him."

She sat back in her chair. "Okay. Tell me more about him."

"He's thirty-four, single, no kids. Has a dog and a house. He's successful, he likes all those fancy restaurants and wine that you like. Obviously a suit guy."

"He sounds interesting."

"Great. I talked to him about you and he wants to meet you. He's actually coming to the bar this afternoon to go over some legal documents with me. How about you come here and I can introduce the two of you tonight?"

Panic dropped like a bomb in her stomach. "Uh, tonight?"

"Do you have plans?"

"Not really."

"Then come on over. How about six?"

She'd have to shower, do her hair and makeup, and find something appropriate to wear. And Bash would introduce them? Wouldn't that be . . . awkward?

Why would it be awkward? They'd shared a kiss, nothing more. This was her goal, so . . . why not? "Sure."

"Great. I've gotta go. I'll see you later."

He hung up, and she found herself staring at her phone.

That was the weirdest conversation ever.

But, whatever. This was what she wanted, right? She took a shower, dried her hair, and put on makeup, then studied her closet. She had no idea what she was going to wear to meet Kris.

It wasn't a date, per se, so she chose a pair of her favorite pants—her skinny black jeans—and a long black button-down silk top, then added her boots. A slinky, slimming effect, and when she topped the look off with her silver jewelry, she thought it added a nice touch.

It was a decent outfit for the bar, and if Kris was wearing his suit she wouldn't look like a slouch, but she also wouldn't be overdressed like she was expecting a date, either.

She actually had enough time to spare to grade more papers before leaving, but found it hard to concentrate, her thoughts straying to her non-date with Kris.

And to Bash.

It was odd he had fixed her up with someone so soon after their talk about her list. And so soon after he'd laid such a hot kiss on her. A kiss that, obviously, had meant nothing to him.

It meant nothing to her, either, because Bash wasn't her type at all. The kiss might have been hot and she might still be thinking about how it had made her feel, but feelings weren't always logical. Her list, however, was.

She put the papers away and headed to the bar, deciding to push all questions and negative thoughts aside so she could eagerly anticipate meeting a new man.

On the drive over, she found herself getting excited. In the parking lot, she applied her favorite lip gloss, looking at herself in the mirror. She smiled and mentally put on her most positive outlook.

"This could be the one, Chelsea," she said to her reflection, then got out of her car and went inside.

Since it was a weeknight, it wasn't too crowded. She spied Bash behind the bar and the guy in the suit across from him.

Oh, yes. He was fine-looking. Dark suit, sandy brown hair. She could tell from across the bar that he was tall and lean, and his suit fit well. Bash motioned to her so she did her sexiest walk, making sure to throw her shoulders back and hold her head up high.

Kris looked her way, smiled and stood. Bash was smiling, too, in that sarcastic, smug way he had.

She was going to ignore him and concentrate instead on the hot lawyer.

"Hey, Chelsea," Bash said.

"Bash."

"This is Kris Steele. Kris, Chelsea Gardner."

"Hello, Chelsea. Bash has told me a lot about you."

She managed a short glance at Bash before turning her attention back to Kris. "All good things, I hope."

"All good things. Would you like a drink?"

"I would, thank you. I'll have a glass of sauvignon blanc, please."

"I'll take care of that," Bash said, still sporting that smug smile.

"Why don't we get a table?" she suggested, hoping to sit somewhere Bash wouldn't eavesdrop.

"That's a great idea." Kris picked up their drinks and followed Chelsea to a booth she selected in a corner—one that would afford them privacy.

They settled into the booth.

"Bash tells me you're a lawyer. Contract law?"

"Yeah. I assume he told you I'm his lawyer."

"He mentioned it."

"We also went to college together. I've known him a lot of years. We hang out at the gym when I can get him to leave the bar, which isn't often."

Chelsea slanted her gaze over to Bash, who at least wasn't staring at them. He was busy carrying several cases of beer from the back of the bar to the front. But that didn't mean she was staring at the way the muscles in his arms bulged with the effort.

She turned her attention back to Kris. "Yes, he does seem to live here most of the time."

"It's a good business, and he's expanding it. But he needs a social life, too."

"He's got a dog now."

Kris smiled. "Yeah, I saw her. She's cute. Now he just needs to get away from the bar. Maybe find a woman and settle down."

She liked that Kris cared about his friends. It said a lot about his character. She sipped her wine and set it down on the table. "Well, maybe you can find a woman for him."

"Maybe I can. I know a lot of women."

There was a warning bell, but she decided to let that one slide. "Yet you're here with me."

He laughed. "I said I know a lot of women. Not women that are right for me."

"Really? Why aren't they right for you?"

"Various reasons. Temperament, likes and dislikes. I'm sure you know how it is. You can date a really nice woman, but realize she's not the right one for you."

What a perfect answer. She liked Kris. "So true. I've had a lot of experience with that."

He picked up his phone. "I'm wondering if you'd be interested in having dinner with me tonight. There's a great Asian fusion place that just opened in Tulsa. Do you like sushi?"

"I do. And I'd love to."

He made a quick call, then hung up. "We have reservations in an hour, so we have time to finish our wine."

They talked some more, about his job, and hers. He asked her a lot of questions about being a teacher, and they finally headed out. She took her car and followed him so he wouldn't have to drive her back to Hope.

The restaurant was in Brookside. Trendy, clean lines, with traditional Asian details yet modern at the same time. And everything smelled fantastic when they walked in. She'd heard about it and was dying to try the food.

They were led to a table for two and handed menus by the waitress. Chelsea ordered a sparkling water and Kris decided on sake. They sipped their drinks and discussed the menu.

"I don't know about you," she said, "but just reading the menu makes me hungry."

"I thought we'd have drinks for a while. Maybe start with some appetizers?"

"Sure." She checked the appetizer menu. "What looks good to you?"

"You choose. I can eat anything."

She decided on a mixed platter for two people, since it contained a combination of several items. And when she ordered the appetizer, Kris ordered more sake.

"Are you sure you don't want something other than water?" he asked.

"No, I'm fine, but thanks."

She asked him about his job. He told her one of the things he liked about contract law was that once he had made partner, his work hours settled and became more regular, which meant his life became his own again.

Score one for her list. Regular work hours.

"Yeah, the associates put in all the long hours at the firm, just like I had to do when I first joined. It's a pain in the ass, but you have to pay your dues."

He signaled the waitress for another drink.

"I'm sure it was hard, having to work so much."

He smiled. "Part of the job, you know? I'm sure you work just as hard."

"Well, I don't pull all-nighters. But there are a lot of nights and weekends spent doing lesson plans and grading papers."

"I'll bet. Still, it's admirable work you do."

The waitress brought their appetizers and Kris's drink.

"This looks amazing," she said.

"Would you like to order dinner now?" their waitress asked.

"I think we're fine for the moment," Kris said. "But you can go ahead and bring me another sake."

Chelsea frowned. There was a full one sitting right in front of him. And he was already ordering another?

He also didn't scoop any of the appetizer onto the plate the waitress had provided.

"Which one would you like to try? A spring roll, maybe?"

"No, I'm good for now. You go ahead."

She decided to go ahead and eat, since she was hungry, but she was going to keep a strong eye on Kris.

Oddly enough, he exhibited no signs of being drunk, despite having had four sakes and the wine at Bash's bar. Granted, she was a lightweight as far as alcohol went, but still, she knew what a powerful punch sake packed. After four and no food, one would think he'd feel the effects.

When she finished the appetizer, the waitress came to clear their plates.

"Would you like to order dinner now?"

Chelsea looked over at Kris.

"Sure."

She was relieved he was going to eat. They placed their orders, and Chelsea cringed when Kris switched his drink to vodka on the rocks.

He had three of those before dinner was served.

It was a weeknight. He had to work tomorrow. If she'd had that much to drink, Kris would have to carry her out of the restaurant.

Still, he conversed normally with her. He seemed totally relaxed, but otherwise didn't appear to be overly drunk.

It was a little unnerving.

And when dinner arrived, she hoped maybe eating some food would suspend the drinking. It didn't. As soon as their waitress delivered the food, he ordered another vodka. He drank all through dinner—which he ate very little of—then ordered an after-dinner port.

The man was an alcohol-imbibing machine.

He walked her outside to her car after dinner. He didn't weave or bob or act in any way like he was drunk. But Chelsea was very concerned about him.

"I had a great time tonight, Chelsea."

She turned to face him. "Kris, I'm a little bit concerned about how much you had to drink tonight. Are you sure you're okay?"

He frowned. "What? Oh, sure. I'm fine. Don't even worry about that. I drink a lot. I think it's a throwback from my college days and all those long nights as an associate. But I can handle it."

Yeah, right. "How about I drive you home?"

He waved his hand. "Nah. I'm good. I just live a couple of blocks away."

"How about I follow you home?"

He laid his hand on the roof of her car. "Is that your way of saying you'd like to come over?"

Not a chance in hell. "Actually, I'm more interested in you making it home safely. Then I need to get home. Tomorrow's a school day, you know."

"That's sweet." He tipped her chin and leaned in for a kiss. The alcohol from his breath nearly knocked her over. "How about I call you tomorrow?"

She couldn't unlock her car quickly enough. "You do that. Thank you again for dinner."

"You're welcome."

She got in her car and followed him to his house. True to his word, he lived only a few blocks from the restaurant. When he pulled into the driveway of a very nice house, she waited long enough for him to drive into the garage and lower his garage door. Then she drove off.

Good God. That was the most bizarre date she'd ever been on. On paper, he was perfect—he ticked off nearly every item on her list.

Except for all the damn alcohol. She wondered if Bash knew.

When she got home, she realized it was only nine thirty and that Bash would still be at the bar. Still, she had to know. She sent him a text message.

Home from date with Kris.

About fifteen minutes later he replied.

How did it go?

She replied with, I'd prefer to talk to you on the phone or in person about it.

Her phone rang about five minutes later. It was Bash.

"What happened?"

"He's a really nice guy, Bash. But did you know he drinks?"

Bash paused before answering her. "Well, yeah. What do you mean, he drinks?"

She told him about all the sakes and vodkas and port.

"Jesus. I didn't know he drank that much. Was he drunk?"

"That's the odd part. He never slurred his words, he walked just fine, and I followed him home to make sure he got there okay. He seems to function all right. But honestly, I was worried."

"Shit. I'm sorry, Chelsea. I had no idea. It's been a long time since he and I have hung out. I knew he could always pound down the alcohol, but not like that. You have to know I'd never set you up with a heavy drinker."

"I know you wouldn't. And he was a great guy. It's not like he treated me badly during the date. It was just the drinking—that's just not normal, Bash."

"I agree. Again, I'm sorry."

"Nothing to be sorry about. I just felt it was something you should know about, since not only is he your friend, he's also your attorney."

"I'll talk to him."

"Oh, don't do that. I'd hate to betray a confidence."

"Okay. I'll do one better. I'll take him out one night soon. If we're drinking together and it's behavior I notice, then I can call him on it, friend to friend."

That sounded like a much better idea. "Thank you."

"Sorry, Chelsea. I'll try to do better the next time I set you up with the perfect guy."

She laughed. "No problem. Good night, Bash."

"Night."

He hung up, and she felt bad for having to tell Bash one of his friends might have a problem. But she would have felt worse if she hadn't told him.

She trusted Bash to do the right thing where Kris was concerned.

Another date, another wrong guy.

She headed into her bedroom to get ready for bed.

Chapter 7

A WEEK AFTER his conversation with Chelsea, Bash took advantage of having a rare night off. He checked the time, knew Chelsea's classes were over for the day, and texted her.

Are you at home?

It took her five minutes to answer with: Still at school. Cheerleading practice.

He grinned at the thought. He knew she coached Hope High's cheerleaders, but an instant mental image of her in a cheerleader outfit flashed in his head.

Yeah, rein it in, Bash.

He grabbed Lou and got in his truck. It was a short drive from his place over to the high school. He parked in the lot, put Lou on her leash, and checked out the football field first. They weren't there, so he headed into the gym, the sounds of girls shouting telling him he'd found them.

He opened the door and walked in. Chelsea was sitting on the bleachers watching the cheerleaders practice.

She'd been a cheerleader in high school—she'd had her first year on the squad during his senior year. He could still vividly remember how she'd looked in her green and white uniform, cheering on the sidelines while he'd played football and basketball.

Chelsea hadn't really been on his radar at the time. Back then, he'd been dating Erin Phillips, another senior. But who could have missed the hot redhead? Even then, she'd been noticeable. Long legs and mouthy as hell. That hadn't changed all these years later.

Now? She was a goddamn knockout.

Still mouthy as hell, too.

Since he was behind the girls and Chelsea, he leaned against the wall and watched for a while.

"Charissa, you need to straighten your form. Your legs are wobbly," Chelsea said, having set her paperwork aside as the girls went through one of their cheer routines. "And Emily, you seem to be one count behind everyone else. Let's go through it again."

The cheerleaders were good. It took a lot of strength to do these routines.

Plus, they were loud. He remembered hearing them on the sidelines when he played. It had always given the players a boost to know the cheerleaders—and the crowd—had been behind them during the games. The one thing Hope High had always had was a lot of spirit. It was good to see it continued all these years later.

"Okay, that's much better," Chelsea said. "Take a five-minute water break, and then we'll go through the second set. You want your form to be perfect for the basketball game Friday night. We want to out-cheer Minnow High."

Bash pushed off the wall and headed toward Chelsea. Her eyes widened.

"What are you doing here?" she asked, then bent down and picked up Lou, petting her as she cradled her in her arms.

"I had the night off, so I thought I'd drop by to talk about Kris."

Chelsea looked around. The girls were all off getting drinks, though Bash noticed several of them glancing their way.

"Did you talk to him?"

"I went out with him the other night. You're right—he's like a functioning alcoholic. I can hold a lot of liquor, but the amount he drinks without showing signs of getting drunk is unbelievable. I told him I was concerned about his drinking."

"What did he say?"

"That he could handle it, and that he's always had that much to drink, which isn't true."

Chelsea sighed. "So what's next?"

"I already called his parents and his brother. They're aware, and they said they've discussed it with him as well. He blew them off, telling them the same thing—that he can handle it."

"I'm sorry, Bash."

He shrugged. "You can't help someone who doesn't want to admit he has a problem. All I can do is let him know I'm there for him if and when he decides he wants help."

She laid her hand on his arm. "You're a good friend."

"So are you. Thanks for letting me know. I don't know how I didn't notice it before. Maybe because he and I haven't been out together lately."

"If you haven't been around him for a long night of drinking, you probably wouldn't notice it."

He laid his hand over hers. "I sure as hell would have never set you up with him. I feel bad about that."

"Don't. Nothing bad happened. It's just something I noticed and thought you'd want to know about."

"Thanks."

"You're welcome." She turned to look at the cheerleaders. "I should get back to the girls."

"Okay. So, you want to have dinner later? I figure I should at least buy you dinner to make up for setting you up with the wrong guy."

She cocked a brow. "You don't owe me dinner, Bash."

"I know I don't. But I want to."

She shrugged. "Okay. I have another hour here, then I'm done."

"Sounds good." He glanced at the clock on the gym wall. "I'll pick you up about six thirty?"

"Perfect." She handed Lou back to Bash, giving the dog a scratch behind its ears. "See you later, sweetheart."

"Okay, honey," Bash said, then winked.

Chelsea shook her head and walked off.

Bash made his way back to the truck and slid Lou inside. She snuggled up on his lap. He smiled down at her. "Guess I should take you home, let you romp outside for a while, then feed you dinner before I have to meet Chelsea," he said, then realized he was starting to have regular conversations with Lou. "And don't tell anyone about our talks, okay?"

Lou stared up at him silently.

"See? I knew I could count on you."

He started the truck and pulled away.

"WHO WAS THE hot guy, Ms. Gardner?"

"Is he your new boyfriend? And how come we didn't know about him?"

"His dog is so cute. A guy with a tiny Chihuahua? Oh, gosh, how adorable is that?"

"You're dating Bash Palmer? My dad knows him. He is so hot."

Chelsea rolled her eyes at the barrage of questions from the girls. "He's not my boyfriend. We're just friends."

Vivian, one of the co-captains of the cheer squad, jutted her hip out and laid her hand there. "Seriously? How could you be just friends with a smokin'-hot dude like that?"

"Easy. I've known him since I was on the cheer squad here at Hope High. And as you know, that was a very long time ago."

Vivian sighed. "Still, he's pretty fresh for an old dude."

Chelsea laughed. "I'll be sure to tell him that."

After practice ended, she went home and changed into a pair of jeans and a long-sleeved top, then slid on a pair of wedges. She checked herself out in the mirror and decided she looked pretty good. After all, it wasn't a date, and Bash was probably just taking her to Bert's diner for dinner anyway.

She saw him pull into the parking lot of her apartment complex, so she grabbed her jacket and purse and headed outside.

"I was planning to park and come to your door," he said, giving her a look of displeasure after she climbed inside his truck.

"No need. It's not like we're dating, Bash. Besides, I'm hungry."

He laughed. "Okay. Let's feed you."

He surprised her by taking her to the Italian restaurant in town instead of Bert's. The place had opened last year and was always packed, mainly because the food was amazing and the service was awesome. It was a family-owned restaurant, and Chelsea sometimes stopped in for some great home-cooked pasta.

They had to wait a few minutes for their table, but she didn't mind at all. She had a chance to stop and talk to the parents of one of her students, much to the student's embarrassment, since he was also there. But the parents were eager to know how their son was doing in her math class, so she took the opportunity to update them.

When the waitress sat them at their table, Bash smiled at her. "I'll bet you get that a lot."

She looked up from her menu. "Get what a lot?"

"Running into either students or parents when you're out."

"Oh. Yes. The drawback of teaching in a small town. So much fun when I run into a student—or their parents—when I'm wearing no makeup, sweaty, and just ran two miles on the track at the gym."

"I can imagine. There's just nowhere to hide around here."

"Not for me. Most of the kids I teach have worked at the grocery store, too. Try having a kid you just gave a C minus to smirk at you when you're buying tampons."

He laughed. "Every woman buys them. It's not like it's a secret, Chelsea."

"Tell that to a fifteen-year-old boy. I don't know which of us was more embarrassed. I guess him, because he had to put the box in the grocery bag."

"Scarred him for life, did you?"

"You'd think so. It's a good thing I wasn't buying condoms, too."

He feigned a look of shock and clutched his chest. "Why, Miss Gardner. You aren't trying to tell me you have an active sex life, too."

"I'd like to. Which is why I keep a supply of condoms around."

"It's good to be prepared, just in case that perfect man shows up."

She nodded. "Exactly."

The waitress brought their salads, and they dug in to eat.

"I'm still working on that, you know."

She looked up. "On what?"

"Your list. And a guy for you."

"Oh. Thank you. I'm sure he's out there somewhere."

"I'm sure he is, too. In the meantime, if you need someone to get you through that supply of condoms before their expiration date, I'm happy to help you out."

She choked out a laugh. "Wow, Bash. That's awfully generous of you."

He waggled his brows. "I'm a generous kind of guy."

"Such a sacrifice for you, too."

He gave her a smoldering-hot look that made her forget all about how hungry she was, and directed that hunger in a new, more interesting direction.

"Believe me, Chelsea. There'd be no sacrifice involved. And I wasn't exactly kidding."

She laid her fork down. "You're offering me sex."

He shrugged. "Why not?"

Just looking at him tempted her, though she should be highly offended.

She paused, waiting to feel insulted. It didn't happen. Maybe because it had been so long since she'd had actual sex that the offer appealed.

Bash definitely appealed. She hadn't exactly forgotten his kiss or the way his hands felt on her.

But . . . no. Not a good idea. For . . . reasons.

"Thanks, but I think I'll hold out awhile longer."

His lips curved, and she had a sudden urge to repeat that kiss and see if it would be as hot as it had been the first time.

"Offer stands. Anytime."

"Thanks."

But that anytime wasn't going to happen. Not with Bash. She was going to stand firm and wait for Mr. Perfect. She had a feeling he was out there, and it was going to happen for her.

Soon.

Chapter 8

"ARE YOU PICKING me up, or am I driving today?" Jane asked when she called Chelsea that afternoon a week after her impromptu non-date with Bash.

A non-date that had her thinking a lot more about Bash than she ever wanted to. Especially since he'd offered to be her sex stud. She'd definitely spent a lot of nights tossing and turning, with sex on her mind. And Bash on her mind, mixed with sex. Which had made sleep a lot more elusive. And made her even more resolved to find Mr. Perfect. A Mr. Perfect she could have mind-blowing sex with, so she could stop thinking about Bash.

"You have the monster minivan, with more storage space for the dresses," Chelsea said to her. "So you're driving."

"I'll pick you up at about six. Then we'll swing by and get Emma."

"Okay. See you then. I can't wait."

She hung up, then sat at the table to work on grading papers for a while until it was time to get ready. She went into the bedroom to fix her hair, put on makeup, and change clothes, selecting an easy-to-get-into-and-out-of dress and the appropriately sized heels. Since it was a little cool today, April being unpredictable in Oklahoma, she grabbed a sweater and went back in the kitchen, where she spied her notebook. She'd been so busy this past week she hadn't had time to focus on her list, or on what she was going to do about it. She flipped it open and stared at the list for the first time in a week.

"Yes, still perfect."

Just like the man who was going to tick off every item on that list.

As soon as she found him.

Though, considering her dating history, she had no idea where the mystery man who met all her criteria was going to materialize from. But she refused to give up hope.

He was out there—somewhere. And all her thoughts about Bash—the wrong man—made her want the right man even more.

She pulled lip gloss out of her purse, opened her compact and applied it, then looked out the window to see Jane pulling up in the parking lot. She headed downstairs and climbed into the backseat of the minivan.

"Are we ready for this?" Chelsea asked Jane and Emma.

"I know I am," Emma said. "The question is, is Des ready?"

Chelsea grinned. "You know she is. I'm so excited for her."

The drive to Tulsa took about twenty minutes. They pulled into the parking lot, climbed out, and headed into the bridal salon.

As they expected, everyone inside was already gathered in the back of the shop. It wasn't every day that a bridal salon received a movie star like Desiree Jenkins. Until last year, none of them had even known Des. Chelsea couldn't believe this was happening already. They'd been so lucky to meet Des when she'd filmed a movie on Logan McCormack's ranch. And even more fortunate to witness Des and Logan falling in love. Getting to know Des had been so much more than getting to know a movie star. She was down-to-earth, fun, and just like the rest of them—a real person.

They all loved her like she'd lived there forever.

And now Des and Logan were getting married. Fun stuff.

And while Des hadn't bought her dress at the bridal salon, she was getting her final alterations at their shop, something the salon had readily agreed to. Plus, the bridesmaids were doing their final fittings at the shop as well.

It was a week before the wedding, and Chelsea couldn't wait. She loved weddings. She hoped to have her own someday.

Of course, that meant finding the right man—something she had yet to do.

Her list was a good first step.

Des walked out of the back room. She wore jeans, a long-sleeved flannel shirt, and high-top tennis shoes, and her hair was tucked under a ball cap.

In other words, she looked nothing like a glamorous movie star.

"You look like a truck driver, Des," Emma said.

Des laughed and pulled the ball cap off, her long raven hair spilling out from under it. "I'm traveling incognito today."

"Hiding from the paparazzi again?" Chelsea asked as they handed off their dresses to one of the salon assistants and made their way toward Des.

"Yes."

"Do you really think you're going to be able to pull off this wedding without the press knowing about it?"

Des took a seat in one of the chairs. "Currently, Amelia, my stand-in, who looks uncannily like me, is having the vacation of her life at a private villa in Tuscany—with my compliments and on my dime. And she just happens to be there with her boyfriend, Max, a stuntman who resembles Logan. Plus, a very prominent member of the press who's a good friend might be leaking details that Logan and I were spotted at a private villa in Tuscany. In return he'll attend our wedding, and he'll get an exclusive interview and photos of the real thing. Anyway, the fake story should put the press hounds on the Italian wedding scent."

Emma laughed. "You've thought of everything, haven't you?"

Des beamed an angelic smile. "I've tried to. At the very least, I don't think anyone's going to be looking for Logan and me to be getting married on the ranch next weekend."

"I don't think so, either. I think they'd expect something splashier," Chelsea said.

"Yes. Like a villa in Tuscany. Plus, we're keeping the

wedding low-key. A few of my Hollywood friends are invited, plus our friends here, and my parents and brother and sister are flying in. Otherwise, not a big deal. At least not by Hollywood standards."

"But by Hope standards?" Jane said. "This is going to be a major spring event."

Des took in a deep breath. "I'm so excited. And this has been such a whirlwind. I can't believe it's already here." She grasped Chelsea's hand. "And that you're all here to help me. Thank you for this."

Chelsea squeezed her hand. "We're your friends, Des. We're practically family now."

And when Des came to them last year around the holidays and told them she wanted to plan a spring wedding, they were all excited for her. Even if it didn't give them a lot of time for planning. But that's what wedding coordinators were for.

Des had a big film coming up that would require four months of filming out of the country, and she'd told them she and Logan didn't want to wait any longer. She wanted to marry him, and she wanted to marry him this spring.

So they knuckled down and did wedding planning as a team, and with the help of Martha, who was Logan's ranch manager/pseudo mother, they had managed to divide up everything that needed to be done. Des had pulled in a wedding planner to deal with all the bigger details, and she'd been a lifesaver.

Des had been finishing up a movie in Paris, and had also somehow managed to sneak into one of the designer shops and buy one hell of a gorgeous wedding dress. And while in Paris, she had also chosen the most amazing dresses for all the bridesmaids to wear.

Des might be getting married on the McCormack ranch, but this wedding was still going to be haute couture.

Chelsea, who had never met a designer dress or shoes she didn't love, couldn't wait.

If she was lucky, some fancy millionaire or movie star would show up at the wedding, and he'd be her Mr. Perfect.

Because so far, she hadn't met him in the small town of

Hope, Oklahoma. And it felt like she'd dated almost every available man who lived in the town. She was nearly certain there wasn't a match for her there.

So maybe perfect guy was on the guest list for Des and Logan's wedding.

Things might just be looking up for her.

BASH MET UP with his best friend, Logan McCormack, at the ranch where Logan had made his living all his life.

They'd often had parties on the ranch and had celebrated a lot here. Though Bash found it hard to believe that lone-wolf, stubborn-as-hell, quiet Logan was going to get married next weekend. And to a fiery, outspoken, wild-to-the-core movie star like Desiree Jenkins, no less. Never in his craziest imaginings would he ever have put those two together.

He knew the old adage that opposites attract. It sure as hell fit for Logan and Des. He'd never seen two people who were so completely different, and yet so much in love.

He pulled his truck in front of the main house at the ranch and put it in park.

Yeah, maybe that love thing did work after all.

For some people. Sure as hell hadn't worked for him and Cathy. He'd tried to be the man she wanted, but in the end, he hadn't been, and it had ended in disaster. The relationship had lasted for a painful two years, and the parting had been ugly. He could still remember the look of disappointment on her face when she'd left him. God knows he'd felt it, too, but it had been directed inward.

He took responsibility for the failure of their marriage, because he hadn't been able to adapt. Cathy had always had big dreams about the guy she was going to spend the rest of her life with—and that guy hadn't been him.

He swore then he'd never get married again. He'd never do to another woman what he'd done to Cathy. He'd never bring that kind of unhappiness into a relationship. Nope. Never again.

Figuring he'd traveled down the road of unpleasant-memory

lane long enough, he pushed open the door of the truck and headed up the stairs into the McCormack house, where laughter always greeted him.

"Well, hello, Bash."

Martha came and greeted him as she always did, her arms open wide for a hug.

"Hey, Martha. How's it goin'?"

"It's wonderful. So glad you could make it. The tuxes just arrived, and everyone's in the main room for the final fitting."

Some kind of designer tux thing. Whatever. So not Bash's idea of a good time, but for Logan—and for Des—he'd do it.

"Okay. And how's Miss Martha doing?"

"Are you serious? It's wedding time, and I couldn't be happier."

"Of course you are." He kissed her on the cheek, happy for her. She and her husband, Ben, the ranch foreman, never had kids of their own, but they'd unofficially adopted the McCormack boys after their mother left and their father died. To Logan, Luke, and Reid, Martha and Ben were parents. Damn good ones, too.

"You go on in there," Martha said, patting him on the back.

"Thanks."

He walked into the living room. Logan was in there, and so were Logan's brother Luke, Carter Richards, and Martha's husband, Ben.

"'Bout time you showed up," Logan said. "Can't do this monkey suit party without you."

"Hey. Some of us work for a living. We don't all lie around on the front porch drinking beer all day."

"Screw you, Bash."

Bash laughed. "Where are Reid and Will?"

"You just missed Will. He had to do something with one of the kids, so he'll meet us at the bar later. Reid is finishing up a job in . . . I don't know," Logan said. "Wherever the hell he is. He'll fly in on Thursday. He's having his tux fitted in Boston. Des is taking care of all those details. Her dad's and her brother's tuxes were done a month ago. Colt is getting his tux done in LA because he's got a final shoot there, so he and Tony will be here midweek. Other than that, we're all here."

Bash was introduced to Daniel, someone from one of the local tux shops, who was taking care of making sure hems and sleeve lengths and all those details were dealt with. Since they were custom tuxes, they'd already been measured once, but they had to make sure everything was perfect.

He'd never owned a tux before. He supposed he was going to now—a gift from Des and Logan.

The tux fit him like—well, he guessed like it had been made for him.

"We're going to look damn good, aren't we?" he asked Logan as they stood side by side looking into the mirror the tailor had brought.

"I guess. This is all for Des. I'm just happy she agreed to marry me. I'd wear a clown suit if that's what she wanted."

"I'd like to see that," Carter said. "The red nose would look good on you. And you definitely have the big feet, Logan."

Logan smirked. "They go with my big dick."

Bash rolled his eyes. "I need a beer."

The tailor's head shot up. "Not until you change out of these tuxes, gentlemen."

"Then let's hurry and get out of these things," Luke said. "Because it's beer time."

The tailor got through his final fittings, and they changed clothes and headed outside where there was a cooler waiting.

They all stuck their hands in and grabbed cans of beer.

"You ready for this, Logan?" Luke asked.

Logan popped the top off his beer. "You mean the wedding, or you all trying your best to get me drunk tonight?"

Luke slapped him on the back. "There is no *trying* about it. You just think you're a hot cowboy who can hold his liquor. We're taking you down tonight."

"Evan already volunteered to be designated driver, since he said he's on police patrol duty tomorrow morning, and I'm shutting the bar down for the party," Bash said. "It's going to be epic. Hard liquor epic."

Logan rolled his eyes. "I'll make sure you all don't cry when you're puking your guts up in the parking lot."

Luke slid a smirk Bash's way. "He thinks we're amateurs, when we know he doesn't drink all that much."

Logan laughed. "Oh, who doesn't do all that much drinking? I think your gullet is all sensitized by that fine wine you and Emma partake of these days."

"Now I'm insulted. And it's on, brother."

Bash couldn't wait for tonight.

Chapter 9

DES HADN'T WANTED an out-of-town bachelorette party because of the possibility of paparazzi following her around, but she was still determined to have a party anyway, so Chelsea and the other women decided the best place to do it and do it up right was at the ranch, where they were assured of privacy.

After all, this was where Des and Logan were going to have their wedding next weekend, which was going to be locked down tight. No one got on the McCormack ranch without the ranch hands and Logan knowing about it.

Not that he was going to be here tonight, but he had made sure the gates were secure, and several of the hands were on tap to provide security for Des.

They wouldn't need it. With Des's master plan in the works, Chelsea hadn't seen a sign of photographers on her way out to the ranch.

Martha had prepared all kinds of fun food, and Chelsea had arrived early to make several signature drinks, including Bellinis. Emma and Jane were in charge of costuming. Samantha and Molly were bringing decorations, and Megan was bringing awesome confections, courtesy of her bakery.

This was going to be a fun party.

"Martha," Chelsea said, pulling her attention away from her drink concoctions to note that Martha had quite the array of food piled up. "Have you been spending your free hours watching the Food Network again?"

Martha beamed a wide grin. "Let's just say I wasn't going to serve fried chicken for Desiree's bachelorette party. We're doing it Hollywood-style tonight."

Chelsea knew Des loved Martha—and her cooking. She wouldn't have cared if fried chicken had been on the menu for tonight.

But from the looks of things, Martha really had been spending some time broadening her culinary horizons.

"Is that caviar?" Chelsea asked.

"It is. I had to drive all the way into that fancy store in Tulsa to find it, too. Which was fine, since I had to pick up crab and lobster there."

"I can't wait to see what you're going to do with the seafood."

"Something magical, no doubt," Des said as she came into the room. She pressed a kiss to Martha's cheek, then hugged Chelsea. "Everything she cooks is magic."

"Don't I know it. Martha, you should give cooking lessons to the rest of us poor mortals who can only dream of whipping up those delicious meals you fix."

"Oh, that's nonsense, Chelsea," Martha said, opening up the oven, which emitted aromas that made Chelsea's senses go haywire with food lust. "You're a good cook as well."

Chelsea laughed. "Oh, sure, if you like brownies. Out of the box."

Des snickered. "Some of my favorite desserts come from a box."

"I think you two are too hard on yourselves. I know for a fact you've brought amazing pies to potluck dinners before, Chelsea."

Chelsea shrugged. "Maybe. When I've taken the time and effort to work at it."

"That's all cooking is about, is taking the time. And doing it with love."

Des put her arm around Martha. "Aww. Thank you. Considering the amazing smells in here, I feel very loved right now."

The front door opened, and Emma, Jane, Megan, and Samantha spilled in, all carrying bags and boxes. Chelsea and Des rushed to help them, and suddenly it was pandemonium, everyone trying to talk at once.

Fortunately, Martha was organized and commanded attention, and she knew how to direct the troops. She sent everyone who didn't have food into the living room to set up—and sent Des and Chelsea with them, with meant Martha and Megan stayed in the kitchen for food prep.

"Wait 'til you see what we got," Samantha said, pulling feather boas and tiaras out of a bag, along with a fancy white sash that had the word *Bride* emblazoned on it.

Chelsea braced herself for Des to say those were the corniest things she'd ever seen. Instead, Des squealed with delight. "This. Is. Awesome. It's what I've always wanted for my bachelorette party."

Des held still while they put the sash and tiara on her, then twirled around. In her hot pink dress and high heels, she was one hell of a sight.

"I need a picture of this." Chelsea fished her phone out of her purse, then snapped a couple of quick shots.

"Oh, take some with my phone, too," Des said, handing her phone to Chelsea. "I'm going to text them to Logan."

"Shouldn't you wait until you're mostly drunk to do that?" Jane asked.

"I promised him I'd send him photos all night long. That way he can watch the progression of the debauchery."

Emma grinned. "Sweet."

"I also told him I intend to get totally trashed tonight. One of you will have to hold my hair when I throw up."

"I volunteer Emma for that duty." Chelsea cast a sweet smile Emma's way.

Emma blinked. "Me? Why me?"

"You're a vet. You deal with blood and guts all day long. What's a little vomit?"

"I think Colt should totally be here with us. He is, after all, the man of honor and your best friend, Des."

Des nodded at Samantha. "This is true. And he would have loved to come, but he's stuck filming. He's flying in on Wednesday."

"When is your sister coming in?" Jane asked.

"She'll be here on Friday, along with my mom, my dad, and my brother. She's working on a research project. Of course she's always doing that, being a biologist. I'm just happy she's going to be in the wedding."

Emma squeezed her hand. "I'm so happy your family is going to be here."

Des grinned. "Me, too."

"Tony's coming with Colt, too, isn't he?" Samantha asked.

"He told me he wouldn't miss it," Des said. "Now that the two of them have outed their relationship, they try to never be apart."

"Great," Chelsea said. "Now, if you'll all excuse me, I need to go mix some of those drinks so we can get our bride-to-be drunk."

She heard Des giggle as she left the room. The one thing Chelsea loved about Des was that even though she was a highly sought-after and successful actress, she defied the image of Hollywood. When she was here on the ranch and around Hope, she was simply one of them. She liked hanging out with them and shopping with them, and she hated having photographers following her around. She preferred her life to be as normal as possible, which is why she loved the ranch so much. It gave her the privacy she craved.

Plus, she loved Logan, she loved his family, and she especially loved Martha. They'd all grown close to Des in a hurry. She'd become best friends with all of them. To Chelsea's way of thinking, that made her part of Hope, even if she hadn't grown up here.

She fixed drinks and put them on a tray.

"You two," she said, casting a stern look at Martha and Megan. "Out of the kitchen and into the living room for cocktails and frivolity right now."

Martha balked, but Megan gave her a gentle shove, and Martha capitulated.

Samantha had brought flowers from her shop, and the room smelled so good. Des looked beautiful, which was no surprise at all, and Emma had decked them all out in boas and tiaras. Molly had put up an adorable sign she'd made with Des and Logan's name and the date of their wedding. Jane had turned on music, and Chelsea started handing out cocktails. She also laid out shot glasses and liquor and started mixing up a few enhanced shots.

They all sat around eating and talking, mostly about the wedding, but it was easy conversation, drifting in and out of several topics. Emma's sister Molly was still working at her boyfriend Carter's auto repair shop, revitalizing his systems and developing sales plans.

"How's that working for you?" she asked Molly.

"Shockingly well, actually."

"There's no friction with the two of you spending so much time together?"

"We don't spend as much time together at work as you might think. With the new computer system in place, Carter has more free time to spend at the different shop locations instead of having to be at one shop for an entire day. Now he's more mobile, which means I don't see him as much since I concentrate most of my time at the main shop in Hope. And if I need something, I can call or text him."

"And soon enough you'll be planning your own wedding," Megan said.

Molly smiled. "This is true. My mother is beside herself with the plans. You all know how she loves the planning. And now that she's completely healed from her injury and back on her feet—"

"More like running back on her feet," Emma added.

Molly laughed. "This is true. She's all over the wedding planning. It's like I don't have to do a thing."

"Which reminds me," Emma said, whipping out her phone. "We're scheduled to meet at Samantha's a week from Wednesday to look at flowers?"

"Yes. I can't believe we're only six months away from my wedding. I can't believe we're doing this so soon."

Emma squeezed Molly's hand. "You two were apart a long time. Why wait any longer?"

Molly gave her sister a loving smile. "That's what Carter said. He proposed so fast it made my head spin."

"And put quite the rock on your finger as well," Chelsea added.

Molly wriggled the fingers of her left hand. "Yes. Totally unnecessary, but who was I to object?"

"What woman in her right mind would?" Since she was a kid, all Chelsea had ever dreamed about was finding a man and getting married. She was an independent woman with a great career—one that satisfied her. But she wanted love.

Maybe it was because she'd had so little of it when she was younger.

Not that she expected a man to be the be-all and end-all of her happily ever after. She created her own satisfaction in life. That's why she'd become a teacher. She loved her kids, even when they were a pain. All it took was one bright mind who reached for the stars, one kid who saw beyond math as something that had to be done, as a class they were required to pass, to the possibilities of a bright future such as engineering or medicine, and she counted it as a success. She'd seen it countless times in the ten years she'd been teaching.

She had a multitude of friends who'd been her lifeline on so many occasions. They'd been there for her, and she'd been there for them. Her life had been full and blessed.

There was her happiness. Or at least it had been.

But now she wanted something more. She'd wanted something more for a few years now—a home and a family of her own. But she wouldn't settle for less than the perfect man.

Her mother had settled for less, and it had left her dissatisfied and bitter. After her father had left them when Chelsea was twelve, her mother had turned that bitterness on Chelsea.

She'd had a long childhood of lectures about how horrible her father was, how men couldn't be counted on, and how it

was best to be independent. The ironic thing was, her mother
hadn't been there for her any more than her father had.

Chelsea had relied on herself, on her own decision making,
refusing to let her mother's bitterness shape her future. She'd
vowed to never do that to her own children. Chelsea intended
to only do the marriage thing one time, which was why she
was so choosy about men.

No losers for her. She'd lived with one for twelve years,
and had lived with the repercussions of one for many years
after that.

She had no intentions of turning into her mother. She had
watched and learned those lessons well.

She'd know when the right one came along.

Megan sat down next to her. "Hey. This is a party, you
know. You're supposed to be smiling, laughing, eating, and
drinking, not staring off into a corner."

Chelsea shook off thoughts of the past and raised her glass.
"I am drinking. And I'm stuffed from the crab and lobster
Martha fed us."

"It was fantastic, wasn't it? But you're looking awfully
quiet and reflective over here." Megan put one of her infamous
cupcakes in front of her. This one was chocolate, with pink
and white frosting piled ridiculously high. "How about something sweet to perk you up?"

Chelsea slid a suspicious look toward Megan. "Your 'something sweets' will make my butt huge."

Megan laughed. "Oh, come on. We'll dance off all those
calories tonight."

She stared down at the cupcake, then shrugged, peeled
down the wrapper, and took a bite. Why not? They were cel-
ebrating, after all. The sweetness exploded in her mouth. "Oh,
God, Megan. This is so good."

Megan wriggled in her chair. "I know, right? I've already
had two. The first I had to taste to make sure they were okay."

Chelsea swallowed, then washed the cupcake down with
champagne. "Honey, everything you bake is more than okay.
It's delicious."

"See? Now you're smiling. There's nothing in this world a good cupcake can't fix."

Chelsea laughed. "I don't know about that, but it definitely doesn't hurt."

"Okay, now that you're feeling better, tell me what you were thinking about."

"My childhood. My parents. Men. Families. Weddings. My future."

Megan leaned back and picked up her glass. "Oh, so light topics."

"Yes."

"Want to get into specifics?"

She didn't, really, but it was probably time she started talking to someone about where her mind was at.

Someone besides Bash, anyway.

"I've made a list."

"Really. What kind of list?"

"You'll think it's stupid."

"I doubt it. Tell me."

"It's a perfect man list."

Megan frowned. "A what?"

"Here. Let me show you." She laid her drink down on the table, then went into the other room to grab her purse. She fished her notebook out of the bag, but was stopped along the way by Des, who had come in from outside.

"Halt. You are not drinking."

Chelsea laughed and hugged her. "I laid my drink down in the living room. I just went to get my notebook."

"Oh?"

"Yes. You might as well come along." Emma and Jane were behind her. "All of you might as well come."

Samantha tailed along, too, as well as Molly. They grabbed Martha, who had snuck into the kitchen in an attempt to do dishes. They all settled into the living room with their drinks.

"So what's in the notebook?" Emma asked. "Secret love notes from some guy you're dating that you haven't told us all about yet?"

"Uh, no. It's a list I was just about to tell Megan about."

"Ooh, a list," Jane said. "I love lists."

"Of course you do. That's because you're a math teacher like me. And you're orderly."

Jane looked at all of them. "Chelsea thinks I'm orderly."

Emma rolled her eyes. "The list, Chelsea."

"It's my perfect man list."

"The one you mentioned a couple of weeks ago?" Emma asked.

"Yes."

"Does it have names on it?" Samantha asked. "And if it does, will you share them with me?"

Chelsea laughed. "No. It's not a list of names. It's a list of qualities I want in my perfect man."

"Oh. Sounds fun. Let's see it," Megan said, taking the notebook from her. She read the list out loud.

"It's an interesting list," Martha said.

"I don't see you with a suit and tie kind of guy," Emma said, regarding her thoughtfully. "I mean, yes, you dress well, and I highly covet the sexy shoes you wear, especially since I'm a veterinarian, so I'm stuck in tennis shoes all day. But I don't know, Chelse."

"Never married? That kind of limits you as well. Lots of great guys have been divorced, honey," Jane said.

Chelsea knew Jane was thinking about Luke, her husband's brother, who'd been married before and was now married to Emma.

"I know that. You have to keep in mind that what might be perfect for all of you might not be the right guy for me. I spent a lot of time thinking about this list, about the kinds of qualities I wanted in a man."

"What about honesty and honor and integrity?" Megan asked.

"Yes, I agree with all those attributes. But that's not what this list is about. It's about the types of things I want—and maybe don't want—in my perfect man."

"You keep saying *perfect*." Samantha looked her straight on. "I don't think I'm the only one who's going to tell you the perfect man doesn't exist."

Chelsea nodded. "I know. This is an idea in my head. Just go with it, for me, okay? I've had my share of dates. I know what I want now, and I'm going to find it."

Megan handed the notebook to her. "That's all you can ask for, then. That's all any of us could ask for, right?"

She knew these women would understand. "Exactly. Now I just have to figure out how to find him."

Emma came over and sat next to her, laying her hand on Chelsea's shoulder. "He's out there, Chelsea. He's probably out there right now, looking for you."

Chelsea wondered if that were true. She could almost picture him in her head, a hazy figure shrouded in darkness.

She felt like he was close, that she was close to meeting him, to having her happily ever after.

But tonight wasn't about her happily ever after. It was about Des.

"I think everyone needs a refill on their drinks." She stood and led them all into the kitchen.

"Now we're talking," Des said as Chelsea fixed them another round of cocktails.

Fortunately, there was amazing food to go with the drinks, because they wanted Des to pace herself. Not that Chelsea felt Des was listening, because within the next few hours Des did a lot more drinking than eating.

"She's doing it up right," Emma said, leaning against Chelsea as they all watched Des dance in the middle of the entryway. "There's nothing like living it up and saying goodbye to your single days."

"That girl hasn't been single since the day she laid eyes on Logan," Chelsea said. "This whole 'last week of being single' thing is a state of mind."

Jane laughed. "Okay, you might be right there. But she's enjoying the heck out of her state of mind tonight."

Des came over and grasped Chelsea's hands. "Come on. You have to dance with me."

"Sure, honey."

At least they weren't in a bar or a nightclub, though everyone was taking a lot of pictures to send to Logan. Either way,

Chelsea intended for Des to have a very good time, so she got out in the middle of the floor and danced her ass off with Des.

"TO LOGAN—AND his dumbass decision to get married, despite all my warnings."

Logan grinned and downed his shot. "Thanks, Bash."

They all downed shots, then several of the guys headed over to the pool tables. Logan hung out at the bar with Bash.

It was good to take a night off, especially on a weekend. And maybe it was costing him money, closing on a Saturday night, but this was for his best friend, and all the guys pitched in to cover the cost of the booze.

Anything for Logan, who'd come to his rescue more than once.

They'd had food and plenty of drinks, and despite their best efforts, Logan didn't yet appear to be drunk.

Logan's phone buzzed—again.

"Another picture of your woman?"

"Yeah." Logan picked up his phone and looked at the picture, his lips ticking up.

"What?"

"Check this one out." He handed the phone to Bash.

Bash couldn't believe what he was seeing. Des, obviously drunk, was dancing with Chelsea. Both of them wore body-clinging dresses, though Bash only had eyes for Chelsea. She had her arms up over her head, which raised her dress up to her thighs. She had long, beautiful legs, and those stiletto heels she wore only made her legs look longer. She'd pulled her hair up tonight, but pieces of it fell across her face. She wore some feathery thing across her neck, but the feathers teased her cleavage. She had her eyes closed, her head thrown back, and she looked like she was in ecstasy.

He'd like to see that look on her face—when the two of them were alone.

Hell, he'd like to put that look on her face.

"Did you even notice Des in the picture, my man, or were you just looking at Chelsea?"

Bash frowned and handed the phone back to Logan. "Des

is shit-faced. And of course I was looking at her. Hardly even noticed Chelsea."

"Uh-huh." Logan gave him a you're-full-of-shit look. "I was big into denial with Des. Didn't help."

"I'm not denying anything. Chelsea and I have nothing together."

"Which doesn't mean you're not into her."

He wasn't about to deny that, so he shrugged and poured Logan another shot, with a beer on the side. "You need to keep drinking."

Logan downed the shot and grabbed the beer, taking a sip. "You're avoiding."

"I'm not avoiding anything, but you're avoiding me kicking your ass in pool."

"Come on." Logan shook his head, and they moved to the pool table and shot a few games.

Though Bash noticed that whenever Logan wasn't up to shoot, he'd pull his phone out of his pocket. And he kept shaking his head and smiling.

Bash sure would like to know if there were any more pictures of Chelsea, though why he was interested, he had no idea. He was perfectly content hanging with all the guys, and Logan was having a great time.

Bash purposely kept his drinking to a minimum because he wanted to make sure to help Evan get all the guys home in one piece tonight—plus, this was his bar. He had a responsibility to everyone here.

There was plenty of food, there were sports on the TV, the guys were playing pool and drinking, and they were all having a good time. This was what Bash lived for—his bar and his friends.

So why the hell did his thoughts keep drifting to Chelsea? Her and her damn list.

He looked around the bar. Carter was engaged to Molly. Luke and Will were both married, Logan was about to get married.

Evan was single, and as far as he knew, Chelsea had never dated him before. Of course, Evan was a cop and he worked odd hours, so that was a strike against him.

There were Caleb and Jared McCormack, Logan and Luke's cousins. Both of them were single, though maybe a little younger than Chelsea. They both worked on the ranch and got up pretty early, but those were kind of regular hours. And they worked around animals all the time, so that was another thing on her list.

But they definitely weren't suit and tie types, and he didn't think either Caleb or Jared would like romantic getaways involving room service. Then again, he didn't know them well enough to find out.

And why the hell was he even thinking about Chelsea's damn list right now?

Her list was moronic. You didn't find the person you were meant to be with by making a list. It just . . . happened.

Then again, he'd tumbled into a marriage with Cathy, and that had just happened. Look how that had turned out.

Maybe he should make a list.

No, he didn't need a damn list, because he wasn't looking for a woman.

Carter came over and slung an arm around him. "Logan wants to go to the ranch and see the girls."

Bash arched a brow. "He does, does he?"

"Okay. I talked him into it. Is he drunk yet? Are you drunk yet?" Carter squinted at him. From the looks of him, Carter had definitely had more than his share of shots and beers.

Bash grinned at him. "What's the matter, Carter? Missing your woman?"

"Maybe. I need to check on her. Make sure she's still there."

Bash knew for a fact those women weren't going anywhere tonight. "I'll check with Logan."

Carter patted his chest and veered off. Bash wandered over to where Logan leaned against the wall in front of the pool tables. He was studying his phone—again.

"More photos?"

Logan shook his head. "These women—my woman . . ."

He let the sentence trail off, but dragged his fingers through his hair.

"Care to elaborate?"

Logan met his gaze, then laughed. "I think they're having a good time."

"Carter said you wanted to go to the ranch and check up on them."

"Oh, Carter said I wanted to, huh? I think Carter is drunk and wants to check on Molly."

"I think you're right."

"But yeah, we can head to the ranch. Let's mash up these parties and see what happens. If nothing else, everyone will have a place to crash tonight."

Bash grinned. "All right."

Chapter 10

IT LOOKED LIKE a crime scene in Logan's house. Bodies were everywhere, draped over furniture and wandering around like zombies. Some were doing movements that resembled dancing, though Bash couldn't be sure that's what it was.

One of those zombies fell into Logan's arms. Fortunately, it was his fiancée, Des.

"Oops." She laughed, and Logan wrapped his arms around her to hold her upright.

"You're drunk, babe," Logan said.

She tipped her head back, her eyes half closed. "And you're not?"

"Nope."

"We tried, Des," Bash said. "He's got an iron gut."

Des blinked, frowned, then laughed, throwing her arms around Logan's neck. "I might throw up on you."

Logan slid a grin in Bash's direction. "I'm putting her to bed."

"Good idea."

Logan hoisted Des up in his arms and disappeared up the stairs.

"I'm going to find my woman," Carter said, weaving into the mass of bodies.

Bash shook his head and made his way into the kitchen.

Martha was in there cleaning up. Ben came in behind him. "How's it going?"

"Good," she said, wiping down the counter. "They made a mess, but had a great time. How about you?"

Ben kissed her cheek.

"We had a good time. About half the guys are blitzed."

Martha looked up at Ben. "Are you one of them?"

"Are you kidding? I can't keep up with these youngsters. It'd take me a week to recover."

Martha laughed. "I feel the same way. I had a couple of cocktails and danced. That was it for me."

"Food smells good," Bash said.

"You want some?" Martha asked.

"I might."

"Everything's in the fridge. You can warm it up yourself. I'm ready to go home and go to bed. Will you make sure all the girls are okay?"

"I will. You two head home."

Ben nodded. "I think we'll do that."

"Good night."

Ben and Martha headed out the door, so Bash waded into the living room. Carter had found Molly. The two of them were tangled up together on the sofa. Molly had wrapped a red feather boa around him and put her tiara on his head, and they were both out cold.

He'd figured Carter wouldn't last much longer.

Samantha and Megan were still dancing, though it was more like a slow weave to a fast song. Will and Jane were picking up, Emma and Luke were helping them, and Chelsea was nowhere to be found.

"We're going to gather up a few things and head out with Will and Jane," Luke said. "Will said he and Jane have to pick the kids up from her parents in the morning, and we have our dogs to deal with."

Bash nodded. "I'll make sure the rest of the ladies are tucked in."

Luke patted his arm. "Okay, buddy. Good night."

So much for the wild party. He made his way into the living room.

"Oh, hi, Bash," Samantha said. "Do you want a feather boa or a tiara?"

He tried not to laugh. "No. But thanks. Hey, have you seen Chelsea?"

"Nope. You jess lemme know if you want some flowers in your hair, then." Samantha turned around and continued her dance.

"Will do." Maybe he'd have better luck with Megan. "Hey, Megan. Have you seen Chelsea?"

Megan pointed wildly in five directions, then rubbed her hand over her face. "Um. Sure. She's over in the fishing cabinet village . . . thingy."

He nodded. Nope, no luck there, either. "Uh-huh. Thanks."

He started out of the room, then stopped, turned around, and waited, wanting to make sure Megan and Samantha didn't go anywhere.

They didn't. They both plopped down on the sofa after the song ended. He figured in about five minutes they'd be asleep.

He rechecked the kitchen, then went down the hall to the bathroom, which was empty. He checked the guest bedrooms upstairs, but those were empty as well.

Huh.

He went out back and found Chelsea curled up on one of the lounge chairs. Sound asleep.

"Jesus, it's freezing out here." It might be spring, but it was still cold at night, especially out here in the country. He kneeled down beside her. "Chelsea. Wake up."

She didn't even budge. He laid his hand on her arm to find it icy cold.

Shit.

He slid his arms underneath her and lifted her out of the

chair. Her body curved into his and she wrapped an arm around him.

Instinct, probably. Whatever. He carried her inside and up the stairs to one of the empty guest bedrooms. He sat her on the edge of the bed long enough to draw back the covers, then he placed her on the bed, slipped off those ridiculous high heels she still had on, and pulled the covers over her.

She should warm up shortly. He was about to turn and walk out of the room when he heard her move.

"Bash?"

"Yeah?"

"I'm cold."

He came over to the side of the bed. "You're under the covers now. You'll be warm in a minute."

"Come lay down with me."

She was obviously drunk and had no idea what she was saying. "How about I get you an extra blanket?"

Instead, she raised up, wrapped her hand around the back of his neck, and brought her lips to his.

It wasn't in his nature to take advantage of a drunk woman. But her lips were cold and he could do something about warming her up. He pressed her to the bed and deepened the kiss, feeling her body respond in a way that made him go hard instantly.

Suddenly, the covers were gone, her dress was hiked up and he was sliding his hands over soft, silky thighs. Chelsea moaned his name across his lips and he knew damn well if he didn't get the hell out of that bedroom, he was going to regret this. And so would she.

He broke the kiss, unable to resist taking one last brush of his lips across hers. She tasted of alcohol and something sugary sweet. His dick was hard and throbbing and he was going to be thinking about that on the long drive back to town.

She laid her head back on the pillow, her eyes half-lidded as she smiled up at him. "It's because I'm drunk, isn't it?"

He brushed her hair away from her face. "Yeah."

"I'd still respect you in the morning, you know."

His lips curved. "But I wouldn't respect myself." He pulled

the covers up and leaned in close to her. "Look, Chelsea. I want to make love to you. But I want you to be fully conscious and stone-cold sober and totally aware of what's going on between us. So you get some sleep tonight, and some other time we'll talk about this."

He heard her sigh as she rolled over on her side. "Okay. Night, Bash."

"Good night, Chelsea."

It took every ounce of restraint he possessed to walk out of that bedroom.

But he did, and after he closed the door, he leaned against it, needing a minute to get his body under control.

Self-respect. What a crock of shit that was.

Chapter 11

ONCE SCHOOL LET out Friday afternoon, Chelsea and Jane drove to the ranch. She'd packed the night before so they could head straight over after school let out, since they had a lot to do. Since Des had stayed on the ranch this past week, Chelsea had made arrangements for the manicurist to do manis and pedis on the ranch today, and the hair and makeup people would be flying in tonight to do their hair tomorrow, courtesy of Des.

She and Jane had talked all through lunch about the wedding preparations. Will was dropping the kids off with Jane's parents, so he'd be heading over later.

"I can't believe Des and Logan are getting married tomorrow," Jane said as they pulled through the ranch gates.

Chelsea nodded. "And so far it looks like no photographers are in sight. We've managed to scatter the arrivals of everyone enough that no one has gotten wind of the upcoming wedding."

"Let's hope all those photographers are still in Italy, sniffing around for possible leads on Des and Logan's whereabouts."

"I know. It was a brilliant idea on Des's part."

Chelsea pulled up and parked in front of the main house. She and Jane grabbed their things and went inside, where the normally quiet house was bustling with activity. She spotted Des in the kitchen with Martha and Tony, Colt's boyfriend, along with a couple of women she didn't recognize. One was older, and another was younger. Those had to be Des's mother and sister. Chelsea could definitely see the resemblance to Des.

"We're here," Chelsea said.

"Oh, great. This is my mother, Cynthia, and my sister, Penny," Des said, introducing her mother and sister to everyone.

"We're so happy you're here," Chelsea said.

"We're delighted to be here," Cynthia said. "And on such a happy occasion."

Penny put her arm around Des. "I never thought I'd see the day that some man would be willing to put up with my little sister for the rest of his life, yet it's actually happening."

Des bumped her sister's hip. "You're so funny. You're right, though."

"Hey," Chelsea said to Tony. "It's so great to see you."

Tony smiled and wrapped his arms around her for a tight hug. "Good to see you, too." After he hugged her, he swept Jane up in a hug as well. "Hi, Jane."

"Where's Colt?"

"He's out riding with Logan, Des's dad and her brother, Teddy, and a few others right now. You know Colt. Any chance he has to get out on a horse."

"Of course. How's the movie business?"

"Great. I just finished cinematography on an amazing drama. I have a month off, then I'm starting a television series that'll keep me busy for about six months in Ireland and Scotland. I'm really looking forward to it."

"Oh, wow," Jane said. "That sounds spectacular."

"Yeah. Colt has a break coming up during my shoot, so he'll be able to fly over and spend some time there with me."

"Sounds romantic," Chelsea said, leaning into Tony. "I'm so happy things are going well for the two of you."

"Thanks. I'm happy it's all turning out so well for Colt. You know how worried he was about coming out. Turns out he didn't have to be. The scripts are still rolling in."

"There was nothing for him to be worried about," Chelsea

said. "He's still a hot leading man. The movie he and Des filmed here? I was fanning myself over their kissing scenes."

Tony laughed. "Yeah. Those were great, weren't they?"

"The entire movie was great," Jane said. "I think I went through two boxes of popcorn during that movie. It filled the seats in the Hope movie theater for months. I think we all saw it at least three times."

"It's because I'm such an irresistible leading man," Colt said as he entered the room.

Chelsea went over and gave him a hug. "You are irresistible. And you're sweaty."

"I know. I had a great ride. It's such a fantastic day out there today. Perfect weather. Plus Des's dad and brother wanted to ride as well. I hear Des had a ride with Logan early this morning." Colt nudged Des. "He tells me you're getting good at it."

Des grinned. "Logan likes to challenge me with these early-morning rides. He thinks I can't keep up with him. Where is he, by the way?" she asked Colt.

"He's showing your dad and Teddy around."

"Okay." Des turned to them. "I'm going to grab a quick shower because I know the nail salon folks will be here shortly. I'll be right back."

"I won't be getting nails done, sorry," Colt said with a wink.

"We'll give you a pass on that one," Jane said. "Is everyone else here?"

"Samantha and Megan are in the barn," Tony said. "With Molly and her mom."

"Okay," Chelsea said. "We'll head on over to see what's up."

"I'll call you when the ladies from the salon get here," Martha said.

Chelsea and Jane trekked across the gravel path toward the main barn, which was where the wedding ceremony was going to take place.

"I've been in the barn before. I can't imagine how they're going to transform it for the wedding," Jane said.

"Trust me. Des has this all planned out. If anyone can make it happen, she can. She brought in an awesome wedding planner who promised to turn the barn into an epic wedding site."

"And Logan didn't mind this, huh?"

Chelsea shook her head. "Logan wants Des to have the wedding of her dreams. I think he's happy they're getting married on the ranch."

They opened the barn doors and Chelsea forgot to breathe. This wasn't the same barn she'd been in a week ago. The cement floor had a lush wood overlay. The wood beams above had been painted white, and stunning white silk fluttered beneath the beams. Lights were everywhere, and Chelsea couldn't believe it, but they'd hung the most stunning chandeliers she'd ever seen. She couldn't wait to see it all lit up tomorrow night. There were tables set up, decorated like Chelsea would expect to see at a Hollywood event, with white and coral linen tablecloths and breathtaking china.

She looked over at Jane, who was equally wide-eyed.

"Wow" was all Chelsea could manage.

"You were right," Jane said. "The transformation is amazing. And so elegant. You'd never know this was a barn."

They made their way to the back of the barn, where Samantha stood talking to Pepper, the wedding planner, whom Chelsea had met several months back when Des had started talking about wanting to do the event in the barn.

Back then, Chelsea had wondered if Des was out of her mind, but she told Pepper—and all of them—that she had a vision. Logan loved this land, and she had fallen in love with it as well. She didn't want a fancy Hollywood wedding or something out of the country. She wanted to get married on this land, with all of Logan's family and friends present. Des thought the barn was big enough to accommodate all their guests and could be converted to a reception area, with the ceremony taking place just outside.

"This looks amazing," Jane said.

Pepper smiled. "Thank you. We're still setting up outside, and flowers won't be brought in until tomorrow, but I think it's fantastic. Des's vision was perfect."

"I can't wait to bring the flowers in," Samantha said. "I'd love to stay and visit, but I need to finish everything up back at the shop. I'll likely be working all night."

Chelsea worried about Samantha. She spent so much time

working, then taking care of her grandmother. And she did it all on her own.

"Do you have someone to help you?"

Samantha nodded. "Yes, I've got a couple of people to assist. I've been working on it awhile now."

Chelsea was relieved to hear that. "If you need anything, Sam, you holler, okay?"

Samantha hugged her. "Thanks. You're a good friend. I'll see you all later."

"If you head out the main doors there," Pepper said to them, pointing, "you can see where the wedding ceremony will take place."

"Great. And this really does look wonderful."

"Thanks. If you'll excuse me, I have a million things to do."

"I'll bet you do," Jane said. "Let's go, Chelsea."

They headed toward the doors and pushed them open.

"Wow again," Jane said. "Look at these stone walking steps. It'll look beautiful tomorrow when Des walks from the barn to the altar."

"And speaking of the altar, have you ever seen anything more beautiful?"

It was a charming, rustic archway, grand in scope and flanked by the most stunning twist of corkscrew willow she'd ever seen. The chairs had been set up, and she could already envision Des walking down the aisle.

"Samantha said she had a flower setting for the top—all coral and white roses. And Penny said they're tying in the white silk along the sides tomorrow. I can't wait to see it."

Jane nodded. "This wedding is going to be perfect."

Chelsea's phone buzzed. She looked at the display. "Martha said the ladies from the nail salon are here."

"Let's get back to the house."

They ran into Callie and Sarah, Colt and Tony's good friends.

"I hear you're doing our hair and makeup for tomorrow," Chelsea said.

Sarah grinned. "We're so excited about this."

"We're excited to have two Hollywood stylists doing our hair and makeup," Jane said.

"But first, nails, so excuse us."

They made their way into one of the back rooms, where Filomena was already setting up with her crew.

Filomena had been doing Chelsea's nails for years. She was one of the best, and, in fact, had originally hailed from New York City. Des had tried her out on numerous occasions and had asked her and her crew to do the manis and pedis for the wedding. Filomena happily agreed. Her own daughter, Connie, had recently gotten married, so she filled them in on her wedding while they sat and were pampered by Filomena's staff.

"What about Jeff Armstrong?" Jane said to Emma while they were getting their nails done.

Emma blinked. "What?"

"The doctor."

"I know who he is, Jane. I just don't know what you're talking about."

"Oh. Sorry. I was just zoning out here and I started thinking about Chelsea's list. What about Jeff?"

"Don't ask me," Emma said. "Ask Chelsea."

Since she'd been listening in anyway, Chelsea thought for a minute. "I hadn't thought about Jeff. He's nice. But he works crazy hours at the hospital."

"What she's trying to say is there's no chemistry there," Megan said. "I just don't see the two of you together. Which doesn't mean it couldn't work. You should ask him out, Chelsea."

"I am not asking him out."

Emma frowned. "Why not?"

Chelsea shrugged. "I don't know. Besides, like I said, he's not on my radar."

"Well, honey, you have that list and you're not dating anyone at the moment, so somebody needs to get on your radar."

She knew that. She'd been trying. "I'll start working on the list after the wedding."

"What are you all talking about?" Penny asked.

"Chelsea has a list of qualities she's looking for in her ideal man," Des explained to her sister.

"Oh. That's very logical. What kinds of qualities?"

Chelsea explained her list of attributes to Penelope and Des's mother.

"It's a good list. You know what you want and you aren't willing to settle," Penny said. "Now me, I'm not even looking. I'm married to my job and I prefer it that way."

Des sighed. "Penny, you're smart and you're beautiful. I want you to be happy."

Penny looked over at Des and smiled. "I am happy, Des. I don't need a man to fulfill me. My life's work does that."

"You know what?" Des said. "I do believe you. And I'm happy you've found the love of your life in biology."

Penny grinned. "Thanks."

"I miss the days when men and women just . . . met each other and fell in love," Cynthia said. "Now it's dating sites and careers and lists. No offense, Chelsea."

Chelsea laughed. "None taken."

"Hey now, Mom," Des said. "Logan and I just . . . met each other. It was kismet. The old-fashioned way."

Cynthia cast a loving smile at Des. "Yes, you did. And we're so happy for you."

Chelsea was so glad to see Des bonding well with her family. She knew her relationship with them had been strained for a while. But Logan had facilitated a reunion of sorts, and Des was happier now than ever.

Especially this weekend. It was like beams of light were shooting from her pores. She practically glowed with sunshine.

As it should be for a woman about to marry the man she loved.

Chelsea sighed. She wanted to feel that way someday. About someone. Right now all she felt was that there was some imaginary guy in her head that would zap her right between the eyes as soon as she met him.

Which could be this weekend.

She always had hope.

After their nails were done, everyone went upstairs to get ready for the rehearsal. Chelsea wasn't even the bride, and still she felt the thrum of excitement fluttering through her as she got ready for tonight's events. She was sharing a bedroom with Megan and Samantha. Neither was in the wedding party, but Sam was doing the flowers and Megan had made the wedding cake, which was currently well put away in one of the refrigerators downstairs. Des still considered both Megan and Sam a huge part of her wedding. Tomorrow night they'd all stay over at the ranch.

Chelsea was looking forward to all of it.

They changed clothes and got ready for the rehearsal. Chelsea had bought a new dress and shoes for the occasion. As she looked in the mirror, she admired her fantastic, fitted blue dress that would show off her legs—and her awesome sparkly shoes. Gorgeous, and she'd bought the entire outfit for less than seventy dollars.

One of her favorite things was bargain shopping. Everyone thought she had an unlimited budget for expensive clothing. Ha. Not on a teacher's salary. She did a lot of online shopping at great sites that offered designer clothes and shoes at discount prices. She could look expensive without actually *being* expensive. She knew how to manage her money—and how not to waste it.

They made their way outside and to the barn, where Des— who looked amazing in a short, beige dress and killer sparkly heels—was holding Logan's hand. They were talking to the minister, and Des's wedding planner was there with her ever-present notebook.

She spotted Bash standing with Carter, Luke, and Evan.

She'd purposely blocked out her last interlude with him out of sheer mortification. She'd had a great time the night of the bachelorette party. She'd also had more than a little too much to drink, but not enough that she didn't remember kissing Bash after he'd so gallantly carried her up to bed.

Or the way he'd so sweetly turned her down. A lot of guys would have taken what she'd so blatantly offered.

Not Bash. And it wasn't because he wasn't interested. She knew better. He'd offered sex to her when they'd had dinner that night. She'd turned him down then. Yet when she'd propositioned him the night of the bachelorette party—oh so drunkenly—he'd said no.

She had no idea what that meant.

Nothing. That's what it meant. He probably thought she was a flake. Saying no one minute then trying to seduce him the next.

She hadn't seen him since the night of the bachelorette party, and she'd prefer to never see him again.

But since at that moment he happened to look her way and smile, she supposed the whole idea of never seeing him again wasn't going to work. So she smiled back.

Not at all awkward.

Much.

Pepper motioned them all to move down to the front of the walkway leading toward the altar.

"Okay, everyone. Let's get this started. I'm going to get all the participants in place in the back, then Reverend Solis will let you all know how the ceremony will happen tomorrow. So if the bridal party can follow me, we'll get into positions."

Des hadn't yet decided who was going to be paired up, so it was going to be a surprise to Chelsea who she was going to be walking with. She was super thrilled that Des had asked her to be in the wedding party at all, but Des had told her she considered them all friends now, and she didn't have a lot of friends.

Chelsea had been touched. She, Molly, Emma, and Jane had grown close to Des in the past several months. Des was as down-to-earth as the rest of her friends, and she was so happy for her.

"Okay. First up will be Molly, and you'll be paired with Carter."

Molly grinned as she slipped her arm in Carter's. "Funny how that worked out," Molly said.

"I like my partner," Carter said.

"You two will walk down the aisle together, then separate at the front of the altar and take your places on the stone markers," Pepper said.

They both nodded, then headed down the aisle.

"Next are Will and Jane."

Jane and Will smiled at each other and headed down the aisle.

Obviously, Des was matching up the couples, which made logical sense. At least those who were coupled up.

"After they go, it's Sebastian and Chelsea."

Her heart did a small leap in her chest, but she masked it by taking a step forward.

"I like my choice of partner, too," Bash said, laying his hand over Chelsea's.

"You'll do. For now," she said, trying her best not to make eye contact with Bash as they stopped at the last row of chairs.

They started walking, and Chelsea was conscious of her hand on Bash's arm, his body so close to hers. She mentally tried not to walk too fast. This wasn't her first time as a bridesmaid. She'd done it for several of her friends over the years. And Bash did a fine job keeping step with her.

She had to admit, though, that she was happy to reach the altar.

"Here, you'll let go of his arm and make your way to your position," Reverend Solis said. "Don't go too fast."

She nodded and made her way over to where Jane and Molly stood, then turned to watch Emma and Reid make their way down the aisle.

Obviously, that would be the only change in couples, since Des's sister was the maid of honor and Logan's brother was the best man, so those two would be paired up.

And last to come up was Colt, whom Des had also included as man of honor. He walked by himself and took his position on Des's side, next to Penny.

After that, the reverend walked them through the ceremony and what would happen. They finished and headed back down the aisle, forcing Chelsea to once again walk with Bash.

At least he was quiet. She wasn't sure whether that was helpful or made it worse, since his silence only made her more conscious of his body. Of what he might be thinking.

Which made her think. Which she shouldn't be doing, because her thoughts were all about him.

Ugh.

But finally, it was over, and everyone headed to the guest lodge near the house, where there was catered food along with rows of tables.

Martha had wanted to cook, but Des had insisted the food tonight be catered.

"You have a big part in the wedding tomorrow," Des told her when Martha frowned at the tablecloths and fancy settings. "Tonight and tomorrow, you get to sit back and enjoy yourself."

Martha shook her head. "It's weird not to cook and serve up the food when we have company."

Logan put his arm around the woman who helped raise him. "Think of it as a vacation."

She lifted her gaze to his and smiled. "I'll try."

They all took to their tables for a fantastic dinner. Pepper had taken care of the seating arrangements, and the wedding party was seated together. Since a lot of the couples were together or married, she ended up seated next to Bash, since they were partners in the wedding party.

She decided not to be uncomfortable with it. So she'd drunkenly kissed him. And he'd turned her down. She was an adult. She could handle this.

Mid-meal, she turned to him and asked, "How's Lou doing?"

"Good. Like she's lived in my house all her life. I took her in to see Emma on Monday for a checkup."

"And?"

"Emma said she's fine. She's a healthy weight, and I managed to wrangle her shot records from Gerri, so she's updated on all that. We're good to go."

Chelsea picked up her glass of wine and took a sip, then nodded. "I'm glad to hear that. I've been thinking a lot about . . . her."

Bash's lips ticked up. "Have you?"

"Yes." She laid her wineglass down and focused her attention on the food.

"And how was your recovery from your night of debauchery?"

She looked around to make sure no one else had heard that. "I have no idea what you're talking about."

"The night of the bachelorette party. When I found you passed out outside in the cold and carried you up to bed."

"I don't remember that at all, but thank you."

He leaned in, his arm brushing hers. "Then you don't remember kissing me."

She turned her head, her gaze colliding with his, sending all her senses haywire. She struggled for balance. "A gentleman wouldn't bring that up."

"But you know I'm not a gentleman, Chelsea."

"You were that night."

He grinned. "So you do remember."

Dammit. "It's hazy. Bits and pieces only."

His lips touched her ear as he leaned in to whisper to her, "I'll be glad to refresh your memory."

His breath was warm, caressing her neck, the left side of his body touching the right side of hers, causing chill bumps to break out all over her skin.

She looked around to see if anyone was watching. They were all engaged in conversation and no one was looking at her and Bash. She turned to face him, their lips only inches apart.

She remembered that kiss, oh so vividly, had replayed it in her head every night this week as she lay in bed, wondering what would have happened if he hadn't been a gentleman, if he'd pressed her to the bed and done what she knew they both had wanted to do.

But he hadn't, and she remembered being oh so disappointed, which was stupid. He'd done the right thing. Just like she was going to do the right thing now, despite the crazy signals her body was throwing at her.

"No."

He shrugged. "Okay." Then he dug into his food as if he hadn't just upended her entire nervous system.

Deciding self-preservation was vital, she turned her attention to Molly, who sat on her other side.

After dinner and toasts, which were lovely, everyone drifted off into groups. The women headed into the house for wine, while the guys moved toward one of the barns to talk horses and ranch stuff or whatever it was that guys talked about when they were in a group.

Chelsea was content to get away from Bash. She'd have to deal with him as her partner tomorrow, at least during the wedding festivities. Other than that, she was going to keep a lookout for men who might fit her list. That was her priority.

She was already looking forward to tomorrow.

For so many reasons that had nothing to do with Bash.

Or so she tried to convince herself.

Chapter 12

CHELSEA STOOD AT the altar, trying to keep her tears in check as Des and Logan said their vows. Des looked stunning in her dress. A cream silk, off-the-shoulder gown that clung to her slender frame, it had long lace sleeves and made her look like a princess. But the back was cut low and sexy. It was one of a kind.

Just like Des.

Chelsea had seen the look on Logan's face as Des had walked down the aisle with her dad. That was a look of pure love, the same look on Des's face. She couldn't be happier for both of her friends.

And as they said their vows, her gaze drifted over to Bash, who at that moment made eye contact with her.

His lips lifted, and she felt that tug of . . . something . . . toward him.

Which was absolutely ridiculous. Sure, he looked amazing in his black tux, his white shirt a perfect complement to his tanned skin, his goatee nicely trimmed, and his mouth . . .

Ridiculous. She was being ridiculous. That "something" she felt was chemistry, and chemistry most definitely was *not* on her list. Chemistry was like the kiss she'd had with Bash. All hot fireworks, but that would eventually burn itself out, and then what would be left?

Nothing.

She was not in the market for nothing. She wanted forever, and Bash was not a forever kind of guy. He was a few hot romps in the sack, then move on to the next woman. She'd never be one of those women.

She shifted her gaze on Des and Logan, forcing herself to listen to the reverend talk about love and commitment, two things Bash obviously wasn't interested in at all.

But she was. And some man would be. That's why he would be perfect.

After a short ceremony, the reverend pronounced the couple husband and wife. Logan scooped Des up in a hot, passionate kiss that made even Chelsea blush—and there wasn't a whole lot that made her blush. Everyone clapped, then Des and Logan led the wedding party down the aisle.

She met Bash at the altar. He gave her his arm, and since both a photographer and videographer were there, she smiled at Bash and slid her hand through his arm. They walked down the aisle together and around the barn.

While the rest of the guests piled into the barn for appetizers and drinks, the wedding party and families spent a half hour or so taking pictures at the altar. It was fun, but Chelsea would be happy when she didn't have to stand next to Bash anymore. He looked too good, and he smelled like her favorite wintergreen-scented candle. Every time he slipped his arm around her waist, she was way too conscious of him—his body and damn near everything about him.

Finally, photos were finished and they headed toward the barn, where Des and Logan were introduced as husband and wife to a round of loud applause.

The bridal party surrounded them while they danced, and then the wedding party all danced so the photographer could take pictures, which meant she and Bash danced together. She absolutely would not notice how tall he was, even though she had on a pair of very high heels.

She also refused to notice how well they fit together, or how perfectly he danced. He wasn't clumsy at all. And he sure did clean up well. He might not be a suit and tie kind of guy, but the man was born to wear a tux.

"You're staring at me," he said. "And I know I don't have spinach in my teeth—yet."

"I was just thinking how great you look in a tux."

He gave her a sexy smile. "That might almost make your list, Chelsea."

She shook her head. "No, it wouldn't, because you don't wear them all the time."

"This is true. These things are uncomfortable as hell. I prefer jeans and a T-shirt."

He also fit those quite well. Not that she paid much attention.

"Where's Lou tonight?"

"My neighbors are watching her. They have a Shih Tzu that Lou sees at the backyard fence, and they've gotten friendly, so Kerry and Bill offered to keep her tonight."

"That's nice of them."

"Yeah."

"What do you do with her when you're working?"

"She comes with me. I bring her crate, but the patrons are getting used to her wandering around. She's pretty well-behaved and she's adjusting to hanging out at the bar. When she gets tired, she wanders into her crate and goes to sleep."

"I'm glad you're both adjusting."

"Me, too. Though we have to work on her not eating things she's not supposed to."

Chelsea tilted her head back. "Like?"

"My tennis shoe, the other day. Now it has gnaw marks on the toe."

She couldn't help but laugh. "Maybe she needs more chew toys."

"That's what Emma told me. But I bought her toys. She still ate my shoe."

Chelsea shrugged. "Don't ask me. I don't have dogs."

He twirled her around, circling the dance floor with ease.

She had to admit she felt comfortable in his arms, almost as if she belonged there. She'd danced with a lot of guys before. Some of them were clumsy, some stepped on her toes, and some—like Bash—danced with confidence. He held her hand firmly, but didn't crush it. He had a good hold on her back, and he directed her, instead of expecting her to lead, like a lot of guys who had no idea how to dance.

She had to admit, she liked that. And the way he looked at her. His gaze didn't wander. He had gorgeous eyes, and amazing lashes. He pulled her closer, her breasts pillowed against his chest.

She shouldn't enjoy being held in his arms, but she did. He had a rock-hard body, and she'd felt every inch of it against hers when he'd kissed her at his house. She also hadn't been so drunk last week that she couldn't remember how good he'd tasted when she'd kissed him again.

Foolish thoughts. He wasn't the right guy for her. Still, that temptation lingered. And his hand roamed along her back . . .

"Place is full," Bash said, drawing her attention away from the way their bodies glided together.

"Yes."

"So are you going to try to find Mr. Perfect here tonight?"

She frowned at his smug smile. How could he be so delicious to look at and to kiss and so utterly wrong for her? "I might."

As the song ended, he took a step back. "I'll be sure to be on the lookout for him. If I see someone who I think fits, I'll send him your way."

There it was again, that feeling of rightness in his arms, while he was trying to find someone else for her.

So. Irritating.

She nodded. "You do that."

She walked away and headed for the main table, where the wedding party would sit for dinner. Where she'd be required to sit next to him again.

But only temporarily. She would be scouting this wedding for Mr. Perfect.

And it sure as hell wouldn't be Bash.

Chapter 13

BASH LEANED AGAINST the bar, nursing a bottle of beer as he watched couples crowd the dance floor.

He'd done his duty and stood up for his best friend tonight. Logan and Des were currently tangled in the crush of bodies on the dance floor doing some kind of line dance to a country song.

Logan couldn't dance for shit, but he was doing his best to keep up with his bride. Bash pondered whipping out his phone to get video of this, but he knew Logan wouldn't be embarrassed like some of his other friends would be. He'd just watch the video and laugh. So what was the point?

But he really was a bad dancer. Good thing Des loved him. She grabbed his arm and kept trying to direct him to the correct foot to lead off on.

Waste of time. Logan would never get it.

Bash slid his empty toward the bartender and asked for another, feeling strange to be on this side of the bar tonight. It was a good thing he had great staff to fill in for him at No Hope at All. He couldn't remember the last time he'd had two Saturday nights off. Probably . . .

Never. He worked weekends. It was his bar, his baby. He took nights off during the week, but weekends were busy, and it was his responsibility to be there. Fortunately, over the past few years he'd hired competent staff, and Hall, his assistant manager, was doing a great job. He knew Hall could handle anything that came up tonight. Bash could relax and enjoy himself.

He pushed off the bar and wandered around, stopping to visit with people he knew, which was pretty much everyone except the handful of Hollywood people in attendance. And he actually had gotten to know a few of those as well. Colt and Tony made regular visits to Hope to hang out with Des and Logan, and they often stopped at the bar to visit, so he'd gotten close to them. They were great guys and a good, solid couple.

His gaze strayed across the room and landed on Chelsea, who was deep in conversation with Jeff Armstrong, one of Hope's ER docs.

Bash frowned. He knew Jeff was single. He mentally compared Jeff with Chelsea's list.

He didn't see a fit there. Maybe according to her list, but Bash just didn't see it.

When Chelsea got up and walked away, Bash met her halfway across the room.

He grasped her arm. "Jeff Armstrong?"

"What about him?"

"I don't see it."

She lifted her chin. "Why not?"

"He works a lot of nights and weekends in the ER, ya know."

"I do know that. And we were just chatting."

"Did he ask you out?"

"And this is your business in what way, Bash?"

In no way. He didn't even know why he cared who she decided to go out with. But he did. "I told you I was going to find men for you that met your list, right?"

"You did say that."

"If you've already found one, I won't waste my time."

Her gaze met his, and that collision of blue green never failed to tighten his gut. "Really, Bash. Either way, don't waste your time."

He slid his hand down her arm, tangling his fingers with hers. "Oh, but I'm interested in your happiness, Chelse."

She let out a laugh. "I'll bet you are."

He shifted in closer. "In ways you can't even imagine."

He caught the wary look in her eyes.

"Stop that, Bash," she whispered.

"Stop what?"

"You know what. Teasing me like that."

His thumb traced the inside of her wrist, felt the rapid beat of her pulse. "I never tease. I only . . . offer."

He liked watching the high wash of color appear on her cheeks, and the way the rhythm of her breathing changed whenever they talked.

There was something going on between them, and he wanted to explore it. He knew Chelsea did, too.

"Wanna take a walk with me?"

She cocked a brow. "Absolutely not."

He gave her a half smile. "You change your mind, you know where to find me."

He let go of her hand and turned around, then walked away.

No, Jeff Armstrong was definitely not the right guy for her.

CHELSEA HEADED INTO the main house, upstairs and into the bedroom she'd stayed in last night. She closed the door and sat on the bed, but her pulse was still racing, so she stood and went into the bathroom and turned on the light.

Her cheeks were pink and her body felt warm despite the night chill in the air. And it wasn't like she was wearing a heavy dress. These strapless bridesmaid dresses were light and airy, and she felt like she was walking on a cloud. So she wasn't overdressed.

She was . . . overheated. And it was all Bash's fault. She'd spent twenty minutes having a very nice conversation with Jeff Armstrong. He was tall, dark haired, good looking, intelligent, attentive, and a great conversationalist. He was a fine doctor, and he'd lived in Hope his entire life, which was why he'd decided to come back there and practice medicine. She'd really enjoyed their conversation. A conversation that left her feeling . . . nothing. She'd so wanted to feel something. Anything. But all she'd left with was the feeling that some woman was going to be very lucky to have him someday.

And that woman was never going to be her, because they'd had absolutely no chemistry. No pop or zing or zap or anything like that.

Three minutes with Bash and she'd been about to self-combust. In the span of one short conversation he'd managed to irritate her and send her libido into overdrive. What *was* it about that man, anyway? Why did she keep allowing him to get to her?

"Chelsea? Are you in here?"

At the sound of Megan's voice, she quickly turned on the water and grabbed a washcloth, dampening it so she could cool down her wrists. Maybe that would help douse the flame.

"In the bathroom."

"Are you all right?"

She rubbed the washcloth over her wrists and arms, then laid it over the sink and turned to her friend with a smile. "I'm fine. I just got a little warm out there."

"Really? I would think the walk over here would have cooled you off. It's a little chilly outside."

"Maybe it's hot flashes."

Samantha peeked her head in as well. "Seriously, Chelsea? You're a little too young for hot flashes."

"Whatever. I had some wine. Maybe I'm drunk."

Megan inspected her. "You are not drunk. I know your drunk look."

The drawback of having friends who knew you all too well. "Whatever. I'm fine now. Did you need me for something?"

"No. We just saw you dash over here and wanted to be sure you were okay."

And that's what happened when you had friends who loved you. She grasped both their hands. "Thank you. I'm fine. Like I said, I just got a little warm."

Sam leaned against the doorway. "So Bash got you hot and bothered when he whispered in your ear again?"

Her knees wobbled. "What? Of course not. What makes you think that?"

"Because we saw him holding your hand, leaning in close, and whispering in your ear," Megan said. "And God, does he look hot tonight or what?"

She refused to comment on the second part of Megan's statement. Instead, she brushed past them and headed into the bedroom. For this, she was going to need to think fast. She took a seat on the bed. "He was asking me about Jeff Armstrong and whether or not Jeff met the criteria of my list."

Sam's eyes widened. "Bash knows about your list?"

"He inadvertently heard me talking to his dog about it."

Megan blinked. "I don't even understand that part, but okay. What does he think about your list?"

"Bash? He thinks it's stupid. But he says he's going to help me find the perfect guy. He already set me up on one date that didn't quite work out."

"You had a date we didn't know about?" Megan asked.

"Really not worth mentioning, if you know what I mean."

Megan nodded. "Understood. And sorry it didn't pan out."

"Bash is going to find a man for you." Sam sat on the bed next to her, then looked over at Megan. "I find that . . . uh . . . interesting."

"You do? Why?"

Sam shrugged. "No reason. Just interesting."

"Now you have to tell me, Sam."

Sam looked over at Megan. It was like the two of them shared a secret and she had no idea what it was. "Come on you two. Tell me."

"I think what Sam means," Megan said, "is that he's single, divorced, rarely has a relationship, and he's going to find you a guy?"

"Sure. That's exactly what I meant," Sam said.

Chelsea was pretty sure that wasn't at all what she meant. "I get it. He's not exactly the right person to go finding the perfect guy for me. But he says he knows a lot of men. And not just through the bar. At this point I'm interested in meeting men I haven't dated before. So if Bash can come up with suitable candidates, then I'm all for it."

Again that look between Sam and Megan.

She huffed out a sigh. "What?"

"Nothing," Megan said. "Anyway, I saw you talking to Jeff. How did that go?"

"Oh, it went great. He's so nice, but you know he's really busy. He's spearheading the opening of the new urgent care clinic on the east side of town, so he was telling me about it."

"I heard about the new clinic," Sam said. "Which means he'll be even busier. So, any sparks fly between you and Dr. Jeff?"

"Unfortunately, no. I think I'm going to have to cross him off my list."

"What list?"

They looked up to see the gorgeous bride leaning against the bedroom doorway.

Chelsea couldn't help but get a little teary-eyed seeing Des standing there looking so elegant with her hair swept up and wearing that gown. Wow, that gown. "You look so beautiful. Are you having a good time, Mrs. McCormack?"

Des grinned. "I sure like hearing that name. And yes, I am. Now, what list?"

"Chelsea's perfect-guy list," Megan said.

"Oh, right." Des came in and took a seat in one of the chairs next to the door. "God, my feet hurt and it feels so good to sit down for like five minutes. I'm going to hide out here for just a few."

"Want me to close the door?" Sam asked.

Des laughed. "No, I'm fine just sitting for a few. So anyway, back to your list. How's that going?"

Chelsea filled her in on what they'd been talking about. Des cocked a brow and shared a look with Megan and Sam.

"Interesting."

She sure would like to know what they all found so interesting. It was like they were telling a joke and she didn't get the punch line.

"So no Dr. Jeff." Des leaned forward. "Hey, I have an idea. Let's go sit you down next to Logan's brother Reid, who is quite the stud and meets all your criteria."

Chelsea thought about Reid for a moment. She knew him—vaguely, from his infrequent trips to town. "This is true. Except he lives in Boston."

Des waved her hand. "A minor drawback. Besides, you're unattached, and so is he. If nothing else, you get someone to dance with tonight."

Chelsea looked at her friends. "All right."

Des took her hand and led her back to the barn. The party was still going strong. And why wouldn't it be? The chandeliers were lit in such a romantic way, music was playing, and Chelsea had a feeling no one was leaving early tonight.

She tried to catch sight of Bash, though for what reason she had no idea. Who cared where he was, anyway? Probably drinking with his buddies somewhere.

Or in the middle of the group of guys—Logan, Luke, Carter, Reid, Will, Colt, and Tony—that Des dragged her to, along with Samantha and Megan.

The men were all gathered around a table, drinking beer and talking.

"You're not all going to break out a poker game, are you?" Des asked. "Because if you are, I'm totally in."

They all stood and Logan came around the table, slipped his arm around his wife, and kissed her. "Not a chance. Not tonight, anyway."

"Too bad," Des said. "Poker sounds fun."

"What are you all doing?" Logan asked.

"Just hanging out with the girls."

Logan pulled a chair out for Des, and the guys made room for the rest of them.

"Where are Molly, Jane, and Emma?" Chelsea asked.

Luke motioned with his head. "On the dance floor."

Chelsea searched the dance floor and finally located the three of them, barefoot and jumping up and down to a popular hip-hop song.

She grinned. "Awesome."

"Reid, I had just started telling the girls about your last job in Boston."

Which she had not, but Des could start and hold a conversation better than anyone.

"Is that right?" Reid arched a brow.

"Yes. But I didn't really get that far into it, so why don't you explain it to them?"

"I renovated a historic building in Boston. It was actually the first historical renovation I've done."

"You're an architect, right?" Chelsea asked.

He nodded. "Yes. Mainly new buildings, so this was a new venture for me. To mix the old with the new."

He started describing the work he'd done, giving her a chance to study him. Reid—who was incredibly good-looking in the oh-my-God-they're-gorgeous McCormack way, was tall. After seeing him at the wedding earlier, standing beside his brothers, she thought it was a wonder it had taken all the McCormacks this long to get married. Though Reid was still single, and since he hadn't brought anyone to the wedding, she assumed he was unattached as well.

His dark hair was cut short, and he had the same bluish-green eyes as Luke. He was a bit leaner than Luke, though, and not quite as tall as Logan. Still, he looked striking in his tux, especially with the tie undone and the shirt unbuttoned at the neck. She could imagine him as quite the lady-killer.

Yet she felt no attraction to him in the least. While she appreciated the masculine vibe and the way he looked, there was no ping to her feminine radar.

Clearly, there was something wrong with her, because as eligible bachelors went, Reid was definitely a catch. And while she was firmly rooted in Hope, she could definitely while away a few hours with a very attractive man. As she listened to him talk about the renovation he'd done in Boston, it was clear he was intelligent, as well as passionate about his work.

"That's fascinating," Samantha said, turning her chair toward his, since she was the one who'd ended up sitting next to Reid. "I'm not sure if you're aware of this or not—you're probably not since you no longer live in Hope—but the old

mercantile building on the corner of Fifth and Main is due
for demolition." She looked around at everyone. "You all
know that old building? It's been standing as long as I can
remember. It's just around the corner from my flower shop.
And from Carter's auto repair shop as well."

"We all know the place," Luke said. "It's one of the first
places that was built in Hope. It's got to be . . . what? A hundred years old?"

"Why are they tearing it down?" Megan asked.

"You know the mayor. It's all about newness and progress."
Sam rolled her eyes. "But this building is beautiful. Do you
remember the one I'm talking about, Reid?"

He leaned back in his chair. "Yeah. The place has great bones."

Sam wriggled in her chair. "It does, doesn't it? My
Grammy Claire did her banking there. Her parents did as
well. She's upset about them tearing it down."

"I think Dad banked there, too," Logan said. "And
Grandad."

Carter nodded. "Probably generations have. I don't know
what kind of shape it's in or if it's even salvageable. The
outside still looks good, but who knows what's going on
inside. Maybe Reid could take a look."

They all turned to Reid. He shrugged. "I'll drive over there
tomorrow. Since it's Sunday, I can take a look, at least at the
outside."

Samantha laid her hand on his arm. "That would be great.
Thanks so much."

Reid definitely looked back at Sam. "It'd be my pleasure."

And that, Chelsea thought, as she saw the way Sam's eyes
sparkled when she looked at Reid, was the chemistry she
didn't have with him. But the way his lips rose when he made
eye contact with Sam? Yeah . . . right there.

Chelsea locked gazes with Bash at just that moment, and
his lips ticked into a knowing smile. The one that said, *Yeah,
I got your chemistry right here, babe.*

Or maybe that was all in her head.

Des gave her a very subtle shrug, but Chelsea just smiled
at her.

It was either there or it wasn't. And with Reid, she'd known it right away.

It wasn't there. Which was fine. She was content to party tonight with her girlfriends. They all ended up kicking off their shoes and joining Molly, Emma, and Jane on the dance floor. It felt good to release a little tension and not worry about her list, or a man.

Tonight, she just wanted to enjoy herself and celebrate her friend Des, who ended up in the center of a circle, surrounded by all her girls, while they danced like crazy until Chelsea couldn't breathe. And when a slow song came on, all the guys came out to dance with their women. Chelsea started to make her exit off the dance floor, until a pair of arms encircled her waist.

"Not so fast."

Before she had a chance to object, she was in his arms, the two of them dangling at the edge of the dance floor.

"I was going to get a drink and catch my breath," she said.

"You can catch your breath in a minute. I'll take it slow."

Was anything with Bash ever slow? Whenever she was with him it always felt like her heart rate doubled its beats per minute. Fast. Faster. A little out of control, and a whole lot of breathless.

Why couldn't she have felt this when she talked to Reid, or to Jeff? Why did she have this incendiary chemistry with Bash, who was all wrong for her?

Maybe that was the problem. It was just chemistry, and she needed to get past it so she could move on. Trying to ignore it wasn't working, because they ran in the same circles. They had the same friends. He was always going to be around, and though they'd known each other for years, there hadn't been this intense . . . desire for him before.

Now there was. And it was getting in the way of her goals.

Maybe she should just sleep with him and get over it. Get over him. Then she could focus on Mr. Perfect. Who she knew—even Bash knew—wasn't him.

The problem was, she wasn't a one-night-stand kind of woman. She wasn't into casual sex. She took sex pretty seriously, and it usually came attached to a relationship.

So could she scratch that sexual itch and then walk away?

"I'm surprised smoke isn't coming out of your ears right now."

She tilted her head to the side. "What?"

"You're staring holes through me, and I can hear the gears turning in your brain. What's on your mind?"

"You, actually."

"Yeah? What about me?"

"I'm pondering having sex with you because you keep showing up on my radar and it's preventing me from finding the perfect man. So if you and I have sex, maybe I'll get you out of my system and I can move on."

Bash blinked. "Uh . . . what?"

Chelsea gave him a look. "You heard me the first time."

Chelsea almost smiled at his confusion as he said, "Yeah, but most women I know wouldn't . . ."

She rolled her eyes. "Bash, most of the women—and I use the word *women* loosely—most of the women you date are too young to have learned to be honest about how they feel. They're still into playing games and using lies and deception to land a man. Like Gemma—"

"Gerri—" he corrected.

"Whatever. Like Gerri, who got an actual, live dog to impress you. That's immaturity. Maybe you should consider reevaluating your standards."

His gaze narrowed, but then he shrugged. "Maybe I should."

"Good."

"But back to you hitting on me."

"Oh, for God's sake, Bash. I wasn't hitting on you. I was pondering a logical way to eliminate this chemistry we seem to have together."

"That sounds analytical and not sexy."

"Exactly."

"Like your list, right?"

"Hey, there's nothing wrong with my list."

"So you say."

He tugged her against his chest and let his hand wander across her back, his fingers dangling dangerously close to her butt. "I can take care of your . . . problem. *And* make it sexy."

She met his dark, promising words with a challenging glare. "That's not what I want."

"You don't want it to be hot, Chelsea? You want it to be boring? Because I don't think I can do that."

That's what she was afraid of. "So sure of yourself, aren't you, Bash?"

He cupped the side of her neck and brought her mouth within a fraction of an inch to his. "Where you're concerned, I'm fucking positive."

Before she could take her next breath, his lips were on hers. Right there in the middle of the dance floor, where everyone could see.

This was so inappropriate. And so damn hot, with his arm wrapped tight around her, his mouth fused to hers.

Everything within her went haywire.

His kiss was a beacon to her fogged senses, drawing her in like a lifeline in a storm. She held on to his arms, and nothing existed in that moment except that kiss. She breathed him in, her synapses on overload as she felt the way his muscles tightened under her hand, heard his groan even through the loud music, and wanted nothing more than to lean in closer and take what he was offering.

Boring? Oh, no. Nothing with Bash could ever be boring. Not the way he kissed, or the way his body felt against hers.

And when he released her, he still kept that firm hold he had of her as he gripped her hand.

"Now we're gonna go have a chat. Away from all these people."

They strolled off the dance floor, stopping only long enough for Bash to grab her shoes.

Thank God her friends were all out on the dance floor and couldn't see her walking out with Bash, though they'd likely witnessed their hot kiss.

Not that she really cared at the moment.

She had no idea where he was taking her and it didn't matter. She was on a mission that had nothing to do with her list.

And everything to do with what she needed right this moment.

Chapter 14

BASH LED HER out of the barn and toward the house. A house that was too damn occupied for his liking. He stopped only long enough to let her slide her feet into those sparkly, fuck-me shoes she was so fond of wearing, slid his hand into his pocket and grabbed his keys, then led her to his truck.

"Where are we going?"

"I don't know. Someplace where there aren't a million people."

She tugged on his hand. "You need a plan, Bash."

"I have a plan. To get you alone."

Now the tug grew harder. "Wait. Let's think about this for a second."

He stilled, let go of her hand, and knew right then it wasn't going to happen between them.

Not tonight, anyway. Probably not ever. Inside, when he'd held her in his arms and kissed her, she'd been right there with him. She'd kissed him back, her sweet, lush body draped against his, every fiber of her filled with passion and abandon.

He'd felt it, had known right then how good it could be between them.

Now, that hot passion had fled and she was crunching numbers, or whatever logical thing it was that math teachers did. Whatever it was that had put her back in her head, he knew she wasn't coming with him.

He slid his keys back in his pocket. "Okay. You'd better go back inside. It's cold out here."

Her head did a slight tilt to the side, as if she was preparing herself to explain it to him. "Bash."

"Don't. I'm not some raging, horny teenager you have to let down easily, Chelsea. I can take a simple no."

Just then the front door of the house opened, and Martha stuck her head out. "Bash? Could you come here for a second?"

"Sure, Martha." He looked over at Chelsea. "See? There's your out."

"Bash, I'm not looking—"

"I gotta go. We'll talk later."

He walked toward the house, leaving her standing there. And maybe that was a shitty thing to do, but she was safe out there, and he needed to get away from her before he did something really stupid, like go back there and kiss her until she changed her mind.

CHELSEA STOOD OUTSIDE in the cold for a few minutes, needing the chill in the air to evaporate the heat that still surrounded her. She needed to clear the confusion from her head and the feel of Bash's body from every cell.

She looked toward the barn, hearing the sounds of partying and people laughing.

She didn't feel like partying anymore, but this night wasn't about her or how she felt. She owed it to Des to be by her side, so she headed back to the barn to join her friends.

She was immediately surrounded by Megan and Sam, who grabbed her arm and hustled her off to a corner.

"What was that kiss all about?" Megan asked her.

"Oh, nothing."

Samantha shot her a look. "Don't *nothing* me. It was definitely something."

She'd hoped they hadn't noticed. "Okay, it was something, but it ended up being nothing because, as you can see, we're not together. Nor will we ever be."

"And why not?" Megan asked.

"You know why not."

"Because of your list?"

"Yes."

Sam took a deep breath and sighed. "Honey, that list—"

"Is important to me," she interrupted. "Please don't tell me it doesn't matter. I'm tired and frustrated from spending years chasing after all the wrong guys. I want the right one."

Megan smoothed her hand over Chelsea's back. "And you're sure Bash is the wrong guy for you?"

"Positive. There might be a lot of chemistry between us, but trust me—he's all wrong for me."

Samantha nodded. "Okay, then. We'll double our efforts and find you the right man."

She felt better knowing she had her friends on her side. They went back to their table, and Chelsea sipped on a glass of wine, determined to enjoy the rest of the night.

She even danced with Reid and with Jeff and with a few other guys while trying her best to avoid Bash, who obviously was doing the same, since he didn't come near her the rest of the night. And maybe there was no electricity with these other men, but at least she didn't feel like a wallflower, either. And if Bash's kiss still burned hot on her lips, well, too bad. She knew the difference between chemistry and choice.

She was still young and attractive and desirable, and she was going to find the right man.

Just not tonight.

Chapter 15

AFTER A LONG, sleepless night at the ranch, Chelsea was awakened way too early the next morning by Sam and Megan, who decided she just had to join them on their drive into town with Reid, who was going to look over the old mercantile building.

"No." She pulled her pillow over her head.

"Oh, come on, Chelsea. It'll be fun."

Nothing about wandering around looking at a dusty old building in town sounded like fun to her. Especially not at whatever early o'clock in the morning it was.

"You have fun. I'm sleeping in."

"You can't sleep in. We neeeeed you."

She opened one eye at Sam's pleading tone, then rolled over, tossing the pillow aside. "You do not need me for this."

"Sure we do. Besides, everyone is going. And Martha said she's got breakfast on the table, so we're all going to eat first."

She smelled coffee downstairs. Martha made great coffee. She had also probably baked something, and Chelsea was a sucker for Martha's blueberry muffins. In response to the thought, her stomach grumbled.

Besides, it wasn't like Megan and Sam were going anywhere.

They currently sat on the edge of the other bed, staring her down.

She threw the covers aside. "Fine. Give me a few minutes to get ready."

Megan grinned. "Awesome."

Sam and Megan left the room and Chelsea took a fast shower, dried her hair, and slipped into a pair of jeans, a long-sleeved shirt, and her canvas shoes, then headed downstairs.

The kitchen was filled with people, some already seated at the table, some gathered around the island deep in conversation. The scent of food made her stomach growl even louder than it had upstairs.

"Good morning, Chelsea," Martha said, coming over to give her a kiss on the cheek.

"Morning, Martha. I see you were here early."

Martha grinned. "Of course. I had to make sure everyone had a decent breakfast. Megan was up early as well, so she helped bake a few things."

Megan sipped from a cup and leaned into Martha. "It was fun baking with you. You know I'm always trying to figure out your muffin recipe." Megan turned to Chelsea. "Unfortunately, she already had them in the oven before I made it into the kitchen."

Martha laughed. "Secret recipe. Handed down from my grandmother. And your blueberry muffins at the bakery are outstanding, Megan."

"Thank you, Martha. But nothing matches yours."

Chelsea shook her head at the two bakers complimenting each other, then made a beeline for the coffee, grabbing one of the available cups. She leaned against the counter and took several sips, letting the caffeine infuse her system and wake her up like nothing else could. As she drank her first cup, she surveyed the activity in the kitchen.

Des and Logan sat at the table, practically glued to each other while they ate. Logan was absently brushing his hand up and down Des's back. It was kind of nauseatingly sweet the way he touched her all the time, and the way Des leaned into him. Then again, Luke and Emma were the same way, always finding ways to hold hands or touch each other. So were Jane and Will.

And now that Molly and Carter were madly in love, they couldn't keep their hands off each other, either.

There really was nothing like a couple in love. As she surveyed the couples, she waited for that pang of envy to strike, but it never did.

It never had where her friends were concerned. While she'd always wanted that for herself, she never resented her friends being happy. In fact, she'd pushed them toward their happily ever afters, even when they'd balked.

That's what friends did. Sometimes love was blind, and her friends hadn't seen it when it was right in front of them.

That was never going to happen to her. When the right man for her came along, she'd know it.

"Are you gonna just drink coffee all mornin', or are you gonna sit down and have breakfast?" Martha asked, pinning her with that motherly look.

She pushed off the counter. "I'm going to sit down and have some of those blueberry muffins you and Megan were talking about."

"Good luck with that," Carter said. "Because we've just about eaten all of them."

Chelsea wedged her way into a spot between Molly and Megan, then glared at Carter. "Don't you dare eat the last one."

"Not to worry," Megan said. "There's another batch hidden away for those who decided to sleep away the morning."

Chelsea rolled her eyes. "It's like eight o'clock."

"Half the day is gone already," Logan said. "We've already milked the cows and fed the chickens."

She grabbed for a muffin from the fresh batch Martha set in front of them. "You're so funny, Logan, in no way whatsoever."

"Yeah, I can't imagine Chelsea getting in the mud with those high heels she wears."

That came from Bash, who sat at the other end of the table. "Fortunately for you, I'm way too much of a lady to throw my shoe at you. Which, by the way, is a tennis shoe today."

"Color me shocked," he said. "Maybe you are intending to feed the chickens."

She bit into the muffin and sighed at the burst of blueberry flavor, deciding not even Bash could ruin her high. "Not on your life. I'll leave that to the experts."

"The chickens are adorable," Des said. "And you're welcome to come feed them with me anytime."

As she poured a glass of orange juice, Chelsea graced Des with one of her thanks-but-no-thanks smiles. "Aren't you so sweet. But I'll take a rain check today since I guess we're all headed into town to check out that old building. Right, Reid?"

"I've been told there's a field trip this morning," Reid said. "Samantha has already called the city to get keys to the building."

"Ever the resourceful one, aren't you, Sam?"

Samantha nodded at Chelsea. "I figured if we were all going to go out to take a look, we should also get a peek inside. And my grandmother is a close friend of the mayor's parents, so he couldn't refuse my request."

It seemed as if they had a plan, and Chelsea had to admit she was curious about the old mercantile, which had been closed up for a couple of years now. It was a shame for it not to be used. It was a gorgeous old building, and she'd hate to see it torn down.

After breakfast she went upstairs to pack her things. She wouldn't be coming back, so Chelsea said her goodbyes to Martha and Ben, then they all loaded up in the cars and made the trek into Hope.

It was a caravan of vehicles, since Colt and Tony and their friends Callie and Sarah had wanted to make the trip as well.

So when they parked on the street, Chelsea counted at least ten vehicles.

It looked like a parade.

She got out of her car and walked nearly a block to meet up with everyone else. She was so used to driving into the main part of Hope and seeing the old mercantile that she never paid much attention to it. It had just . . . always been there on the corner. But now she studied it, since they had to wait for Sam, who was stopping off to get the keys.

It was a beautiful redbrick building, two stories. It was old and worn, but she couldn't imagine some fast-food joint or one of those fancy new drugstores replacing it.

"I didn't know you even cared about what went on in downtown Hope."

She really wanted to ignore Bash today. Or like . . . forever. "I care about a lot of things. This place is my home. Of course I love the old mercantile building. I'd hate to see it torn down." She turned to face him. "And what about you? I wouldn't think you'd care."

"Of course I care. What's good for the town is good for my business. It's not like I tore down the old bar and replaced it with a franchise. I like the history of our town. The mercantile is one of the oldest buildings still standing. Why they want to tear it down makes no sense to me."

At least they were in agreement on something.

"I love downtown," Colt said. "It's one of my favorite places to visit. I wish everyone was open today so we could shop."

"I could open the bakery for you, Colt," Megan said. "But it might take me a few hours to fix you some croissants."

"Please," Colt said, rubbing his stomach. "I'm already going to have to do some brutal gym time next week after all the food I've eaten the past few days."

Megan laughed. "Then no croissants for you."

When Sam arrived with the keys, she headed to the front door, and they all followed. She unlocked the door, then turned the knob to open it.

It stuck.

"Okay, that didn't work," she said.

Reid stepped beside her. "Let me try."

He turned the knob and gave the door a gentle shove with his shoulder. The door gave with a high-pitched squeal that made Chelsea wince.

Reid turned to them and shrugged. "Obviously it's been a while since anyone's been in here. I assume there's power."

Sam nodded. "Yes. I asked the mayor to have the city turn the electricity on here for the day."

Reid looked impressed. "You do have some stroke."

Sam laughed. "My grandmother does. She can be formidable."

"Let me find the light switch." Reid disappeared inside for a few minutes, and then Chelsea saw the lights come on through the door. He returned.

"It's pretty dusty inside, and since the windows are boarded up, if anyone has asthma issues, you might want to sit this one out."

Reid moved into the building, and Sam was the first one in after him, so Chelsea followed her.

The building was filled with old boxes and junk. Reid was right. It smelled musty, and a layer of dust coated everything.

It was a mess.

"Wow, this is amazing," Sam said as they made their way through the piles of junk.

"You think so?"

Sam nodded. "Look at the wood posts. And the staircase over there. Those handrails are stunning."

"Besides the dust and clutter, the place has a beautiful old antique feel to it," Tony said. "Do you have any original photos of it?"

"My grandmother does," Sam said. "She has photos of the original facade—a picture of her as a little girl standing outside the store. Her parents were visiting with the owners at the time."

"I'll bet that's an awesome photo," Colt said.

"It is. There used to be a soda shop inside here," Sam explained. "Grandma said she used to come in here all the time for ice cream and sodas."

"I'd like to see what's under these ceiling panels," Reid said, then grabbed a ladder that was leaning against the wall. He climbed up and popped one of the drop panels out. "Huh. There's a tin tile ceiling under here. Needs some refurbishing, but I'm sure it's the original ceiling."

"Amazing," Sam said. "Can I see?"

He climbed down and held his hand out to help her climb up. "Sure. Be careful."

"I think Reid's checking out her butt," Megan whispered as they watched Sam examine the ceiling.

Chelsea stifled a giggle. "You might be right about that."

The two of them certainly made a striking pair. Reid was tanned and incredibly masculine, and Samantha was petite and blond and so peaches and cream. Plus she was incredibly passionate about the mercantile. As Reid made his way through the building, the two of them stuck together like glue, talking about each piece of wood or what new treasure they might locate behind what old wall.

Chelsea found the old business fascinating, but it wasn't like her life depended on whether it was refurbished or not. She knew Samantha loved old buildings—her flower shop was located in one of Hope's older buildings, and she knew Sam adored her shop. It appeared she and Reid had a lot in common.

Interesting.

But, she had to admit after they made their way upstairs and looked at the potential of the old mercantile, the building had a lot to offer. She could already envision the possibilities, and as they left and made their way back outside—and thankfully, to fresh air—everyone was chattering about it. Especially the McCormack brothers.

"What's the verdict, Reid?" Logan asked. "Do you think it's possible to refurbish it?"

Reid tilted his head back to study the outside of the structure. "It would take a lot of work to restore, but it's definitely doable. The question is, what do we do with it?"

"You could do a retail establishment downstairs, and maybe office space upstairs," Samantha suggested. "Or office space downstairs, and condos upstairs. You have so much space, I think the possibilities are limitless."

"Sam has a point," Luke said. "I think there are a lot of possibilities for this place. It sure as hell shouldn't be torn down."

"Yeah, I can't see something new here in place of what's sitting here now." Logan grimaced. "I can still remember Dad bringing us here when we were kids. Remember?"

"I remember," Luke said.

"So what do you want to do?" Reid asked, turning to Logan and Luke. "Make an offer on it and buy it back from the city?"

Logan nodded. "I like the idea. And I think we could get the people of Hope invested in the idea. They might take to restoring it much more than some new drugstore or commercial building or whatever the mayor and city council have in mind."

"Agreed," Luke said. "It's a good investment."

"It's an amazing old building," Tony said. "It would be a shame to lose it."

Colt nodded. "Old buildings like this need a second chance."

"I think if you make a case for having it named a historical building, the city would have no choice but to sell it to you," Bash said. "Then they wouldn't be able to tear it down. I know someone at the historical society who'd get right to work on it."

Chelsea loved that idea. "And there are a lot of people who work in downtown Hope who don't want the mercantile torn down. Once word gets out that the McCormack brothers are going to make an offer to buy the building, they'll start putting pressure on the city council."

"Agreed," Megan said. "If you're serious, I'll start making some calls."

"All I have to do is let my mom know about this," Molly said. "I can guarantee you that within hours the entire town will know."

Emma laughed. "This is true. Mom will get the word out fast."

"But what about your job in Boston, Reid?" Samantha asked. "How would that work for you doing both?"

Reid frowned. "I don't understand what you're asking."

"You'd design and spearhead the refurbishment of this building, right?"

He shook his head. "I can't do that. It's a great building, but I don't live here anymore. I'm sure there are some great architects who could handle the redesign."

Sam crossed her arms. "Seriously? So you'd just walk away and abandon her?"

"Samantha, I have a job."

"So?" She pointed at the building. "This could be a job. A moneymaking endeavor."

"Look, I'm willing to pitch in with my brothers and make an offer on the building. I'd even be willing to draw up preliminary plans or make suggestions. But I can't oversee this project. I have too many other things going on."

"You own the company, Reid," Luke said. "Surely you could shift some projects off to other people while you spent some time here. Might be nice having you around again for a while."

"This is a great old building. And while we don't really like you, we could maybe stomach having you around—as long as it isn't permanent." Logan shot a smirk in his brother's direction.

Reid studied both his brothers, then turned to everyone else, who were all giving him expectant looks. "It's not as easy as you all think. I have responsibilities."

"It's not like this is happening tomorrow. But we need you, Reid. The town needs you." Sam sent him an imploring look.

He focused his attention on Samantha, then sighed. "I'll think about it."

Sam grinned. "Awesome. So now we have an action plan in place. And all of you McCormack brothers rock for doing this."

She gave Logan and Luke hugs, then Reid, who she clung to a little bit tighter.

"Thanks. You won't regret this."

"I already regret it. But it is a great old building. I might enjoy sinking my teeth into this."

"Well. Now that that's settled, I'm going home," Chelsea said. "Des and Logan's big party last night exhausted me."

Des came over and gave her a hug. "Thank you for everything."

Chelsea gave Des a tight squeeze. "I did nothing except enjoy being part of your happy day. Thank you for including me. I wish you and Logan a hundred years of happiness."

Des laughed. "I'm looking forward to that hundred years. And to our honeymoon, which I need to run home and get packed for. That long movie shoot is hanging over my head, so I can't wait for some alone time with my new husband before we're separated for a bit."

Chelsea hugged Logan, then said her goodbyes to Colt and Tony and their friends.

"I'll call you later tonight," Emma said.

"Sure."

"I'll walk you to your car. I think we're all parked pretty tightly together," Bash said.

She hadn't paid any attention to that when they'd arrived. "Okay."

"So what do you think?" he asked.

"About?"

"The whole building thing."

"I think it's a great idea. I hope Reid decides to come back to Hope to work on it. Mainly because I think Logan and Luke would like to have him around more often."

Bash nodded. "Agreed. Would be nice to see him more."

She stopped at her car. "Okay, so, I'll see you later."

He barely paused long enough to give her a half wave. "Sure. See you later, Chelsea."

She didn't know what she was expecting, but she knew it wasn't this wave of disappointment as Bash headed toward his truck and climbed in. Did she think he was going to sweep her into his arms and plant a passionate kiss on her like he had last night at the wedding? She'd been the one who'd put a stop to that and made it clear she was hesitant to enter into a—whatever it was they had been about to enter into together.

So why did she care that they were now going their separate ways, that he hadn't lingered or said more than a few sentences to her this morning?

She got into her car and started it up, then waited for Bash to back up and pull away so she could do the same.

Obviously she was tired and in need of a nap. She'd had very little sleep last night, and it was clouding her normally clear judgment. Thinking about him all the time, and being around him even more, wasn't helping.

It was time to start focusing more on her list and less on Bash. Then these feelings she was having for him would go away.

Chapter 16

SINCE REID WAS in town for a few extra days, Bash sat down with him over a few beers at the bar and went over his plans to add in a kitchen.

Lou enjoyed the run of the place while it was empty. After playing with her ball, which Reid had thrown for her what seemed about a hundred times, she ended up passed out by Bash's feet.

Bash supplied the free beer while Reid looked over the blueprints. It was still early and the bar wasn't open yet, so the two of them sat at a table to talk and go over Bash's plans.

"It looks solid to me," Reid said, taking a long swallow of the ale Bash had poured for him. "The only thing you might want to consider is the space out back. You could open a terrace area for the summer and serve outside as well." He put a piece of white paper over the existing blueprint and drew it out in such a hurry Bash had a hard time keeping up. "It might cost a little on the front end, but it gives you room for expansion."

Bash studied the blueprints. "I do own the land next to and behind the bar."

Reid nodded. "Exactly. And you might not want to do anything with it right away, but something to consider in stages."

"One of my ideas . . . for down the road, anyway, is to open a restaurant."

Reid grabbed his beer and leaned back in the chair. "Attached to the bar or somewhere else?"

"Somewhere else. Still in Hope, but yeah, someplace new."

Reid's brows rose. "Expanding your empire. I like it. Do you have blueprints for that?"

"Not yet."

"Hmm." He sipped his ale, then grabbed his sketchbook from his bag. "Do you have ideas?"

"Yeah."

"Let's get to work."

An hour later, he and Reid had roughed out a sketch of Bash's restaurant idea, which up to this point had mostly been in his head. To see it on paper was very cool, and he was glad to have Reid there to sketch out his vision. He could already picture the tables, the booths, the way the kitchen would look, and how many people the restaurant would seat.

"I think if you start by expanding here at the bar and serving meals—and it's a success—"

"Which it will be."

Reid grinned. "Of course it will be, because you're getting a great chef. Anyway, once you've planted the seed that you serve food as well as drinks, it's a natural progression to opening a restaurant."

"I've already talked to Jason about that. It's the reason he's willing to come aboard and cook for me at the bar."

Reid smiled and nodded. "My man. You've got a business plan."

"I do. Hard to believe when I was cutting high school classes with your brother all those years ago that I'd end up employed, let alone maybe a little successful."

Reid grinned. "Yeah. Hard to believe. I thought I was the only one who'd end up without a jail record."

Bash laughed. "You were always the smart one. Stayed in school, head down and focused. Look at you now."

"Look at all of us now. We're doing okay."

"We are." He poured another ale for Reid and grabbed a bottle for himself, since he had plenty of time before the bar opened this afternoon.

"One of the things I'm thinking about when all this starts is to open for lunch."

Reid propped his feet up on a nearby chair. "Don't you already work enough hours?"

"I'd have someone else work the lunch shift and I'd come in later in the day, like I do now."

"Must make it hard on your dating life to work late at night."

Bash took a sip of his beer. "I do all right."

"I don't know, man. You're getting up there in years, like Logan, and I don't see a wedding ring on your finger yet."

"Hey, I've been down that road before and don't intend to do it again. The single life is fine for me, and believe me, I'm not hurting for dates."

"Yeah? Who've you been dating?"

"Uh . . . the last one was a girl named Gerri. She dumped her Chihuahua on me." Bash looked down at Lou. "That's how I ended up with Lou."

Reid arched a brow. "Lou was her dog?"

Bash recounted the story of how he'd ended up with Lou, and Reid shook his head. "I don't understand women. It's all good in the beginning, and then after three dates they're planning your wedding. That's some scary shit."

"Sounds like you've had some experience."

"Let's just say I don't know how to pick 'em and leave it at that." Reid took a long swallow of his beer.

"Well, join the club."

Reid laughed. "So how's it working out with Lou so far?"

"Actually, I like her. She chewed my shoe, but otherwise, we're getting along fine."

"At least you got a great dog out of the deal. Women-wise, anyone else on the horizon?"

Bash's thoughts immediately strayed to Chelsea, but that was obviously going nowhere. "Not right now."

"You've got your hands full with the bar, anyway."

"True. And what about you?"

"I see plenty of women. After a couple relationships I can only classify as disasters, I'm content to keep things low-key. I have a heavy travel schedule anyway, and a lot of women don't have patience for that. So I tend to get dumped a lot."

"Too bad."

Reid shrugged. "I'm okay with that. I like my work."

"Speaking of work, what do you think about the mercantile?"

"It's . . . intriguing."

"Just intriguing?"

"Yeah. Under all those layers of dust, old walls, and shit ceilings, she's a beauty just waiting to be rediscovered. I'd be lying if I said I wouldn't like to dig in and make her shine again." Reid studied his glass of ale, as if he might be considering the idea. "I don't know. I've kind of gotten used to living in Boston."

Bash noticed he didn't say he loved living there, though. "But you are the boss. If you had to shuffle some things around and work here for a while, you could do that, right?"

"Maybe. I'll leave the politics and making an offer on the building to Luke and Logan. We'll see what happens after that." He left it there and finished his beer, then took off.

Bash cleaned up and readied the bar for opening, thinking a lot about his conversation with Reid as he did so. He wondered if Reid missed home, and if maybe the mercantile was his opportunity to spend more time in Hope—and with his family.

Bash didn't have family anymore. His mom had died several years back, and his father—they didn't talk anymore. His mother had been the glue holding the family together. He and his father had had a rocky relationship at best when his mom had been alive. Once she had passed, there was no reason for him and his dad to maintain contact. When his dad moved to Arizona, that had pretty much ended things between them. Bash was fine with that.

He had his friends, and they were enough family for him.

He sure as hell didn't know what he'd do without them. Some weaved in and out of his life and he didn't see them a lot. Like Reid. But when he needed them, they were there for him.

He was a pretty lucky guy. And maybe the whole relationship-with-a-woman thing hadn't worked out so well for him, but that was okay.

He had plenty to keep him busy.

After spending an hour doing liquor inventory, he looked down to find Lou asleep on his foot, which seemed to be her favorite nap spot. He scooped her up and cradled her against his chest. She yawned, then licked his chin.

Yeah, a guy could do worse than having great friends and a pretty loyal dog.

He picked up his phone to check the time.

"What do you think, Lou? Time for a quick walk outside so you can pee, then let the hordes in?"

She blinked and gave him a blank stare.

And even better, this female always agreed with him. "That's what I think, too."

He hooked Lou up on her leash and led her out the back door.

Chapter 17

AFTER SHOWERING, DOING her makeup and hair, and spending at least a half hour staring down the contents of her closet, Chelsea had chosen what she thought was the perfect outfit for her date tonight.

"What was wrong with the red dress?" Molly asked.

"Too short. I don't want to look easy."

"Why not?" Molly cast a grin in her direction.

"Not on the first date. Maybe the third."

Molly laughed. "Okay, I can see your point."

Chelsea finally settled on the black. It went right to the knee and had three-quarter-length sleeves, but with a bit of a sexy neckline. So she'd give him a taste of the goods without showcasing everything. And, of course, killer heels.

When she came out of the bedroom, Molly's eyes widened.

"Dell is going to swallow his tongue."

Molly had set her up on a blind date, which wasn't ideal, but she had insisted Dell was perfect. He was a new manager at one of Carter's shops in Tulsa, and Molly had been working with him for a while, getting him acclimated to all the business systems. Molly said he was to-die-for good-looking. And since Carter knew him pretty well and vouched for him, Chelsea agreed to the date.

"You don't think I'm overdressed?" she asked.

Molly shook her head. "I told you, Dell's a pretty classy guy. He might manage an auto repair shop, but trust me, he's not a mess. And he's totally unattached. I've spent a lot of time talking to him. He got out of a long-term relationship about six months ago and he hasn't really been dating anyone. He's thirty-two, he owns his own place in Tulsa, and he's a hell of a nice guy, Chelsea."

She fastened her bracelet on her arm, then looked over at Molly. "Sounds too good to be true."

"He said the same thing when I was telling him about you."

Chelsea smiled. "Really?"

"Yes."

As a plus, he was driving into Hope to pick her up, which was awfully nice of him, since he lived and worked in Tulsa. Not that it was that far to drive into Hope, but still, she'd had to drive into Tulsa several times to meet dates there because the guy hadn't wanted to make the trip to Hope.

Points for Dell already.

Molly grabbed her keys and her purse. "Okay, I'm going to get out of here before Dell shows up and thinks we were talking about him."

"Which we were."

"Of course. But he doesn't have to know that." Molly gave her a hug. "Have a great time, and please, don't think about your list while you're out with him?"

Chelsea frowned. "Why? Does he not meet the criteria?"

"Oh, he definitely meets the criteria. I just don't want you making lists in your head instead of having fun with a wonderful guy."

"You have a point. And I promise, I won't make lists."

"Awesome. Text me tomorrow and let me know how it went."

"I will."

After Molly left, Chelsea dashed into the bathroom to apply her lipstick, making a stop to check her dress in the mirror one last time. When she heard the doorbell, she hurried out to the living room, surprised that her heart was doing a double-time beat.

It was just a date, and it wasn't like she hadn't had more than a thousand of those before.

But she really wanted a good date. Because she hadn't had a lot of those.

Taking a deep breath, she turned the knob and opened the front door.

Molly hadn't been lying. This man was fine-looking.

"Chelsea? I'm Dell West."

She held out her hand and he shook it. She took in his nice dark suit. He'd even worn a tie. And a white shirt. And they all fit him perfectly. He was tall, with broad shoulders, dark hair, and the most striking blue eyes she'd ever seen.

"Come in, Dell, please."

"Thanks. You look beautiful, by the way. I'm glad I decided on the suit. Otherwise, we'd have had to make a pit stop back at my place so I could change clothes. I'd hate to lose my gorgeous date before we even make it to dinner."

"Thank you." He knew how to compliment a woman without it sounding cheesy or rehearsed, as well.

She led him into her apartment, feeling it necessary to give him a tour. "It's not much, but it's close to school, and that's convenient."

"It's a really nice place, Chelsea. Molly said you were a teacher. What an admirable job. And high school—you must love what you do. I was a terror in high school. How do you handle it?"

She laughed and grabbed her purse and sweater. "With a very firm voice and a lot of help from administration at times. But I do love it."

They walked outside to the parking lot. He also had a really nice car. A sleek black Lexus, which meant she didn't have to hike up her dress to climb into a truck.

How very convenient.

* * *

DELL HAD CHOSEN a nice restaurant downtown, so he got points for that as well. He even knew how to read the wine list, and they talked about various wines before settling on a very nice bottle of pinot noir, which they enjoyed together.

As they ate, the conversation continued smoothly, a lot of it back and forth with no awkward silences. Dell didn't monopolize the conversation talking about himself. He asked a lot of questions about her job and her life in Hope, but still filled in the blanks about himself as well.

"How's the new job going with Carter's place?"

"It's good. I'm glad he made the offer. I was ready to make a move from the place I'd been working, and Carter and Molly have made great strides in modernizing their business. Molly has updated all of their computer systems and has a knack for marketing as well. She and I are working closely on some new sales tactics, so business is picking up at my store."

"I'm glad to hear that."

He obviously took his work seriously. She liked that about him.

"It can't be all about work, though, so what are some of your favorite vacation spots?"

He smiled, leaning back in the booth. "I took a great vacation to the Caribbean a few years back. I had several weeks off, so I hit a few islands."

"Mmm. That sounds delightful. I do like the beach."

"Do you? What are your favorites?"

"I have this dream about the Seychelles. I've never been, but I'd love to go."

"I've never been either. I've heard the islands are amazing."

She tried not to think about her list, but it was hard when he was ticking off a lot of the items on it.

He was a nice guy. He was extraordinarily good-looking. He wore a suit. He had a great job, owned a house, and could carry on a conversation through the car ride, dinner, and dessert. And they'd spent at least an hour after dinner just sitting in the restaurant talking about all kinds of topics.

She liked this guy—a lot.

When he brought her home and walked her to her door, he maintained a respectable distance, so it was clear he had no expectation of being invited in. She liked that, too.

She unlocked her door, then turned to face him. "I had a really nice time tonight, Dell."

He smiled at her. "I did, too."

Obviously, if she was going to get a kiss tonight, she was going to have to be the one to initiate it. She stepped in closer to him. "Thank you for dinner."

He was clearly good at reading signals as well. "Thanks for coming with me. I hope we get to do this again."

She laid her palm on his chest. "I hope so, too."

He leaned in and brushed his lips against hers—easy at first, but when she didn't back away, he wrapped his arms around her and really laid a good kiss on her.

And that's when disappointment set in. It was a hot, passionate kiss, and after the perfection of tonight's date, it should have made her toes curl inside her shoes. But all she could think about was Bash's mouth, and the way it felt when his body was pressed up against hers. Why in the hell would she think about Bash when a delicious man was kissing her?

Dell pulled away and smiled. "Good night, Chelsea."

"Good night, Dell."

She was crushed. She'd had an amazing date, with incredible conversation, and the kiss was . . . wow. Or it should have been wow.

But she'd felt nothing.

She watched Dell walk away, irritated with Bash for so many reasons.

She wanted good-looking, friendly, desirable Dell in her head. She didn't want Bash or his smirk or his rock-hard body or the way he kissed on her mind. And especially not when she was kissing the best date she'd had in months.

This was unacceptable.

Chapter 18

IT WASN'T CHELSEA'S choice to find herself at the No Hope at All bar on Saturday night, but that's where everyone had agreed to meet up. Luke was getting off work a little later than usual. And with Des out of town, they invited Logan as well. Jane had told her they had a sitter for Tabitha and Ryan, but not until seven, and because the sitter was only thirteen, they'd have to be home by eleven, so they wanted to stay close. Carter and Molly had put in some hours in the auto repair shop during the day, and everyone wanted a fun night out. Chelsea had suggested a bar in Tulsa, but no one liked that idea when Bash's bar was closer to home.

She'd been outvoted by everyone, and short of telling them she didn't want to be anywhere near Bash and then having to explain why, she'd agreed to meet them all at the bar at seven thirty.

Which probably wasn't a big deal anyway. It was Saturday night and the bar would be crowded. Bash would be busy and she'd barely even see him. Plus, it sounded like a lot of people were coming and it was going to be a big group, so she intended to get lost in that crowd.

She deliberately showed up at seven forty-five to make sure she wasn't the first one there, which meant she had to park in the farthest part of the lot.

And it was still early for bar standards. Was he giving stuff away tonight or what? There wasn't even a championship game on tonight, at least not that she was aware of.

Wishing she'd worn her canvas shoes instead of heels, she trudged the distance through the gravel part of the lot until she hit the asphalt. Her hair was blowing in a million directions because it was late April and windy as hell, and a storm was brewing. She hoped it wasn't pouring rain by the time she left the bar tonight.

She made her way through the front door, her eyes trying to focus in the darkness of the bar. The televisions were on, the music was loud, and she scanned the room to try to find her friends.

She spotted them at a large table in the center of the room, pausing midway there when Lou scurried over to greet her. She crouched down to scoop up the dog.

"Well, hi there, sweetheart. How are you doing?"

Lou wriggled in her arms and tried to lick her face.

"Not a chance, punkin. It takes a while to get this makeup on, and only seconds for you to lick it off." She carried Lou to the table with her, running her hands over the dog's back.

"You finally made it," Emma said. "I thought you were going to stand us up."

"Would I do that?" She set Lou down, and the dog scampered off. Chelsea took the seat Emma offered. "Sorry, I had a last-minute phone call."

Which was a total lie, but she didn't want to tell them she'd deliberately delayed her arrival for no good reason.

"Oh, yeah? Hopefully with a hot new boyfriend," Jane said.

"Unfortunately, no."

"What about Dell?" Molly asked. "He said he had a great time with you last week."

"We did. He's such a great guy, Molly. Thanks for setting us up."

"Are you going out with him again?"

It would be a waste of time. "Maybe."

Emma studied her, then leaned over to whisper in her ear. "Obviously there's something you're not saying."

"You think so?"

"I know so. We need to talk."

"No, we don't."

"Yes, we do." Emma stood. "Bathroom break."

"But I just sat—"

Emma grabbed her hand and hauled her out of her chair.

"I guess I'll be right back. Someone order me a martini."

She was dragged along to the ladies' room, where Emma shut the door.

"Okay, spill."

Chelsea leaned against the bathroom counter. "Nothing to spill. Dell was a great guy. We had a nice date."

"But?"

"No buts."

Emma crossed her arms. "But you're not going to see him again."

"How do you know that?"

"Because I know you. Now I want to know why."

Chelsea sighed. "I don't know, Em. He was perfect. He ticked off so many items on my list. He was funny and charming. He works a nine-to-five job. He likes good wine and takes great vacations. We talked about goals for the future. He wants to settle down and raise a family."

"Okay, so far so good, as far as your list."

"I know, right? We had a wonderful time and we really clicked. And then he took me home and kissed me good night—a really awesome kiss."

"And?"

"And . . . nothing. No sparks."

Emma wrinkled her nose. "Oh. There kinda have to be sparks."

"Yeah, there does. I was so disappointed. I mean, he's fantastic-looking, and he has everything I want in a guy. But there's just no chemistry."

"Well, that's too bad." Emma laid her hand on Chelsea's arm. "It'll happen for you, Chelsea. I know it will."

"Sure it will."

They left the restroom, and Chelsea started to follow Emma back to her table.

"Ms. Burnett?"

She stopped and turned around. No one called her Ms. Burnett except her students, and none of her students should be at a bar.

She frowned. "Yes?"

The guy towered over her, and she didn't recognize him.

"You probably don't remember me. Aaron Goodwin. I had you for three math classes my sophomore through senior years. That was like . . . five years ago, though."

Oh, shit. Former student. And Aaron had to be a college graduate now. "Of course. Hi, Aaron. It's so nice to see you again."

He was standing at a table with four of his friends, who all looked to be either in college or recent graduates. All very nice-looking young men, too. She might have taught some of them as well.

"So . . . how are you doing?" he asked, leaning casually against the table.

"I'm great. And you? Are you finished with school now?"

"Yeah. Got my degree in business and I'm working for my dad."

"Oh, Aaron. That's wonderful. I'm so proud of you. I'm sure your parents are very proud as well."

"Thanks. They are. Oh, these are my friends." He introduced her to them and she shook hands with all of them.

"So, are you here with a date?" he asked.

She blinked, certain she was reading him wrong. "No, I'm just here with friends."

He grinned. "Great. Then can I buy you a drink?"

She hadn't been wrong. Her former student was definitely hitting on her. That was a first. He couldn't be more than twenty-four at most, which put him firmly in the way-too-young-for-her category. He might be amazing-looking, but she did not date former students. Ever. "Oh, well isn't that sweet of you, Aaron, but I can't. I should get back to my friends."

He looked over at the table where she'd motioned with her

head, then moved in a little closer. "They don't look like they'd miss you if you just had one drink with me."

He was persistent, like a lot of young guys. And then he put his arm around her.

Bold, too. A little too bold. She thought she'd smelled alcohol on his breath, but she'd hoped he was sober. Apparently not. She plucked his arm from her shoulder. "I don't think so, but thanks for the offer."

Obviously he wasn't taking no for an answer, because he came back with, "Just one drink, Chelsea. We can rehash high school."

Now he was overstepping. She was going to have to shut him down in a very firm way. "No. Good night, Aaron."

And then he grabbed hold of her wrist, tugging her forward. It hurt. She was about to pull away, but suddenly Bash was there, and he had extricated her from Aaron's grip. He had grabbed Aaron's arm in a firm hold. Aaron winced.

"When a lady says no, buddy, she means no. The first time. She shouldn't have to say it three fucking times."

"Hey. Let go," Aaron said, trying to fight off Bash.

Bash had twisted Aaron's arm around his back. "Your night at the bar is over. And you can take your friends with you."

Aaron's friends didn't take kindly to Bash's treatment of him. Chairs got pushed back in a hurry, but Bash didn't look concerned. Especially when Will, Luke, Logan, Carter, and the other two bartenders quickly appeared to back him up.

One look at Will and Luke's badges on their belt buckles put an end to any possible skirmish that might have erupted. Aaron's friends put their hands up in surrender.

"All right, all right," Aaron said, his teeth clenched tightly together. "We're going."

"Damn right, you are." Bash let go of Aaron, who rubbed his wrist, but he and his friends made their exits. Will and Luke went out the door to make sure they all took off.

And now Chelsea had the entire bar staring at her.

"Okay, so much for your free entertainment," Bash said. "Next round of drinks is on the bar."

That took care of everyone gawking at her, because there

was a rush of drink orders. Bash's bartenders and waitresses hurried to fill the orders, but he turned to her.

"Are you okay?"

She nodded, though she was a little more shaken than she would have expected. "I had it handled. Or I thought I did, until the idiot jerked at my wrist."

Bash picked up her hand. "Dumbass. I should have punched him for touching you like that." He gently rubbed at the spot where Aaron had grabbed her.

She looked from her wrist to Bash. That eye contact was electrifying, and her wrist no longer throbbed. Just him touching her gave her that ping of awareness she always got whenever he was near.

"Thank you."

"No problem. Are you sure you're okay? I can get some ice for your wrist."

"It's fine. I'm fine. And I appreciate you stepping in."

"I'd still like to go find that punk and beat the shit out of him. What was he thinking? Did you know him?"

She nodded. "Vaguely. He's a former student."

Bash's lips curved. "Hot for teacher, huh?"

She laughed. "I guess so."

"Can't say as I blame him for that part. But the manhandling part? Absolutely not."

He picked up her hand and pressed a kiss to her wrist, causing flutters of awareness to skitter across her skin. "I need to get back to the bar. If you need anything, you let me know."

"Okay. Thanks again."

His gaze met hers, and the heat she saw there nearly melted her to the floor.

"Anytime."

Gathering in a deep breath, she made her way back to the table and took her seat.

"Are you all right, honey?" Emma asked, rubbing her back.

"Fine now."

"I can't believe that jerk," Jane said. "I had him for math his freshman year and I'd like to kick his butt. I'm going to talk to his parents."

"Oh, God, Jane, don't do that. I think he's likely embarrassed enough that Bash threw him out. And Luke and Will followed him. He was likely terrified he was going to be arrested."

"And he had tears in his eyes, too," Samantha said with a triumphant gleam in her eyes. "That was quite the move Bash put on him."

"I think Bash has had his share of bar drunks to deal with," Carter said. "He knows how to handle himself."

"You all helped. Thanks for that," Chelsea said, giving a loving smile to every man there.

"Too bad we couldn't arrest him. I would have liked to throw him in a cell," Luke said. "Him and all his belligerent friends."

Will nodded. "Fortunately for them, one of the guys was sober, and he piled them all in the car and promised us he was going to take them all home."

"Yeah, let's hope they don't end up hitting another bar tonight," Megan said. "What idiots."

Emma checked her phone. "And it's still early, too. Not even eight thirty. I wonder what time they got started on the drinking today?"

One of the waitresses set a fresh martini in front of Chelsea. "Bash said these are all on the house for you tonight. Whatever you'd like."

Chelsea beamed at the waitress. "Thank you."

The guys went to shoot some pool, so all the women scooted their chairs over.

"Okay, so let's talk about Bash," Emma said.

"Clearly the reason you and Dell didn't hit it off."

Chelsea looked over at Molly. "But I liked Dell."

"I know you did, Chelsea, but there's something going on between you and Bash. A woman—any woman—would have to be blind not to see it."

"And none of us are blind," Samantha said.

Chelsea shook her head. "There's nothing going on with Bash and me."

"Are you sure about that?" Megan asked. "Because he's tending bar with one eye and has the other firmly fixed on you."

She didn't want to look. She didn't have to look, because she felt the heat of his gaze like a caress on her skin.

So, instead, she took a long drink of her martini, which of course had been made perfectly. Just the way she liked it. Dirty, with three olives. He knew what she liked. She'd bet he'd know everything she liked. Dirty or otherwise.

"Are you all right, Chelsea?" Megan asked. "Because your cheeks are pink."

Even from across the room the man affected her. It was uncanny and downright annoying. She put her cool hands up to her hot face. "No, I'm fine. It's just a little warm in here."

"When are you going to stop denying how you feel about Bash and do something about it?" Emma asked.

She slanted her gaze at her best friend. "He's all wrong for me."

Emma shrugged. "So? Sometimes all wrong can be oh so right."

"He meets none of the criteria on my list."

"But I'd bet he'd be fun in bed."

Chelsea's eyes widened as she looked at Jane.

"I said that out loud, didn't I?" Jane asked, then slapped her hands over her mouth.

Samantha laughed and dragged Jane's hands away from her mouth. "You only said what the rest of us are thinking. So you haven't found your perfect man yet, Chelsea. You keep looking for him, and maybe have some fun with Bash in the meantime?"

She shifted her focus onto Bash. Fortunately, he was busy filling drink orders, and didn't see that she couldn't help but notice how utterly amazing he looked tonight. He wore a black polo shirt that fit tight against his oh-so-fine chest. A chest she wanted to touch without the shirt being present.

"Okay, so maybe I might want to get him naked."

"Finally we're getting to some fun truths," Molly said.

She downed the contents of her martini, then fished the olives out of the glass and feasted on them while she pondered her options regarding Bash.

"You're considering it, aren't you?" Emma asked.

"I might be. He's not a forever kind of guy, or even a dating kind of guy. But a between-the-sheets kind of guy? Yeah, definitely."

"Now you're talking. If anyone needs to have some fun, Chelsea, it's you," Megan said.

She took a deep breath and sighed. They were right about that. She couldn't even count the number of first dates she'd been on. Though lately she could—three. With no result. She was so damn tired of . . . dating. She wanted something different.

She wanted a relationship and she wasn't having one, so what was wrong with at least having a good time while she was waiting for the right guy to come along?

The waitress delivered another martini and Chelsea took a long swallow of it, then played with the stick holding the olives, her attention drawn to Bash, who must have felt those sexual psychic vibes she was throwing out, because he lifted his attention from the bar and leveled his gaze on her.

She could feel him—his touch—all the way across the room. She didn't have that with anyone else and hadn't felt anything like it in so long. That promise of something sensual, something so spectacular she'd be a fool to pass it up.

Okay, so . . . maybe. She'd think about it.

She turned her attention to her friends, but Bash stayed in her mind the rest of the night.

They all had a great time hanging out until well after midnight. And when she got home and changed into her yoga pants and tank top, Bash was still there in her head. So much so that she felt unsettled and jittery and, despite the two martinis she'd had earlier in the night, not at all relaxed and ready for bed.

Maybe she should have had more to drink. But then Luke or Will would have had to drive her home, and that would have been a logistical nightmare. She liked her independence too much and didn't want to rely on other people. So she'd switched to soda after the two martinis and driven herself home.

She curled up on the sofa and grabbed the remote, surfing for something that might help relax her. She found a romantic comedy and settled in to watch, hoping a great movie and a cup of tea would wind her down.

Two hours later, she was well satisfied with the movie, but still not tired.

"This is stupid," she said to the television, which obviously didn't reply.

It was too bad she lived in an apartment that didn't allow pets. It would be nice to at least have a cat to talk to. Though she really wanted a dog.

Even a dog like Lou, who was the cutest little thing Chelsea had ever seen, though she'd always had her mind set on a big dog, like Emma and Luke's dogs.

Right now, she'd be very happy to have Lou to snuggle up with.

Or Lou's owner.

"Okay, enough of this." She picked up her phone. It was two thirty and clearly she wasn't going to sleep tonight. She sent a text message to Bash.

Are you closing up yet?

Ten minutes later, he texted back.

Just finishing up here. Are you okay?

She smiled at that and replied.

I'm fine. Just wide awake for some reason. Are you heading home?

Yeah. Want me to come over?

Her stomach did a leap at his suggestion, but this was what she wanted, so she sent the text before she changed her mind.

You have Lou to deal with. How about I come to your place?

She rubbed her stomach, feeling ridiculously nervous as she waited for him to reply.

Sounds good. I'll be home in about twenty minutes. See you there.

Now she'd made a decision, and she wasn't going to change her mind.

She laid her phone down and went into her bedroom, put on her clothes, brushed her teeth and hair, and fixed her makeup.

Taking a deep breath, she grabbed her keys and walked out the door.

Chapter 19

ONCE HE GOT home, Bash took a quick shower, then put on a pair of sweats and a T-shirt, not at all sure what Chelsea had in mind.

Maybe she was still freaked out over her encounter with those assholes in the bar tonight and she didn't want to be at home. He couldn't blame her for that. Some men were jerks. He was still pissed about it, and if it had been anywhere but his bar, he'd have taken it outside and given those young punks a lesson they wouldn't forget.

But as the bar owner, he bore a certain responsibility, and beating the shit out of customers wasn't something he could get away with, so the only thing he could do was throw them out. He'd make sure they never came back, too.

Will had told him Jane knew the kid's parents, who were great people. He had an idea a message would be delivered to the parents and that the kid would be in deep trouble. That gave him some satisfaction.

In the meantime, he'd do whatever it took to ease Chelsea's mind. Women had a right to feel safe no matter where they went and not be subject to harassment by men who thought they had a right to take whatever they wanted. That it had happened in his bar made him feel responsible, and he felt really shitty about it. If the bar hadn't been so crowded he'd have taken her home and sat with her all night. So he was glad she texted.

He'd just come inside after taking Lou out when the doorbell rang. Lou, who'd taken to barking at the slightest provocation, was proving to be one hell of a tiny guard dog. She wagged her tail and ran to the door in a yapping frenzy.

"I've got this, Lou. Thanks for the heads-up."

He opened the door and Chelsea was there, wearing tight jeans, a red Henley, and high heels.

Jesus. Those heels. They made her legs look miles long.

Something he should not be thinking about right now, when his intent was to simply be there for her. Not seduce her.

"Obviously you knew I was here," she said, coming in and then bending down so Lou could check her out. When Lou wagged her tail and licked her hand, Chelsea picked her up and cradled her close.

"I definitely knew you were here. Now that she's comfortable with me and with the house, she thinks she's fierce."

"She is fierce, aren't you, honey?" Chelsea followed him into the living room and took a seat on the sofa. Lou settled in on Chelsea's lap.

"Something to drink?" he asked.

She shook her head. "No, I'm good right now, but thanks."

"I'm gonna have a beer."

"You go right ahead."

He grabbed a beer out of the fridge and unscrewed the top, then went to sit down next to her.

She looked okay as he watched her pet Lou, but he knew looks could be deceiving.

"How are you?" he asked.

She lifted her head and met his gaze. "I'm fine. Why?"

"I've been thinking about you all night."

"You were? Again . . . why?"

"I thought maybe you were upset about that guy who gave you a hard time at the bar."

"Oh. No. At the time he freaked me out a little, but honestly,

I don't think he was dangerous. Just a little drunk and too full of himself. I was intending to shut him down when you came over. Thanks again for doing that."

"I was really pissed off, Chelsea. I'm sorry about what happened."

"It's not your fault. You can't take responsibility for every drunken douchebag who hits on a woman."

"He went beyond hitting on you. He got physical, and I won't accept that from anyone in my bar."

"It's still not your responsibility to police their behavior. You threw him and his friends out, and I appreciated it. End of story."

She didn't seem distressed and her voice wasn't shaky, so maybe that wasn't the reason she'd come over. "Okay. I'm glad you're not upset."

She cocked her head to the side. "You thought I came over because I needed comforting."

"Yeah. Which I would have been happy to provide."

Her lips tilted. "Thanks. But I'm tough, Bash."

"I've never doubted it. But you know, it's okay to lean on someone, too."

"Is that what you do?"

He laughed. "I don't need to."

She twisted to face him. "Why? Because you're a guy?"

"Something like that."

"Totally sexist statement, Bash. You think I'm going to crumple when I have a bad day, so I'd need to be held and comforted. But a man would never need that?"

He had no idea where this conversation was going, but maybe she needed to let off some steam, and he was always up for a good debate. "I'm not the fold-and-crumple type. But yeah, I can see how a man could benefit from having a partner to talk to when he's had a shit day. Who wouldn't?"

"So who do you go to when you've had a bad day?"

"My friends. Same as you, right?"

She leaned back against the sofa. "Yes."

"Look, neither of us are close with our families. We rely on our friends to be our support systems and always have."

"Somehow I don't see you calling Carter or Logan to cry on their shoulders when you've had a particularly rough night at the bar."

His lips curved. "You don't, huh?"

"No. But men are wired differently. You internalize and work out your issues in other ways."

"Such as?"

"I have no idea. Maybe you sweat out your frustrations at the gym. Or do a home-improvement project to get your mind off of what's bothering you."

He nodded. "That works."

"Or maybe sex."

He laughed. "Yeah, that'll work, too."

"Whereas women tend to want to talk things through. I'll call up one of my girlfriends and rant. Then I'll feel better."

"You should try sex. Better endorphin rush, and you'll forget all about your problems."

She stared at him for a few seconds. "You're right. I should try sex."

Bash didn't know where to go with that statement. "Okay. Got a guy in mind?"

"As a matter of fact, I do."

Now it was getting awkward. While he was more than happy to sit and talk with her about what had happened earlier tonight and help her through any issues that might be bothering her, he was going to have to draw the line at her sex life. Just thinking about her being with another guy made him uncomfortable. Though he didn't know why. It shouldn't bother him. She was an adult, and she could have sex with whomever she damn well wanted to.

Problem was, he'd been spending a lot of time lately thinking about having sex with Chelsea. They'd kissed—more than once. He'd made his intentions clear. She'd backed off—making her intentions clear. But it didn't mean they couldn't be friends. He'd just have to suck it up and deal with it, because that's what friends did.

"Is there someone you'd like me to set you up with?"

"No, and I realize I'm not handling this well because I backed away the night of the wedding. I want you, Bash."

He blinked. "You do."

"Yes. But not in a relationship kind of way."

"So you just want sex."

"Yes. Are you okay with that?"

He was having a hard time coming to grips with the fact that Chelsea had just propositioned him. It didn't seem to be her style at all. She was after a relationship—the happily-ever-after kind. But here she was, sitting on his sofa in the middle of the night, asking him for sex.

"I'm totally okay with it. But we talked about it before and you changed your mind, if you remember."

"I do. I'm bringing it up again."

"Okay." This time, he was going to let her carry the conversation without him pushing her on it. Because he wanted her to be sure it's what she wanted. So he waited for her to continue.

She looked down at her fingernails before meeting his gaze again. "There's this thing between us. I need to get rid of it before I can continue my search for the perfect man."

He wanted to laugh, but he could tell she was taking this seriously. "Yeah, that thing. Kind of a pain in the ass, huh?"

"Yes. I figured we should sleep together and eliminate this lurking chemistry, and then I could move on. I hope you don't find that insulting."

"Nope. Not in the least." He wouldn't mind at all being used by Chelsea. It might help him get rid of the lust he'd been carrying around for her for these past several months, too. Then they could both move on.

It'd be a win-win for both of them.

She looked at him, and he didn't think he'd ever seen a more honest expression on her face. "I'll bet you think I'm cold."

"Honey, I've never thought of you as cold."

"But I'm here tonight propositioning you about sex. That seems, I don't know, cold, somehow. Doesn't it? You and me having sex for no other reason that to eliminate a lurking passion we feel for each other."

He needed to communicate to her how much he was in this. Hell, he was getting hard just thinking about being with her. He put his arm over the sofa and leaned in, brushing his hand over her hair. "Trust me, Chelsea. What we have together feels anything but cold to me."

She inhaled, then let it out. "You're right. And that's the problem. There's an intense heat between us. Very distracting. But in a good way. And also in a bad way."

His lips curved.

"I'm not making much sense, am I? See, this is why we have to have sex."

"Obviously."

"I need to stop overanalyzing it. So . . . we're agreed then? Sex with no strings?"

He stood and reached for her hand. "It's a deal."

CHELSEA FINALLY EXHALED, moved a sleeping Lou to the sofa, then took Bash's hand. The contact of their fingers touching was electrifying.

What was it about him that got to her like that? A simple touch and her nerve endings were frazzled.

Tonight was going to take care of that. She was going to finally stop thinking about it, dreaming about it. She was ready.

More than ready, actually.

He pulled her to stand, then skimmed his hand down her back. His touch made her shiver in all the right ways, the wickedly, deliberately hot look he gave her making her damp in all the right places.

"All night, Chelsea. And all day tomorrow. No running. You're either in or you're out. Decide before we get started."

Her eyes widened. "All day tomorrow?"

His lips curved in a sexy smile that melted her feet to the floor.

"I'm very thorough. This isn't going to be a once-and-done thing."

She swallowed, her throat gone dry. She was already imagining the things they could do together with all that time. "Oh. Okay, then. All day tomorrow, too."

"Good." He slid his hand into her hair, gripped a handful of it like he meant business, and put his mouth on hers. At the same time his other hand slid down to her butt, cupping it and drawing her body close to his.

It shocked her senseless. There was nothing tentative about the kiss. It was a man taking possession of a woman, and it was everything she'd fantasized about. Her heart pounded, she felt damp and weak and all those things she'd read about when she read the love scenes in her favorite romance novels, but had never experienced before. She'd been kissed, but not like this. Not the kind of kiss that made her feel light-headed, that made her clutch Bash's shirt and hold on for dear life as he plundered her senses with relentless intent. She felt feverish with desire, with the need to tear off all their clothes and get to the really good stuff, but at the same time she wanted to linger, to feel his lips on hers, his tongue sliding against hers, to feel the way his body pressed into hers as he moved them toward the sofa.

He pulled away from the kiss only long enough to bend down, scoop Lou off the sofa, and gently set her on the floor. Lou scampered out of the room, and Bash pressed Chelsea down to the sofa.

"Shouldn't we head to the bedroom?" she asked as Bash lay on top of her.

"We'll get there. Eventually. I've had fantasies about you on this couch ever since I kissed you here that night."

She palmed his chest, felt his raging heartbeat against her hand. "Is that right? What kind of fantasies?"

"Lots of them. Like getting you naked and licking you all over. Or bending you over the sofa and taking you that way. You have a great ass, Chelsea. Have I ever mentioned that?"

Could a woman die from hearing a man talking dirty to her? Or how about her heart exploding when he pulled her shirt up and laid his hand on her stomach, then inched his fingers up to cup her breast over her bra?

They hadn't even gotten to the really good stuff yet and she was already close to hyperventilating. She let out a whimper.

"Shh," he said, hovering over her as he pulled one of the

cups of her bra down, his thumb brushing over her nipple. "We'll take it slow so you can breathe a little."

She gasped as he teased and tweaked her nipple. "That . . . is not taking it slow."

One corner of his mouth lifted. "It's not?"

In a flash he had her top lifted over her head. He was straddling her hips and she had an opportunity to look her fill at the way his T-shirt fit so tightly over his chiseled chest, and the oh-so-prominent erection that wasn't concealed by his sweats.

"Shirt off," she managed in between breaths.

"Yes, ma'am." He pulled his shirt off and tossed it in the nearby chair where he'd thrown hers.

She couldn't resist sitting up to span her hands over his flat, muscled abs, his wide chest, and his amazing shoulders.

And, suddenly, he'd unhooked her bra and slid the straps down her arms.

"Now, we're going to have some fun," he said, resting her back against one arm. "You're so beautiful, Chelsea."

He swept his hand over her neck, her collarbone, then her breasts, touching her, inflaming her as he teased her nipples to tight, hard points. He put his mouth on one of the throbbing buds, making her moan his name. She was his for the taking, and damn if she cared.

She arched up toward him, needing more of the pull to temptation, of his wet, hot mouth on her.

It had been so long since her body had been worshipped like this, since a man had wholly focused his attention on her. Bash was a man on a mission, and as he slid off the sofa and removed her shoes, then undid the button and zipper of her jeans and pulled them off, she felt his undivided attention.

But there was no hurry, just a slow, languorous inspection of her body as he took off her clothes.

He grabbed her hand and drew her up to stand. She thought he'd lead them to the bedroom, but all he did was turn her around.

"Your back is this beautiful canvas of soft, creamy skin, Chelsea," he said. "Do you know how much I've thought about getting you undressed and touching you?"

She'd had no idea. But she loved his hands on her.

He swept her hair to the side and put his mouth on the nape of her neck, kissing his way along her shoulder and using his hands to map the skin of her back. When he cupped her butt, she laid her head on his shoulder.

"I like your hands."

"You're going to like them a lot more when I make you come." He swept his hand around, teasing her stomach and the rim of her underwear with his fingers. When he tucked his hand inside her panties and cupped her sex, she gasped, arched, her body damp with need and desire.

She shuddered. This was what she needed. This was what she came for. To be touched by Bash, to delve into this mind-numbing response. She'd danced around him for years, watching him date all the wrong women.

She wasn't the right woman for him, either. They weren't right for each other.

But tonight she was his, and she intended to take everything he offered.

And what he offered was pure, unadulterated erotic bliss. His fingers slipping inside of her while his other hand caressed her breasts. His hard body rocking against her. His mouth on her neck making her tingle all over. It was sensory overload in the best possible way. And as Bash whispered in her ear, dark words coaxing her to give in, she was connected to him in ways she had never imagined.

She climaxed in a wild rush of quivering sensation, grasping his wrist to hold his fingers in place while she rode the wildly out-of-control pulses that threatened to drop her to the floor. But Bash was right there, continuing to hold her, caress her, and murmur dark, sexy words to her until she finally settled and found some semblance of calm.

Then he turned her around and claimed possession of her mouth in a wild, passionate kiss that took that calm and shattered it. She wound her arms around his neck and held on, diving deep into the pleasure he gave her, the crazy lust he'd awakened inside of her.

This was just the beginning, and she wanted so much more.

Chapter 20

_____

BASH HAD BARELY touched on the flame burning deep inside Chelsea. She was a carefully banked fire and he intended to ignite her into an inferno tonight.

As he kissed her, he could feel the tightly coiled passion she held in check. Even after one orgasm, he knew she had more. He wanted to give her more. He also wanted all of her for himself. Selfish, he knew, but if she hadn't found some guy to release that tension, then he intended to benefit.

He pulled away and looked into her eyes. Fiery green, and yeah, there was that fire.

He rubbed his thumb over her bottom lip. "Pretty mouth. Sassy mouth. I like the things that come out of it when you talk."

Her lips curved. "I can do a lot more with this mouth."

His cock tightened. "Yeah, I'll just bet you can. Come on. I need to stretch you out on my bed and get you naked."

After a quick search for Lou, who he found in the kitchen next to the island, asleep on the kitchen towel that she'd pulled off the cabinet door, he led Chelsea down the hall and into his bedroom.

It wasn't a fancy room, but he wasn't a fancy guy. He had

a king-sized bed, because he liked to sprawl. There was a dresser, and enough room for him to walk around in there. That was pretty much it.

He yanked the comforter down to the end of the bed, and Chelsea sat on the edge of the bed.

"No, that's not good enough," he said, then used his hand to give her shoulder a gentle push. "Lie down in the center of the bed."

She did, and he shrugged out of his sweats and underwear.

She was up on her elbows eyeing him when he came back to the bed.

"You have one hell of a body, Bash," she said.

He grinned. "Thanks. So do you."

He grasped her panties and pulled them down her legs, shaking his head in awe at the thatch of red hair covering her sex.

So damn sexy. So hot. And he was so damn hard and eager to be inside of her, but he knew she was picky about men, and she'd chosen him. So he was going to take this slow. Make it good for her. They had all night. And, because he'd bargained with her, they had all day tomorrow, too.

He was going to need it, because he wanted a lot of time with her. Chelsea was not a one-time-only kind of woman. Or maybe he just wanted more than once with her. He knew he was only going to have tonight—and tomorrow. He was going to make good use of his time with her.

He stood at the edge of the bed and grasped her ankles, absorbing the soft, silken feel of her skin under his work-roughened hands before sliding them up her legs, memorizing the feel of her strong calves, her sweet thighs, spreading her open.

He sucked in a breath at how beautiful, how utterly sexy she was. He pulled her legs forward, letting them dangle over the bed, then dropped to his knees and draped those gorgeous legs over his shoulders so he could align her sweet sex with his mouth.

Chelsea rose up on her elbows again to watch him. He liked that she was bold, that she wanted to see what he was doing. He put his mouth on her, breathing her in as he took a long, slow swipe of her sex. The sounds she made told him he was in the right place, so he followed the map of her responses.

Chelsea was vocal about what she liked and where she wanted him, which not only drove him crazy with lust—it also helped him spiral her up. She had her hand in his hair, her hips working overtime arching into him.

There was nothing he loved more than a sexually enthusiastic partner. A woman lying there limp while he tried to pleasure her made him think he was doing it all wrong. But as Chelsea's cries increased and she writhed against him, he figured he was doing something right. And when she let loose with a loud cry of completion, he knew he'd hit the right buttons.

And damn near tore himself apart in the process, because a turned-on woman made his dick harder than stone.

After her quivers died down, he crawled up her body and kissed her. She grasped the sides of his face with her hands and held him still for a deep, hot kiss that left him in no doubt that she appreciated the orgasm.

He rolled over onto his side, petting her nipple as he let her come down and relax.

"If I'd known you were so good at that, we'd have been doing this a lot sooner."

He laughed. "It was my pleasure."

"Oh, hell no, it wasn't. That, Bash, was all about my pleasure."

She climbed on top of him, and he had to admit, seeing her fully naked and sitting on his body was sweet as hell. "Now, we need to see about your pleasure."

She slid down onto his thighs and grasped his cock in her hands. He had to hold his breath for a few seconds, because just looking at her and feeling her sweet, soft hands touching him was almost more than he could bear.

Though if she kept her hands on him, he could definitely bear it for a long, long time.

"You know what your problem is, Bash?"

He grasped her hips. "What's my problem?"

"Your problem is you've been dating girls. Girls who are way too young for you. What you need is a woman. Someone who knows what she's doing, who's had some . . . experience."

He arched a brow. "Is that right?"

"Yes."

She wedged herself onto her belly between his legs.

"I'm interested now."

"A woman who knows how to pleasure a man. The right way."

She got up on her hands and knees, then took his cock between her lips and showed him all the reasons he should have had her in his bed a long damn time ago. The visual of her beautiful breasts dangling in front of him, her hot, wet mouth going down on his throbbing cock, coupled with the way she made him feel, blew his goddamned mind, and nearly his control as well. It took every ounce of restraint he possessed not to let go and release.

The way she teased him, taking him deep, then letting go, giving him a saucy smile before enveloping his cock between her lips again, made him grab tight to the sheets and hold on, because in this, Chelsea held all the control.

Yeah, she was all woman, and she knew exactly what she was doing. And he wasn't the only one doing the moaning, which only heightened the experience for him.

"Chelsea," he said, reaching forward to sweep her hair off her face. "You're gonna make me come."

Her only response was to hum against his cock. After that he lost all control and lifted against her mouth, grasped her hair, and gave her everything. When he came, she held on to the base of his cock and took everything. And that was so damn hot, so damn sweet, and all he could do was hold on and watch, because he was shaking all over.

Now he was the one who needed a few minutes to get his head on straight. Chelsea crawled up his body and planted a kiss on his lips. He tangled his fingers in her hair and lingered on the kiss, needing to hold her there, still unable to believe she was really in his bed in the middle of the night.

She snuggled against him and he felt the *thump thump* of her heart against his ribs. He was just going to close his eyes for a minute, then he was going to rock her ever-loving world again.

He was asleep within a minute.

Chapter 21

"SHIT."

Chelsea blinked her eyes open, unaccustomed to hearing a man cuss first thing in the morning.

She was also not used to being wrapped up in a tangled puzzle of naked body parts. She was on her side, and Bash's warm body was pressed against hers, their legs intertwined.

She rolled over to face him.

"What's wrong?"

"I fell asleep."

She smiled at him. "So did I. We had quite a bit going on before that."

"Yeah, but not the main event. Sorry about that." He brushed his lips over hers. "Good morning."

"Good morning. As I recall, I hit you up pretty late last night to start with. And we had some rather entertaining pre-main-events."

He laughed. "We did, didn't we? I just don't want you to question my stamina. I have plenty."

"Your secret is safe with me. I won't let the female population of Hope and the surrounding communities know that you're unable to keep it up after a long night at work and pre-pleasuring your female company with two orgasms at four in the morning. Though I'm sure the city newsletter would be *very* interested in that juicy tidbit of gossip."

He kissed her shoulder, then took a little love bite, which made all her feminine parts tingle.

"Which part? The two orgasms? I'll be happy to give an interview about that."

She laughed. "You *would* latch on to that part."

He turned her over, then cupped one of her breasts, lazily teasing her nipple with his fingers. "Well, yeah. My intent is to make you happy."

Her stomach tightened at his words. This was a one-time deal. Just today. Then it was over. But she'd had a wonderful time last night, and she'd slept better than she had in a long time. She and Bash had both instantly drifted off, and then he'd held her all night long. Or for however many hours they'd slept.

"What time is it?"

He paused. "I'm playing with your nipple and you're asking the time? Do you have somewhere you need to go?"

She laughed. "No. I'm worried about you getting enough sleep."

He rolled over on top of her. "Trust me. I get plenty of sleep."

Chelsea heard a bark and rather urgent whine at the foot of the bed.

Bash sighed, then rested his forehead against hers. "Lou needs to go outside." He gave her a quick kiss. "I'll be right back."

He hopped out of bed, grabbed a pair of jeans, and climbed into them, but not before giving her a stellar view of his naked ass.

"Come on, princess. Let's go pee."

The dog wasn't the only one with urgent bladder needs, so Chelsea got out of bed and used the bathroom, then came out and grabbed one of Bash's T-shirts and put it on. It was miles too long for her. She didn't care. She had a sudden need for coffee, which trumped sex.

They had all day anyway.

She went into the kitchen and started a pot of coffee, then

scrounged around for sugar and found cream—thank God—in his refrigerator.

"You are not in my bed."

She looked up to see him leaning against the doorway.

"I am not, because I need coffee."

He pushed off the wall and headed into the kitchen. "That does sound good. And I'm glad you're not bashful about rummaging."

"Not much will get in the way of my need for caffeine. And if you have an issue about me going through your drawers and cabinets, I guess that's too bad, because it's already a done deal."

He laughed. "I don't have anything to hide. No dead bodies, no love letters from former girlfriends. The only thing I have lying around is a dog that some crazy ex foisted on me."

Chelsea bent and petted Lou. "She's such a sweetheart, too." She looked up at Bash. "The dog, not the crazy ex-girlfriend."

He smiled down at her. "I knew which one you meant."

When the coffee was finally ready, Bash poured both of them a cup. Chelsea fixed hers up with cream and sugar, then took a long couple of swallows, letting the caffeine do its job.

"Ahh. Now this is exactly what I needed."

Bash put his cup aside to pour food in Lou's bowl. She attacked her food like she hadn't eaten in three days, tossing nuggets around on the floor.

"Is she always like that?"

"Yeah. She's kind of sloppy. But she'll get the remnants after she finishes up what's in the bowl."

"The two of you have bonded well."

Bash looked down at Lou. "I guess so. Never thought I'd end up with a Chihuahua, but now that she's here, I can't imagine not having her around all the time."

This was a new side to Bash. She'd always seen him so . . . solitary, so alone. And he'd always seemed to prefer it that way. Now, though, while he didn't have a person in his life, at least he had a dog. And he was so good with her, taking her to work with him and being so caring with her. She'd put Bash in this "big and tough" box in her head. He'd always been kind of a badass, in her opinion. It turned out that while he was big and tough, and definitely a badass, he was also caring and tender.

Like last night, when he'd gone all badass on that guy who'd harassed her, then immediately tender when he thought she'd been hurt.

She'd also always thought of him as incredibly sexy and hot as hell. She'd pictured their coupling would be fast and furious and over in a hurry. Yet here she was, the proverbial morning after, having coffee in his kitchen, she'd had two orgasms, and, technically, they hadn't actually had sex yet.

He constantly surprised her.

She stood and reached for her cup, leaning over the counter to take a sip.

"You wearing anything under that shirt?" he asked.

She shook her head.

"Good." He took the cup from her hand and laid it on the other side of the counter, then grasped her waist and hoisted her up, setting her down on the kitchen island, lifting the shirt over her hips.

"You do realize I'm naked, and this counter is cold."

He gripped her thighs and spread her legs. "You'll warm up fast."

He was right, because heat spread through her when he stepped between her legs, cupped her neck, then kissed her, a soft, sweet, exploratory kiss that quickly turned passionate. She wrapped her legs around his hips to draw him in closer, the naked part of her making contact with denim—and the quickly hardening part of him making her forget all about the cold counter.

Her sex brushed his jeans, and all she could think was that if he was naked, too, he could already be inside of her.

"Bash," she said, her lips making contact with his neck. "I want . . ."

"Yeah, I know what you want, Chelsea. And we have all day to get to it. But right now this is what I want."

He pushed back and bent down, then put his mouth on her. She gripped the edge of the counter and held on while he took her to heaven and back again with his lips and tongue.

This was so much better than any caffeine, an awakening

jolt to her senses in the best possible way. His dark head nestled between her thighs, his soft hair tickling her skin as his tongue performed magic and brought her right to the edge of reason in record time.

Her orgasm hit her like a shock wave, rocking her nearly right off the counter. Only Bash's hold on her hips held her there while she rode that wave of pleasure to its conclusion.

She barely had time to catch her breath before Bash scooped her off the counter, her legs wrapping around him as he carried her to the bedroom.

He fused his mouth to hers as he laid her on the bed, his body coming down on top of hers. She made free use of her hands, sliding her fingertips over the smooth muscle of his shoulders and down his arms, then lifted against him, letting him know what she wanted. But he continued to kiss her, using his mouth to drive her absolutely crazy until she couldn't take it anymore. Her body was on fire, and there was only one way to douse the flames.

She pushed on his chest, and when he lifted to look down at her, she said, "No more preliminaries, Bash. I want to feel you inside me."

His eyes were pure wicked desire as he pushed himself off of her and dropped his jeans. Just gazing at the pure perfection of his naked body created a spiral of deep, dark need that demanded satisfaction. And only Bash could satisfy her.

She took off the T-shirt she'd been wearing and cast it aside, while he reached into his nightstand drawer and pulled out a condom. He made quick work of putting it on, then he was right with her again.

"I've been waiting a long time for this," he said.

"So have I." She brushed his hair away from his face, feeling an emotional tenderness that was probably inappropriate right now, but she couldn't hold it back.

He grasped her hand and kissed her palm, then placed her hand around his neck, nestled in between her legs, and slid into her.

He kept eye contact with her as he seated himself fully inside her.

Tears pricked her eyes at the convergence of emotion and physicality of the moment. There was so much going on with the way her body felt, the absolute perfection of the way they were joined, and the look in Bash's eyes as he began to move against her, that she almost couldn't handle it.

But this wasn't meant to be an emotional moment—just physical. She squeezed her eyes shut, determined to wash away the emotion and let the physical take over.

"Chelsea." His words were a whispered caress, a lover's touch on her senses. "Look at me."

She couldn't not obey the sweet words of his command. She opened her eyes, and met his gaze as he thrust, slow and easy, the two of them connected so intimately it seared her, connected her to him in ways she'd never imagined.

She was awash in sensation, from the way his chest rubbed her breasts to the absolutely perfect way his body touched hers. She swept her foot along his leg, feeling the crisp hairs there. Everything about him, from the hardness of his thighs to the softness of his hair, made her tingle all over. He had a powerful body, a body made to do amazing things to her body. And as she quivered around him, she was glad she'd made this decision.

It might only be a physical response, but they just . . . fit. It was so right and it felt so good to be in this moment with Bash, to lose herself in this wild roller coaster of insane pleasure, to let go and fall helplessly as he dropped fully on top of her, cupped her butt, and tilted her pelvis up, grinding against her and spiraling her right out of control.

She reached up to grab a handful of his hair, needing that lifeline connection to him as she released. It was a mind-numbing experience to feel that burst of orgasm, her gaze locked with his, watching him as he went with her.

She'd never expected something this crazy good, but there it was, and she had no hope of tamping down the emotions that came along with the explosion of pleasure that rocked her to her core.

When he kissed her, it didn't help ground her at all. It only served to lift her even higher. She grabbed on to his arms, locked her legs around his hips, and continued the journey until she felt out of her body, floating on an endless cloud of deep pleasure.

Panting and out of breath, she smoothed her hands over Bash's back and down his arms, needing to feel for herself that this was actually real—that he was real and not some made-up version of a fantasy she'd created in her mind.

He lifted his head and looked down at her, smiling in that sexy way he had about him.

"That was good for a start."

Now there was some reality. "A start, huh?"

"Yeah. Now I'm hungry. How about we get dressed and go out for breakfast?"

She wasn't sure how she felt about being seen with him in public on a Sunday morning. It seemed an awful lot like a morning-after. And then if she ran into anyone she knew, there'd be questions—ones she wasn't prepared to answer.

"I could cook you breakfast," she said.

He arched a brow. "Nah. Then there's dishes, and who wants that?" He rolled out of bed. "Come on."

Deciding her concerns were probably a little ridiculous, she followed him into the bathroom, cleaned up, then got dressed, already preparing in her head how to answer any questions people might ask.

She and Bash could have run into each other on the way to breakfast, then decided to eat together. A perfectly reasonable explanation.

She left the bedroom and found her shoes in the living room next to the sofa. Her body tightened at the thought of how Bash had taken off her shoes and undressed her there last night, along with all the other delicious things he'd done to her.

One would think that after the amazing orgasms he'd given her, she'd have had her fill and be more than satisfied. But as he came up to stand beside her, she had a sudden urge to fling herself against him and kiss him, say, "Screw breakfast," and go for more.

Okay, so maybe she hadn't had her fill just yet. And he had asked for the entire day, hadn't he?

"Ready?" he asked.

She was definitely ready. "Yes."

They walked outside, and she had her keys in her hand. Bash stopped. "You're driving?"

"Oh. I thought we might drive separately."

He frowned. "Why the hell would we do that? Bert's is only a few blocks away. And you're coming back here after. Right?"

"Yes, but . . ."

He gave her a confused look. "But what?"

How was she going to explain her reasoning to him. "Um . . ."

He laughed. "Come on. We'll take my truck."

She had no logical reason for taking her car. Not one that made sense anyway. But it also blew her we-just-ran-into-each-other plan right out of the water. "Okay."

They didn't say much on the ride to Bert's, but Bash reached across the truck and held her hand. It was nice. A little too nice—a bit too much like they were dating, or a couple.

The problem was, the simple gesture felt good.

They arrived at Bert's, and Chelsea cringed at the packed parking lot.

"Looks crowded," she said. "Maybe we should go somewhere else."

Like a restaurant in Tulsa, where there was a chance she wouldn't know everyone in the place like she would at Bert's.

"Nah. We'll be able to get a table."

With a resigned sigh, she got out of the truck, then lagged a little behind Bash as he started toward the door, trying to appear as if she and Bash weren't walking in together. Unfortunately, he waited for her; even held the door for her.

Dammit.

There were people waiting inside for a table, and of course she knew several of them. So did Bash, so after the waitress wrote Bash's name down, they engaged folks in conversation.

And just as she feared, the inevitable questions surfaced.

"Why, Chelsea, honey, I didn't know you and Bash were dating."

"How long have you and Bash been going out?"

"Are you and Bash . . . together? As in a couple?"

Bash took it all in stride, laughing and saying they were just friends having breakfast together. He clearly had no idea what the gossip mill in Hope was like. It only took one person to start spreading the word—even a false rumor. By Monday it would be all over town that she and Bash were a couple.

They finally got their table and placed their orders. Chelsea found herself staring at her phone, just waiting for the rumors to start spreading and for one of her friends to call or text her.

"Hey," Bash said.

She looked up at him.

"You expecting a call?"

"Probably any minute now."

"From?"

"One of my friends, who will have heard from one of their friends or some relative that you and I are now the hot item in Hope."

He took a sip of his coffee, then leaned back in the booth. "And that bothers you?"

"Yes. No. I don't know. It might. You know how gossips are. Doesn't it bother you that people assume that just because we're having breakfast together, we're a couple?"

"Not really. People are going to think what they want to think, Chelsea. I'm surprised it upsets you. It's not like I'm Hope's resident serial killer."

She gave him a look.

"That you know of," he added, wriggling his brows.

She rolled her eyes. "Come on. This has nothing to do with you."

"Doesn't it?" He leaned forward, wrapping his hands around his coffee cup. "Say you and some random guy you'd been out with on a few dates decided to spend the night together, and he wanted to go out for breakfast the next morning. Wouldn't the same thing happen?"

"I suppose."

"And would you be this upset about it if people started talking about you and Random Guy?"

She shrugged. "I don't know."

"So maybe it does have a lot more to do with me than you think."

"I guess it's because we're not dating and we haven't been dating. But now there will be a rumor that we are."

"Oh." He nodded. "And you think this will hurt your chances with other men, that they'll see you as off the market."

Was that what she'd been thinking about? She had no idea. She only knew that people assuming a relationship where none existed bothered her. "I don't think that's it."

"Then what is it?"

"I don't know!"

She'd raised her voice enough that people at the nearby tables turned to look.

"Uh-oh. And now we've had our first fight. I'll bet that makes the rounds, too," he said, grinning at her.

She narrowed her gaze at him. "Now you really are pissing me off."

"We should kiss and make up." He got up and came over to her side of the booth.

Chelsea scooted away. "Bash, what are you doing?"

"Making sure they have something more to talk about."

Before she could object, he'd gathered her into his arms and pressed his lips to hers, giving her a hot, melt-your-panties kind of kiss that should not be given in a public place.

He pulled back only when someone cleared their throat.

Chelsea's heart pounded, and she was all too aware they had an audience. Like . . . the entire restaurant was staring at them.

Bash smiled at her, then rubbed her bottom lip with his thumb.

"Now there's no rumor. It's fact," he said, staying put on her side of the booth and smiling up at the waitress who stood there, full tray in hand, gaping at them.

"Uh, your breakfast is ready."

"Awesome," Bash said, seeming to be perfectly fine with being the center of attention.

Chelsea, on the other hand, wanted to crawl under the table and hide.

Though if she did crawl under the table, that would start another kind of rumor. And she had enough to deal with as it was, thanks to Bash.

He added salt and pepper to his eggs and started eating, while Chelsea had totally lost her appetite.

"I can't believe you did that," she finally said.

He swallowed and took a drink of orange juice. "Did what?"

"You know what. Kissed me like that."

He turned to look at her. "You don't like the way I kiss?"

"You know I do."

He pressed his lips to hers. "I like kissing you, too."

She scooted away from him. "Dammit, Bash. Stop doing that."

He laughed. "Eat your breakfast, Chelsea."

She was beyond irritated with him at the moment, but hunger finally won out and she decided to eat. Besides, eventually everyone else decided to eat as well, though she was certain she and Bash were the topic of every conversation in the place.

And when her phone started pinging with texts during her meal, she took a quick glance.

One from Samantha: Heard Bash laid a hot one on you in Bert's. Can't wait for deets.

Another from Megan: So I guess Bash kissing you at Bert's means . . . what? Call me!

And from Emma: My mother had to tell me Bash kissed you at Bert's. What's going on?!

There were more, but Chelsea finally turned her phone off.

"I take it from the nonstop vibrating of your phone that the rumor mill has started spreading the word."

She finished off her toast and took a drink of coffee. "You could say that."

"Huh."

She laid her fork and knife on the plate, then pushed it aside. "You don't even seem . . . upset."

"Why would I be? It's not the Dark Age, Chelsea. We're both single and unattached. We're allowed to see each other if we want to."

"I guess. Maybe I am making a big deal out of it for nothing."

"Hey, if you don't want to be seen with me, I understand. I'm gonna go pay the bill."

She'd hurt his feelings. Sometimes she could be such a bitch without realizing it. "Hey, Bash?"

He stopped. "Yeah?"

"Wait for me. I'm ready to go, too."

She grabbed her purse and got up, then laced her fingers through his.

He looked down at where their fingers were twined together.

"I would never be ashamed to be seen with you," she said. "Sometimes it just takes a minute for my head to get on board with what my body already knows."

He smiled at her. "Let's go."

She walked out with her head held high and her hand firmly in Bash's grasp.

The gossips could suck it.

Chapter 22

IT MIGHT TAKE a while for Bash to figure Chelsea out. She was definitely complicated. But not in a bad way.

The truth of the matter was, he liked how complicated she was. He couldn't predict her reactions, and that made her fun. And she sure as hell was sexy, smart, and smokin' hot. It was a pretty lethal combination.

Plus, she was all his for the day.

Now he just had to figure out what to do with her. Besides undress her and spend the day in bed.

He figured that's what she'd expect, but he wanted to keep her off balance.

So he stopped at her place, holding back a smile when she frowned at him.

"What are we doing here?"

"So you can get a change of clothes."

"For what?"

"I thought when we got back to my place, we'd take Lou for a walk. It's supposed to be a really nice day today. You don't want to spend it all cooped up in the house, do you?"

"But I thought—"

He purposely gave her a blank stare. "What?"

"Never mind. I'll be right back."

He knew exactly what she thought. That they were going to spend the entire time in bed.

Yeah, he'd like that a lot, but that's what she expected.

He wanted to give her the unexpected, and to show her this was more than just about sex.

She came outside about five minutes later carrying a large bag that she threw in the back of the truck, then climbed inside.

"Staying a week?" he asked.

"Funny. And no. But I might need a shower and a change of clothes. And makeup. I like to be prepared."

He grinned at her.

She shoved at him and laughed. "Just drive."

Chelsea took her bag into the bedroom to change. He went and changed, too, into his workout pants and a sleeveless shirt. It was supposed to be in the mid-eighties today, really warm weather for early May. He intended to take advantage of it with a nice walk. Lou was in good shape, and he'd already taken her to the park for long walks, so he knew she had great endurance for a small dog. He grabbed her harness and leash and put on his tennis shoes. By then, Chelsea had changed into a pair of tight capris and a short-sleeved shirt and put on her tennis shoes as well.

She always looked good, and God, she looked hot as hell in those heels she wore. But casual like this, with her hair in a ponytail and wearing workout clothes and tennis shoes? That did it for him, too.

Once he got the harness on Lou, they piled into the truck.

"Where are we going?" Chelsea asked.

"I thought we'd head to the park by the lake. There's a dog park over there that Lou likes."

"Awesome," she said. "I love it over there. I can't remember the last time I took a walk out that way. I usually take my walks over by my apartment."

He frowned. "There's no park that way."

"No. But I like to walk downtown. And now that the town square project is finished, I wander around that way. Plus, I can stop into the shops and browse on my way back."

"That's not a walk. That's a stroll."

She laughed. "Maybe."

He pulled into the parking lot at the entrance to the park, scooped Lou into his arms and set her on the ground, then attached the leash. She was already running forward, tugging on her leash.

Chelsea glanced down at Lou. "Obviously, she's ready."

"She is."

"Then let's go."

"If you don't mind, we'll head to the fenced-off dog park to start. It'll let Lou run off some frenzy before we walk."

"I'm fine with that."

The dog park was a short distance from the parking lot, so Bash led them there. It looked like there were quite a few people with their dogs already at the park, which would be good for Lou. They entered through the gate, and he let Lou off her leash. She didn't even hesitate, making a mad dash for a German shepherd nearby.

"She has no fear, does she?" Chelsea asked as they slowly followed along.

"She's turned out to be pretty feisty. I've brought her here a few times since I got her. She's friendly and not mean to other dogs or to people. She's a great dog."

Chelsea turned to him. "You're in love."

He couldn't fight the smile. "I might be."

"I can't blame you. She's irresistible. Look at her, tumbling around with that Shih Tzu."

"Oh, that's Barney. He's been here the past few times we have. They're good friends."

He waved to Victoria, Barney's owner. She waved back and headed their way.

"Hi, Bash. How's it going?"

"Good. Victoria, this is Chelsea."

Chelsea shook her hand. "Nice to meet you, Victoria."

"You too, Chelsea." She turned back to Bash. "So what are you up to today?"

"Just hanging out with Chelsea and Lou. You?"

"Letting Barney run off some energy for a bit." Victoria

turned around to look at the dogs. "The two of them sure do get along well, don't they?"

"Yeah, they do."

Chelsea stood back and watched the interplay between Victoria and Bash. Bash was being friendly, but not overly so. Victoria, on the other hand, was quite obviously interested in Bash.

And she was gorgeous, with long, brown hair and big brown eyes. She had long lashes that she was definitely batting in Bash's direction, too.

And when she slid her hands in the back pockets of her very short shorts, the action thrust her breasts right toward Bash, who didn't appear to notice. Or, if he did, he was polite enough not to ogle.

"It's like they're best friends already," Victoria said. "I'm glad you bring Lou around. A lot of the dogs that come here are big and play too rough for him, but Lou is the perfect size."

"They are a good fit, aren't they?"

"Yes. Perfect."

Yeah, there was some play on words going on, because Victoria's *perfect* sounded all breathy and sexy.

Very interesting. And Chelsea decided to ignore the twinge of jealousy, because Bash wasn't hers.

"By the way," Victoria said, "I was talking to Jay, the trainer who brings his dogs here. He's setting up an agility class. He's going to run it at the pet store in Tulsa. I thought you might be interested?"

"That sounds good."

"Great." She took out her phone. "Why don't you give me your number and I'll pass it along to Jay? He's talking about starting it in June."

"Okay." He gave Victoria his number.

Well played, Victoria.

Bash clearly had no idea he'd been maneuvered.

"Awesome. I need to get going, but I'll call you later. Nice to meet you, Chelsea."

"You, too, Victoria."

She walked away—slowly—the sway of her hips obviously

exaggerated. The interesting thing was, Bash hadn't even been watching, because he'd already turned his attention back to her.

"You could come with me."

"Where?"

"To the agility class."

She shook her head. "You didn't even notice it, did you?"

"Notice what?"

"Victoria. She was hitting on you."

He shifted his gaze briefly on Victoria, who had gathered Barney up and was heading out of the dog park. "Uh, no she wasn't."

"Yes, Bash, she was."

"No, she wasn't. In what way was she hitting on me?"

"First, she barely said anything to me other than hello and goodbye. Second, body language."

His brows rose. "Body language?"

"Yes. She leaned into you, and thrust her breasts out, and you totally missed her seductive walk away."

"I guess I didn't clue in to all of that. But come on. I'm with you. Surely another woman wouldn't do that."

She let out a short laugh. "You don't know women. We can be very competitive when it comes to men. And then she got you to give her your phone number."

"That was for the agility class."

"No."

"No?"

"No. For someone of your advanced dating age, I would've thought you'd be able to read all the obvious signs. I'm kind of disappointed in you."

She walked away, but he caught up in a hurry and grabbed her hand.

"Hey, I'm not clueless."

"If you say so. But I'll bet you ten bucks Victoria calls you by tomorrow night. And not about the agility class."

He turned to face her, determination set on his features. "I'll take that bet."

Chelsea shook her head. "It'll be the easiest ten bucks I ever make."

He cocked his head to the side. "You're just so damn sure of yourself, aren't you?"

"About everything? No. About this? Absolutely."

"You'll be sorry when you're wrong."

Before she could say anything else, he kissed her. Just a light, easy kiss, and not too passionate, since they definitely weren't alone in the dog park. She supposed she was getting used to these public displays from Bash, because when he pulled back and took her hand to wander around and watch the dogs, she didn't try to disengage.

Screw the gossips. They could think what they wanted. For today, at least, she enjoyed being with him.

After about thirty minutes, Lou came over, her tongue hanging sideways out of her mouth. They went and got her a drink, then Bash tethered her and they left the dog park.

Lou was much more subdued as they made their way along the path toward the lake.

Bash had been right. It was a beautiful day today, and while she sure wouldn't have minded spending it in bed with him, the weather was too nice to spend the day inside.

He stopped at the truck and pulled out a blanket, then walked them over to a shady spot on a hill overlooking the lake. He spread out the blanket and they sat. Lou settled in and promptly curled up next to her and went to sleep.

Chelsea looked out over the water. A flock of geese flew in and landed on the lake, creating waves along the surface. She watched the geese for a while, a little surprised when a couple of them ventured out of the water and toward them.

"People feed them, so they're not afraid of humans," Bash said. "Once they realize you don't have any food, they'll go away."

She was fascinated, having never been that close to geese before. They were so beautiful, with their long necks and shiny feathers. It made her wish she had some sort of geese food so she could entice them to linger, but, true to what Bash had said, they only ventured a couple of feet closer, then wandered off.

"Do you come here a lot on your days off?" she asked.

"Sometimes, when the weather's decent, I'll take a run around the park. Now that I have Lou it's more of a walking thing. If I want to run I have to leave her at home."

She looked down at Lou, snoozing peacefully by her side. She smoothed her hand over the dog. "I've always wanted a dog. Or even a cat. I mean, I had a dog when I was a kid, but not since then."

"You could buy a house, then you could have whatever animal you wanted."

"True. I just didn't want to make that kind of commitment. I figured I'd wait until I got married, or at least was in a long-term relationship. So far that hasn't happened. The longest relationship I had was a year, and we never got to the moving-in-together part before we broke up."

"That was Elliott, right?"

She was surprised he remembered, it was so long ago. "Yes."

"He was an asshole for letting you go."

She laughed. "In the beginning it was good. He just loved his career more than me. And I need someone who'll put me first."

"That's not on your list."

"True, but I think that's a given in any relationship."

"I guess so."

"What about your marriage? What went wrong there?"

He looked out over the water. "I don't know. We wanted different things, I guess. She wanted a different person than the person I was. I don't think I could ever fit into the mold of the kind of man she envisioned." He looked over at her. "Maybe she needed a list like yours."

For some reason that stung, but she didn't know why. "I don't think the list thing is for everyone. Some relationships don't work out for a multitude of reasons."

"You're right about that."

He went quiet, and Chelsea felt bad for bringing up his marriage. She'd always known it was a sore spot for Bash, but she'd never known why. It had been a lot of years since his marriage had ended, yet he never talked about it.

"I'm sorry," she said.

He looked over at her. "For what?"

"For bringing up your marriage. It's obviously still painful for you."

"Actually, it's not. I just can't ever seem to give anyone a good explanation for why it ended. It wasn't her fault and it wasn't my fault. We just didn't . . . fit. You know?"

"I do know. But you shouldn't give up on the idea of being with someone just because it didn't work the first time."

His gaze was direct. "Maybe you're right about that."

The air hung heavy between them, and she suddenly felt like she'd waded into pretty serious waters. She was drowning in the depths of his eyes, and needed to find a way to back herself out.

But before she could, he advanced on her, pushed her down on the blanket, and covered her mouth with his. Passion exploded, and she wrapped her leg around his, exploring the fullness of his lips, the way his tongue licked against hers, and the unleashing of her desires she felt whenever she was in his arms.

Until a hot, wet tongue lapped the side of her face.

She leaped up and laughed. "Ew. Thanks for the kiss, Lou."

Bash laughed, too. "Talk about a mood-killer."

Lou barked, got down on her haunches, and wiggled her butt, thinking it was playtime. Chelsea would rather play with Bash, but that was a different kind of game.

They wrestled with Lou for a while, now that she was awake. She'd advance and bark, then back away. Bash took her ball out of the bag he'd brought and she fetched it a few times, until she got tired and finally sat next to Bash's knee.

"Okay, fine," Bash said. "Time to go." He grasped Chelsea's hand and hauled her up, but wrapped an arm around her and gave her a quick kiss "We'll finish what we started once we get back to my place."

She grabbed hold of his shirt and pressed her nails into his chest. "I'm counting on it."

Because she wasn't nearly finished with him yet. And it was still daylight. There was a lot of time left before the sun set.

He was still hers, until the end of the day.

Chapter 23

BASH WATCHED CHELSEA play with Lou on the way home, wondering if she would want to bolt as soon as they got back to his place. It was getting late, and he knew his time with her was limited.

He pulled the truck into the garage.

"Do you want me to take Lou out back?" she asked.

He shook his head. "She should be fine, since she had a good run at the park."

"Okay."

He held the door and Chelsea came inside, then put Lou on the floor. The dog scampered over to her bowl, took a long, sloppy drink of water, then ran over to her toys, picked one out, and ran into the living room.

"She'll be happy playing for about five minutes," he said. "My guess is she'll be passed out shortly."

"She was pretty active today. It's good you exercise her."

He nodded. "She likes the park. She's made some friends."

Chelsea laughed. "You sound like a dad."

"I do not."

"Whatever you say . . . Dad." She wandered over to his cabinet and grabbed a glass. "Water?"

"Sure." And maybe he was interested in making sure Lou stayed active, but that didn't mean he was acting parental toward her. Chelsea brought his glass to him. "Thanks. And I'm not her dad, ya know."

"Whose dad? The dog's? Of course not. But you're really sweet with her."

"I feel sorry for her because she was stuck with Gerri. I might be overcompensating a little."

She took a sip of her water. "I can't blame you for that. You need to date less crazy women."

"You might have a point about that." He laid his glass on the kitchen counter, then took hers from her hand and put it next to his. He wound his arms around her waist, drawing her close. "Now, where were we before Lou slobbered all over our faces?"

She tilted her head up to meet his gaze, palming his chest. "I was on my back. You were kissing me."

He shifted, cupping her around her thighs to lift her. "Oh, yeah. I like the sound of that."

He took her to the bedroom and placed her on the bed. She rolled onto her side and he laid next to her, facing her, breathing her in. She smelled of the outdoors and something sweet, like cookies. He dragged her on top of him, just so he could nuzzle that sweet scent in her neck.

"What are you wearing?" he asked.

"Uh . . . clothes?"

"No." He kissed her neck, dragged his tongue over her skin. "Perfume."

"I'm not wearing perfume."

"Mmm. Must be your soap. Smells like cookies. I like it."

"If it makes you lick my neck like that, I'm washing with it every time."

He lifted her, so he could make eye contact. "You like that?"

"My neck is very sensitive."

"I'll keep that in mind."

He rolled her over again, this time following her, sliding

his hand under her T-shirt to palm the skin of her stomach. She was so soft, yet her muscles were firm—and quivered under his touch.

"Bash."

He lifted his head to see her watching him with a pensive expression. He wanted to know what she was thinking, what kind of deep thoughts put that look on her face. But he also didn't want to stop this train, so instead, he kissed her. He liked kissing her, loved the way she always eagerly fell into kissing him, matching him with passion. Her fingers dove into his hair, and damn, he liked the way she tugged at it, as if she wanted to claim possession of him when they kissed.

He moved his hand down, mapping her body. He enjoyed touching her, too, the way she sparked hot when he put his hands on her. He lifted her shirt and bent to press a kiss to her stomach, and was rewarded with her soft sigh.

He made quick work of removing her pants and underwear as well as her T-shirt and bra, then shed his clothes as well, needing to be skin to skin with her. When he pulled her on top of him, her hair fell against her cheek, soft red waves framing her face. He tucked her hair behind her cheek as she sat and straddled him.

He ached for her, his cock hard as she rolled against him, teasing him with her beautiful body. He reached up to cup her breasts, and when she covered his hands with hers, he lifted up to show her just how much he wanted her.

She slid back and forth over him, and he'd had enough of her teasing.

"Condoms."

"I know," she said. "Drawer." She climbed off and went over to his nightstand to take a condom out, then waved the packet back and forth as a tease as she stood beside the bed.

"Chelsea."

"I like the way you say my name." She crawled onto the bed, slid the package between her teeth, and grabbed hold of his cock.

There was nothing Bash liked better than to have his dick in a woman's hands. Other than having it in her mouth, of course. Or being inside of her. Those were kind of his top three awesome things. But Chelsea sitting on his thighs and sliding her hands over his shaft felt really damn good. Just watching her naked and having the time of her life teasing the hell out of him was entertaining, especially when she made slow work out of putting the condom on him. It might be one hell of a torture, but hey, it was her hands on him, so he could endure it.

And when she lifted, then came down on him, sliding her sweet sex over his cock, he took a deep breath, held on to her hips, and brought her forward, wanting to give her the same pleasure she was giving him.

She tilted her head back and closed her eyes, a naked goddess in his bed as she rode them both with soft, rhythmic movements.

"Mmm" was all she said as she rocked back and forth.

Yeah, he definitely understood what she meant, because it was exactly how he felt. Being able to look at her and feel her at the same time tightened him, made him want to thrust deeply inside her and give her everything he had.

But not yet, not when he could enjoy this view for a while longer. Especially when she leaned forward and dug her nails into his chest, then lengthened her body onto his.

His breath caught as he felt the full effect of her positioning herself on him that way, her entire body draped over his, her sweet sex capturing his cock in a tight, gripping sheath.

He slid his fingers into her hair and caught her lips in a kiss as he was caught in a vortex of sensation. She moaned against his lips as he thrust upward, rotating to take her with him.

And when she came, whimpering against him, he let go, too, gripping her butt as he lost control. He held tightly to her as his world turned on its axis so hard he thought for a few seconds there he might have stopped breathing.

But Chelsea was right there, her heart beating against his chest, her warm breath against his neck, and all was right again.

He disappeared for only a few seconds, then came back and pulled her to him.

She lay against him and he stroked her back, feeling more content than he could remember feeling in a long time.

That had been crazy, and yet oh-so-perfect at the same time. It was like she'd been right there with him the whole way, as out of control as he'd been. They'd needed no words—just each other and their bodies to communicate what they both needed.

Which didn't make a whole lot of sense, since it had just been sex, right? Really phenomenal sex.

He needed to stop thinking about just how good it had been with Chelsea. Because they weren't in a relationship and weren't going to be. It's not what she wanted, and it sure as hell wasn't what he wanted.

"Hungry?" he asked.

She didn't move. "Getting there."

"Okay. We'll go cook some burgers on the grill."

She lifted her head, resting it in her hands. "Now I'm definitely hungry."

He patted her butt, smoothing his hand over the curve there.

"Keep doing that and it'll be a war between two different hungers," she said.

"Which would win?"

"Not sure. But at the moment, my stomach is growling."

"Okay, we'd better get up, or I'm never letting you out of my bed."

She gave him a bright smile. "My students might miss me. And finals are coming up for my seniors. I kind of have to go to work tomorrow."

"You're ruining all my fantasies, princess." He gave her a quick kiss, then they slid out of bed and got dressed.

Bash heated up the grill while Chelsea got the patties ready. While he cooked the burgers and corn on the cob, she fixed a pretty delicious-looking salad.

Lou, who'd woken up after they'd climbed out of bed, spent time wandering around out back while he cooked. She was on the trail of something in the corner of the yard.

Probably a frog or a turtle, because she'd stuck her nose by the fence and was barking her head off.

"Get away from whatever it is, Lou."

"She's just excited she found something smaller than her," Chelsea said after she'd come out to keep him company.

He laughed. "You might be right about that. Though I don't think she cares if something is smaller. She thinks she's tough."

The barking continued, with Lou inching away from whatever it was, then charging it. Advance, retreat, over and over again.

Bash took the burgers off the grill, slid them onto the waiting plate, and handed them to Chelsea to take inside.

"Come on, Lou, let's go."

The dog ignored him.

"Lou. Inside."

Still nothing. Rolling his eyes, he walked toward the back of the yard to investigate. Sure enough, a turtle was lodged back there, stuck way inside his shell and probably highly offended by Lou's barking.

"Don't pick on things smaller than you, Lou," he said, then picked up the turtle and relocated it to his neighbor's backyard. His neighbor didn't have a dog, so he figured the turtle would be a lot more content over there. Then he shuffled Lou into the house.

They ate dinner, then washed dishes together.

"I forgot to ask you earlier. Did you figure out what Lou was barking at?" Chelsea asked while Bash put the last of the pots in the dish rack.

"Yeah. A turtle. Who's now living in my neighbor's yard."

"Aww. That was sweet of you." She came around to the sink and put her arms around him, laying her cheek against his back.

He stilled for a minute, absorbing her warmth and the tight way she hugged him.

He hadn't had a lot of love in his life, or a lot of people who had given a shit about him or what he did. His mom had loved him, but she was gone now, which left . . .

Pretty much no one.

Which didn't mean Chelsea cared. They'd just had one night, and today. No sense in making more out of it than it was.

He dried his hands and turned around. "Hey, I was only thinking of the turtle. Lou's not big enough to do any damage, but she was annoying the hell out of it."

She stepped into his arms, wrapping hers around him. "You're uncomfortable with people thinking you're a nice guy."

"What are you talking about?"

"I never noticed that about you. You taking care of me at the bar the other night and thanking you for it, and me complimenting you about being so sweet with Lou. It makes you uncomfortable when people notice you being nice."

"No, it doesn't. Hey, you want to watch some TV after dinner? Or even better, we could go back to bed." He waggled his brows.

"You also tend to change the subject when it's about you. Why is that, Bash?"

"I don't do that."

"Yes, you do. You're not a bad guy, you know."

"For someone who doesn't meet the criteria on your list?"

Her lips lifted. "Yes. For someone who doesn't meet the criteria on my list."

He cupped the side of her neck and kissed her, lost for words around her. There was something about Chelsea that got to him, and he didn't know what to do about her. So he did the only thing he knew how to do around her—show her how she turned him on, and how happy he was when she was near.

She molded her body to his, which meant he just had to cup her butt, drawing her closer. He lost himself in the softness of her lips, and the sounds she made when they kissed.

A sudden urge to have her, to be inside of her, flashed through him.

He turned her around and bent her over the counter, his hands all over her, and once again heat flared in an instant as she wriggled her butt against him, her drive equaling his. They shed their clothes and he left only long enough to grab a condom, and then he drove inside of her, taking in the sounds she made, the way she moved against him as he thrust deep, then retreated. He reached around to rub her clit, which caused her to moan long and loud as he brought her to a quick orgasm.

Her body tightening around him took him there in a hurry, and he finished off with his legs shaking, his arm wrapped around her.

The things Chelsea did to him made him question his sanity. She shook him to the core and made him want her over and over again.

He flipped her around and kissed her, his tongue diving in as he realized his passion for her hadn't waned at all.

When he pulled back, she touched her forehead to his. "I need to go."

"I know."

She grabbed her clothes and headed into the bathroom to clean up and get dressed. He ducked into the spare bathroom and did the same, giving her some time to catch her breath. Hell, he needed time to catch *his* breath, too.

When she came out, he was leaning against the kitchen counter drinking a glass of water. She had her bag packed and laid it on the sofa. She came over and grabbed the belt loop of his jeans.

"I had fun," she said.

"Yeah, me, too."

He picked up her bag and walked her to her car, opened the door, and slid her bag into the backseat.

This time she grabbed his shirt and hauled him against her, planting a blistering hot kiss on him. It seemed neither of them wanted this night to end, but he took a step back, because if he didn't walk away he was going to pick her up and carry her inside his house.

And she had her students to think about.

"I'll see you around, Chelsea," he said.

She got into her car and closed the door, but rolled the window down.

"Thanks, Bash," she said.

He nodded, then she backed down his driveway and drove away.

He'd never missed any woman who'd ever left him. Ashamedly, not even his ex-wife.

But once Chelsea left, he realized he already missed her.

That wasn't a good thing.

Chapter 24

THE FIRST ONE of her friends Chelsea ran into was Megan, because she stopped at the bakery before school on Monday.

"You have to tell me everything about Bash," Megan said as she slipped a croissant into a bag and then made Chelsea a tall caramel macchiato, which she would then have to spend about six hours working off this week. But she didn't care. Today called for a caramel macchiato.

"I promise to fill you in, but you have a long line of customers waiting, and I'm going to be late," Chelsea said, begging off and dashing to school.

Of course, then she had to face Jane, who caught up with her in the teacher's lounge before school started. Chelsea had hoped she'd actually be able to enjoy her croissant and drink and have some quiet time to reflect on yesterday and the day before.

"You didn't answer my text messages. Or my e-mails. Or my phone calls."

Chelsea looked up from her very appealing croissant to give Jane a blank stare. "I did text you."

Jane cocked her head to the side. "Your text said: *Occupied.*

We'll talk Monday. What does that even mean? Occupied with Bash, I assume. And how was it?"

She took a long sip of her drink before answering. "We had a good time."

Jane pulled up a chair next to her. "Oh no. You don't get to give me a non-answer like that."

She stuffed her face with a giant piece of croissant, and then she thanked the stars for timeliness, because the bell rang. She pointed to her full mouth, then the clock, and shrugged in apology, then grabbed her bag and her coffee and backed away from her friend.

Jane pointed a finger at her. "This conversation is far from over, Chelsea Gardner."

She knew it wasn't, but she honestly had nothing to say. She'd had an amazing day and a half with Bash. But they weren't an item, or a couple, or even dating.

They'd had sex, and that was it. And now it was over.

Which made her feel kind of empty inside. But she wasn't going to think about how she felt, especially as it related to Bash.

Not that her friends would let her forget about Bash, because several days later she was forced into a summit meeting.

Emma had called it dinner at her place. Luke was pulling night-shift duty for one of the guys on the squad and Emma had said Molly was hanging out with her. She said they were going to make it a girls' night. Will was working as well, which meant Jane would be there. Samantha and Megan were coming over, too.

Chelsea knew she shouldn't be suspicious of her friends' motives, but she hadn't told any of them details of her time with Bash, even though everyone had asked. And maybe they'd respect that, but she kind of doubted it. If the shoe were on any of these other women's feet, she'd hound them incessantly until they gave up the info, so why should she assume they'd leave her alone?

She'd slept with Bash. That made her fair game for gossip. And she'd spent the past few days—and nights—prepping for finals. She was tired of doing schoolwork. A girls' night sounded like a great idea.

She stopped at the liquor store after school and picked up a couple bottles of wine, then hit up the grocery store after that. She made a chilled crab salad that would pair exceptionally well with the crackers she'd bought.

After changing into a pair of capris and a long top, she slid into her wedge sandals and headed over to Emma's.

Emma answered the door and took the tray she was balancing on her hand.

"Whatever you've made, I'm going to love it," Emma said.

"You don't even know what I made."

"I don't care. I'm starving."

It looked like everyone but Samantha had arrived, so she gave them all hugs.

"I made chocolate-covered strawberries today," Megan said. "Oh, and baklava."

"You made baklava?" Chelsea asked. "In your spare time, when you're not running a bakery?"

Megan grinned. "Of course I did. I also picked up some champagne to go with the strawberries. That's dessert. Now what did all of you bring to entice me for our snacking-for-dinner soiree?"

"I made pasta," Jane said. "Thankfully, my parents picked up the kids after school, so I had time to cook."

"Awesome," Chelsea said. "Too bad you and Will couldn't have had the night alone."

"That is too bad. But we get plenty of alone nights together. The grandparents always want the kids."

The doorbell rang, so Emma left to answer it.

"I'll put the rest of the food on the counter," Molly said.

Chelsea opened up the paper plates and set them out. It was nearly seven, so she knew everyone was hungry.

"Sorry I'm late," Samantha said, placing her bowl on the counter next to everyone else's. "I had a late flower delivery. I hope the homemade meatballs make up for my tardiness."

Chelsea's stomach grumbled. "I love your meatballs. And actually, I just came in right before you, so I don't think you're late."

"No one's late," Emma said. "But I'm hungry, so let's grab plates and eat."

Bottles of wine were opened and plates were filled. Emma

had moved extra chairs to her table, and Chelsea filled her plate with pasta, several different salads, and, of course, meatballs. She knew her eyes were bigger than her stomach, but she wanted to try a little bit of everything. The wine was fantastic and helped her wind down some, which she'd desperately needed.

"I'm so not ready for finals," Jane said. "The end of school has come faster than normal this year. Or at least it seems that way. And Ryan and Tabby are already in summer mode. They're driving me crazy."

"All the kids are crazy," Chelsea said. "They're over school, and the whole idea of finals is tipping the scales for them."

Jane nodded. "Especially the seniors. Several of mine are so nervous."

"Yes. I'll be glad when the next week and a half is over."

"Are you teaching this summer, Jane?" Molly asked.

She shook her head. "Will wants to take a vacation with the kids, so I opted out. It'll be nice to have the time off."

"How about you, Chelsea?"

"I'm not certain yet. They had another math teacher lined up, but he might need surgery. I told them I'd fill in if necessary. It's not like I have any big plans this summer."

"Not even with Bash?" Sam asked, smiling at her over the rim of her wineglass.

She had known the question was coming. "Especially not with Bash."

"So he was lousy in the sack?" Megan asked. "That must have been disappointing."

"I didn't say that."

"What are you saying, then?" Emma asked.

"Nothing yet."

Everyone went quiet. And stared, obviously waiting for the lowdown on her weekend with Bash.

"Fine. We had sex."

"Woo!" Megan shouted. "I knew it. You always answer my texts right away, and when you didn't, I knew it was because you were with Bash."

She lifted her chin. "It could have been another guy."

"Really. What guy?"

"I don't know. Someone else."

"Is there someone else?" Samantha asked.

"Well, no. But there could be. There will be someday."

"Which means what, exactly?" Molly asked. "You and Bash didn't hit it off?"

She took a deep breath, then let it out. "It was fine."

Megan pinned her with a glare. "*Fine* is the word men use when they don't want to say, 'Yes, that dress does make your butt look big.' Women should never use the word *fine*."

She deserved this for butting in on all her friends' lives over the years. Now they were exacting revenge by butting in on hers. "Okay, it was awesome. He was amazing, and it was the best sex I've ever had."

Emma grinned. "Now you're talking. When are you seeing him again?"

"I'm not. We're not dating, Em. We're just friends."

"With benefits, now," Jane added. "Your weekend of awesome sex changed things between you, right?"

"No. It scratched an itch, that's all."

"Seriously?" Samantha arched a brow. "That sounds like a line a guy would use. You're the one who wants a relationship, Chelsea."

She had no idea how to explain this. Mainly because she didn't know how she felt. Nothing had changed between her and Bash.

Right? She'd made it clear to him. She didn't want things to change. They'd always been friends, and she didn't want to lose that.

"I do want a relationship. Just not with Bash."

"What's wrong with Bash?" Molly asked. "He has a great job, he owns a house, and he has the cutest dog ever."

"Hey," Emma said, resting one hand on Daisy the Labrador's head, the other on Annie the pit bull's. "I can't believe you said that in front of my dogs. And you're my sister. Talk about sticking the knife in deep."

Molly laughed. "Your dogs are my family. I wasn't referring to them. I was talking about one very hot guy and his adorable Chihuahua."

"Okay, then. But back to you, Chelsea. You seriously think nothing will change between the two of you? And you felt nothing for him?"

She'd be lying if she said otherwise. "Of course I did. We had fun together. Bash is a great guy. A decent guy. And so incredibly sexy."

"But . . ." Samantha said for her.

"But, there's my list."

Jane sighed. "Yes, your list."

These were her friends and she knew they all loved her. If they couldn't understand how important her list was, she'd just have to keep reminding them. "I made that list for a reason."

Emma squeezed her hand. "We all know you did. But you might be missing out on the right guy for you because of it. Maybe you're being a little too rigid in your thinking?"

She shrugged. "I don't think so. I'm sticking to my guns on this. Bash and I both agreed it was just sex, and nothing was going to happen otherwise."

Fortunately, they didn't press her further, and the topic changed, for which Chelsea was grateful. They spent the rest of the evening catching up on one another's lives. Chelsea left around eleven, but she wasn't tired or ready to go home.

For some reason, she found herself in the parking lot of the No Hope at All bar—again—wondering what in the world she was doing there. For a fraction of a second she pondered pulling out of the lot and going home. But she always listened to her instincts, and something told her she should be there. So now that she'd parked her car, she might as well go in.

No Hope was crowded, of course, because it was a Friday night. She didn't want to sit at a table by herself, so she headed to the bar. There was a single open spot at one of the corners. She sat and tossed her purse on the bar. Bash was busy at the other end, so it gave her a few minutes to watch him. Tonight he wore worn, loose-fit jeans and a dark green T-shirt that fit him so well it made all her feminine parts clench in appreciation, especially now that she'd seen him naked and knew just how good he looked without the shirt. And without the jeans.

Get a grip, Chelsea. Not happening again.

Megan had tried fixing her up with one of her regular customers from the bakery this week. She'd turned her down, saying she was too busy with finals. It was unusual for her to turn down a date. But she really had been busy.

Or maybe she was still riding that high from last weekend with Bash.

Still not happening again.

Lou was curled up in her crate at the far end of the bar, sound asleep. Something about that dog just got to her. Maybe because she was so tiny and Bash was so . . . big. Lou didn't seem like the type of dog Bash would have. She'd always pictured him with a Great Dane or a German shepherd, or even a golden retriever. Yet he'd taken to Lou right away, as if he and Lou belonged together. The two of them just seemed right for each other, even though on paper they just didn't fit.

Kind of like . . .

No. Not the same thing at all.

Bash turned, saw her, and smiled, then headed her way, his big body stretched out as he leaned across the bar.

She instinctively wanted to reach out and run her hands over his forearms, to feel that hard muscle she knew was there.

She resisted the urge.

"Hey, there," he said. "What brings you here so late?"

"I was over at Emma's tonight with all the girls, and I didn't feel like going home so I thought I'd stop in here for a nightcap."

"I'm glad you did. What can I get for you?"

She thought about it for a few seconds. "How about you fix something for me?"

"Something to keep you awake, or something to settle you down so you can go home and get some sleep?"

"Hmmm." She tapped her fingers on the bar. "I'll let you decide that one, too."

She was playing with him, flirting with him. She shouldn't be, but he gave her that sexy, teasing smile she found irresistible. So, why not?

"Okay. I'll be right back."

He wandered off and she flipped around on the barstool

to survey the room. Music was on, and sports recaps were displayed on the televisions. Men and women were playing at all the pool tables. Business was good for Bash. Chelsea was happy he was doing so well.

"Here you go," he said, setting a blue concoction down in front of her. It was in a margarita glass, so she assumed it had tequila in it.

She took a sip, licking the salt. It was rich and delicious, and not too sweet.

"I taste Chambord in there."

"Yeah. And some of my best tequila."

She felt the kick sliding down into her belly, but it was a smooth roar. "Whoa. You're right about that. It's yummy. Thanks."

She made it a point to drink the wickedly tasty cocktail slowly, because she could tell after she'd taken a couple swallows it packed quite a punch. Deceptively pretty little sucker.

She asked Bash for some water and took sips of that in between. She still had to drive home, and the liquor content in this was high.

She also had to fend off a couple guys who decided the suddenly vacant seat next to her was an invitation. One asked her if she was looking for a date. She politely declined, and when he continued to talk to her, motioned with her head toward Bash and said he was her boyfriend and she was waiting for him. That, at least, got rid of him. The second guy slid onto the barstool not too long after guy number one left. Based on his slurring speech, he appeared to be on about his tenth beer, and he was a leaner. He kept brushing her shoulder, obviously thought he was the funniest guy on the planet, and loved talking about himself.

Twenty minutes into their conversation he still hadn't asked Chelsea's name. But she knew all about his job, his friends, and his last two ex-girlfriends. Chelsea knew exactly why they were *ex*-girlfriends, too.

Bash kept looking her way, and she knew he would have gotten rid of the guy for her, but she had this one handled. He might be annoying, but he was pretty harmless.

"So, how about it," the guy finally asked. "Wanna get out of here and go someplace more . . . private?"

She tried not to laugh at the invitation. Instead, she pivoted on the barstool to face him. "What's my name?"

The guy frowned. "Huh?"

"What's my name?"

He blinked. "Uh . . . I dunno. Why don't you tell me?"

"I don't think so. And no, I'm not going anywhere with you, so you should stop wasting your time with me."

At least he was laid-back about it. He shrugged, mumbled something unintelligible, then slid off the barstool and wandered off. Chelsea shook her head and took a drink of water.

"Sorry about that," Bash said, coming over to replace her glass with a fresh one filled with ice.

"It's not your fault. Besides, I get hit on by men like him a lot. It's what you sign up for if you're going to sit in the bar by yourself late at night."

"Then I apologize on behalf of my gender."

She laughed. "Apology accepted."

After that, whenever any guy sat down next to her, Bash gave the guy a look that made it very clear she wasn't to be bothered. It was amusing to her that with one glare, he'd made her off-limits to the rest of the men in the bar.

Not that she had any complaints about that. She was tired of fending off men who thought a single woman in a bar was fair game. It was nice to have someone like Bash to run interference for her.

She ended up hanging out with him until closing. She had a soda and a couple of waters, and she took Lou out back for a walk. Which reminded her of a question she wanted to ask Bash. She brought the dog back inside, then wandered over toward the back of the bar, where he was putting bottles back in order.

"Did you ever hear from . . . hmm, what was her name again?"

He straightened to face her, then frowned. "What was whose name?"

"That woman from the dog park."

His lips curved. "Victoria. And yeah, I did. The next day."

"About the agility class, or something else?"

"She started off talking about the agility class, but then she asked me if I wanted to come over for some home cooking. She said I looked a little lean and probably needed a woman to cook for me."

She laughed. "I knew it." She held out her hand. "You owe me ten bucks."

He pulled out his wallet, took out a ten-dollar bill, and slapped it into her hand. "I hate when you're right."

"Hey, I know women. She definitely wanted you."

He gave her a very deliberate look. "Well, she didn't get me."

He walked away with a couple of empty bottles, leaving her standing there to consider what he'd said.

Victoria was quite a beautiful woman, plus her dog and Lou got along well.

She wondered why Bash wasn't interested.

Sometimes the right fit just wasn't there. Nobody knew that better than her.

Shrugging it off, she helped Bash shut down the bar. Why she stayed that long, she didn't know.

Or maybe she did know, because after his staff left, it was just the two of them.

Alone.

Maybe that's what she'd wanted all along, though she wasn't about to try and figure out why. She was tired of questioning her motivations for anything these days. Right now she was just going on instinct.

Bash finished up in the back and grabbed a zippered bag that he laid on top of the bar. "Other than needing to drop off this deposit at the bank, I'm done."

Chelsea was leaning against the front of the bar watching Bash close all the blinds. "You had a good night. It was crowded."

"It's been that way lately on the weekends. I think once we start serving food it'll be even better."

"When's that going to start?"

"I think I've finalized what I want. Reid helped me make some changes to the blueprints, so now I've got to file for new permits."

"A delay, huh?"

"Slight one, but that's okay. We'll get started within the next couple of months."

She could tell he was excited about making changes to the bar. "I'm happy for you."

"Thanks."

He came toward her, caging her between him and the bar. Despite having worked all night, he still smelled good—like a man who worked—and there was something very heady about that. She rested her palms on his chest, her nails digging into the material of his shirt. "So."

He slid his hand up her arm, and a shiver of pleasure raised goose bumps on her skin. Without the crowd packing in and raising the temperature in the bar, it was cooler now. But she knew her prickled skin was due more to his touch than to the air conditioning.

"So, Ms. Gardner, what would you like to do now?"

She raised her gaze to his, saw the desire written all over his face, and soaked it in. There was something so compelling about knowing a man wanted you.

It had been a long time since she'd been the subject of so much want and need. Maybe that's what had drawn her back to Bash. She knew the chemistry here. She was . . . *comfortable* wasn't the right word, because being with Bash was anything but comfortable. He made her decidedly uncomfortable.

He made her feel all sorts of things. Hot. Damp. Pulse-pounding desire. Things she knew she shouldn't feel for him, but couldn't seem to help herself from feeling whenever she was around him.

She pushed off the bar and leaned against him, sliding her hand upward to trace her fingers around his goatee, then his lower lip. "I think we should just wing it, Mr. Palmer."

His lips curved, and he bent to brush them across hers. A soft, exploratory kiss that soon turned more passionate. She breathed him in, felt his body align against hers as he wrapped his arm around her to tug her close.

Yes. That's what she'd waited all night for—to feel him, to be able to touch him freely. Ogling him from afar as he worked just hadn't done it for her. While she'd appreciated the view, she realized that hands-off had only whet her appetite for more. She wanted hands-on. She pulled his shirt out of his jeans and slid her palms up his back, loving the warm feel of his skin against her hands.

He groaned against her lips and rocked against her, his erection evident as he pushed her back against the bar.

Oh, yes. He fed her cravings by cupping her butt and drawing her even closer to her desire.

And when he rained kisses along her jaw and her neck, she shivered, especially when he turned her around and pressed her against the bar.

"Ever make love in a bar, Chelsea?" he asked, raising her shirt to fill his hands with her breasts.

She shuddered, barely able to form a coherent thought, let alone an answer. "Not yet, but I have a feeling I'm about to."

He unbuttoned her jeans and slid the zipper down. His warm hand cupped her sex. She pulsed, desperate for him to release the ache that pounded incessantly between her legs. He massaged her with rhythmic strokes, rocking his erection against her as he took her right to the edge, only to back off and bring her there once again.

And when she came, she cried out his name, throwing her head back against his shoulder and arching against his hand until she thought she might lose her mind.

He kissed her temple and released her, turning her around to take her mouth in a scorching kiss that blinded her senses, making her whimper and beg for more.

They shed their clothes, and Bash surprised the hell out of her by lifting her and laying her on top of the bar. He grabbed a condom out of his pocket and put it on, then climbed onto the bar and lay on top of her, sliding into her in one hot thrust.

She wrapped her legs around him and lifted against him as he plunged into her, a hot, passionate dance that made them both sweat. She swept his hair away from his face as he looked down at her while he drove into her.

She thought it would be over quick, but he slowed the tempo to an achingly sweet, torturous dance where she felt every part of him. He lifted himself off of her so she could only feel where they were connected, only see the way he looked at her.

She could barely breathe, could only feel, and what she felt in this moment swept her away.

He brushed his lips over hers, a soft, sweet moment, achingly tender as he moved within her. She was lost in him. She tried to hold back the overwhelming sensations, but she couldn't, and when he swept his hand underneath her to bring her closer to him, she lost all sense of reality. She clutched his shoulders, tightened around him, and cried out as her climax shattered her. And this time, she took Bash with her, the two of them shuddering as they fell off the never-ending cliff of bliss together.

She felt like she might never be right again, that this time, things might have gone too far. Because that had felt like a lot more than just sex. She'd seen it in his eyes, but maybe it had just been a crazy reflection of some really good physical lovemaking.

And maybe she'd just made more out of it than she should. She'd have to get her senses back to figure it out.

"I'm sweaty," he said. "And now I'm going to have to sanitize the top of the bar."

She laughed, grateful to Bash that he hadn't said something profound or emotional in the moment.

He hopped off the bar, then helped her climb down. The two of them went into the bathroom to clean up and get dressed. Then she helped him clean the bar, and they gathered up Lou, who, through it all, had slept peacefully in her crate.

Chelsea grabbed her keys. "I guess I'll head home."

Bash frowned, then scooped his arm around her waist. "I don't think so. Follow me home."

She couldn't help the warm feeling that surrounded her at his words. "Okay."

He walked her to her car and waited while she got in. Then he put Lou's crate in there with her. "Wait for me and I'll pull the truck around."

She nodded, still full of those idiotic warm fuzzies.

She was going to have to do something about all these . . . feelings.

Because sex was one thing. Emotions were something else entirely.

Chapter 25

IT HAD BEEN a really good night last night.

A damn good night. First, business was looking up. Second, Chelsea had shown up, and stayed, and then they'd had some phenomenal sex.

Then she'd come home with him and they'd had even more amazing sex.

Nights didn't get much better than that.

Chelsea was currently asleep on her stomach next to him. He rolled over to his side to watch her. Her gorgeous red hair had fallen over half her face, but her mouth was open and she was breathing deeply.

God, this woman was gorgeous. He didn't know if she realized how goddamn beautiful she was.

She'd kicked the covers halfway off, so her back was visible, as was half her butt. He'd like to have a picture of her like this, even with her hair messed up, and her mouth open in sleep.

She'd stayed up pretty damn late for him last night, considering she'd worked yesterday, and he knew how early she had to get up for school. Plus, they'd stayed up even later playing after they'd gotten home last night. He smiled thinking about how well she played, too. Sexually, she was adventurous and up for anything. He liked that a lot.

She also had to be exhausted, but she never complained.

She was a lot tougher than most of the women he knew. He gave her a lot of points for that.

She might come across as someone who was picky and particular, but in his heart he knew she would be game for just about anything.

But was he?

Maybe it was time he tried it out.

He heard Lou stirring, so he slid out of bed and put on his jeans, closed the bedroom door, then took Lou outside. He fed the dog, then grabbed his keys and made a quick drive over to Bert's. When he got back, Chelsea was in the kitchen drinking a cup of coffee and wearing one of his T-shirts.

Man, he'd never get tired of that sexy sight. Just seeing her in one of his T-shirts made his dick hard.

"Where'd you go?" she asked.

He laid the bag from Bert's down on the counter. "I made breakfast."

Her lips curved. "You're my hero."

He went to fix a cup of coffee. "I hope you like it. I made it especially for you."

She put her arms around him and kissed him. "Whatever it is, I'll like it. I'm starving."

They ate breakfast together—egg sandwiches, as it turned out—and Bash asked her about finals.

"Graduation is next weekend, so I'm almost finished for the year. Unless I have to teach summer school."

"When will you know?"

"By next week. If the scheduled teacher has to have surgery, I'll fill in for him. If not, I'll have the summer off."

He bit into his sandwich, chewed, then swallowed. "Whatever will you do with an entire summer off?"

"Read. Go to the pool. Shop. Maybe take a vacation somewhere."

"Sounds fun."

"Doesn't it? What about you? Do you ever take a vacation?"

"It's hard to be a business owner and take vacations, but yeah, I take time off now and then. I like to go camping in the summer."

She wrinkled her nose. "Sounds like so much fun."

He laughed. "I know you don't mean that, but it actually is a lot of fun. You should try it sometime."

"If my blow-dryer can't go with me, then it's not a vacation."

"Where I camp, there are actual bathrooms. With outlets for your blow-dryer."

She gave him a disbelieving look. "You're lying."

"I am not." He leaned back in his chair and took a sip of coffee. "I was thinking, actually . . ."

He didn't finish.

"Thinking what?"

He shrugged. "You wouldn't go for it."

"Wouldn't go for what, Bash?"

He wanted her to want this, but if she didn't, things between them would likely end. He didn't know how he felt about that. But the only way he'd find out was to say it, and he wasn't a coward. "You and I have been sleeping together. Why don't we try actually dating?"

She stared at him. "Dating?"

"Yeah. Dating. You know, go out. Do things together."

"Oh."

"You might be surprised to find we have more in common than you think."

She arched a brow. "You've seen my list, right?"

"I have. And you know what I think about your list."

She rested her chin in her hand. "I believe you said it was stupid."

"Did I?"

"You did."

"Hmm. Maybe I did. Either way, let's try this. I might surprise you."

"You really want to date me? You know how picky I am."

"Yeah. But I'm willing to take you out anyway."

She laughed. He loved her laugh, because it was always genuine, and never forced. "Okay, Bash. You asked for it, and now you've got me."

He liked the sound of that. As prickly as she was, she was also fun. "Good. Would you like to go out to dinner?"

"When?"

He thought about it. It might take some rearranging of his staff, but Hall had been pressing him for more responsibility—along with giving him shit for not taking more weekends off.

"How about tonight?"

Chelsea cocked her head to the side. "On a Saturday night?"

"Sure."

"It's your busiest night of the week."

"Yeah, but Hall's been doing a great job as assistant manager at the bar. I'll let him know I'm not coming in tonight."

She looked him over.

"What?"

"I'm trying to figure out if you're going to break out in a sweat—or maybe hives—at the thought of not being there on a Saturday night."

"Hey now. I've missed weekends. Just last month, as a matter of fact, when Logan and Des got married."

"True."

"So are we on for tonight?"

She hesitated, and he wondered if she'd turn him down—if she'd changed her mind.

But, finally, she smiled. "We're on."

Chapter 26

CHELSEA HAD SEVERAL things to do, so after breakfast, she went home, did some laundry, prepped her test list for Monday, and took a shower. After that, she tried to decide what she was going to wear for dinner.

She'd forgotten to ask Bash where they were going, but, knowing Bash, it wouldn't be any place fancy. Still, she hated assuming. She supposed she could ask him. She sent him a text message.

Where are we going for dinner?

He answered about ten minutes later.

It's a surprise.

She rolled her eyes. Typical man. She typed a response.

How am I supposed to know what to wear? Jeans or a dress?

Wear a dress. Mainly because you have great legs.

Interesting. Was he taking her someplace nice, or did he just want to ogle her legs?

She already knew the answer. Bash was a burger and fries kind of man. Maybe they'd go to a restaurant in Tulsa, or maybe to one of the steak joints, but it wasn't going to be anywhere fancy.

He didn't do fancy. He was a simple kind of guy. She could work with that.

The weather was warming, which she loved, because it meant her clothing options broadened. She chose a sleeveless black dress, low cut in the front, with high-heeled black sandals, and topped it off with a silver pendant that hung in the V between her breasts.

He might be taking her for steak or burgers, but she'd make sure he had something else delectable to look at besides the food.

She did her hair in soft waves and left it down so it caressed her shoulders, put on her favorite pair of diamond stud earrings, and left her wrists bare.

Then she examined herself in the mirror, turning back and forth to make sure the effect was as she intended. Her breasts were nicely accentuated in the dress, but not overly exposed. The dress hit just below her thighs, showing off the right amount of leg, and as she turned around, she was satisfied it highlighted her butt to perfection.

She was ready to knock Bash on his ass. She pulled out a cardigan, because the nights were still a little cool and she wasn't sure where they were going.

The doorbell rang, so she grabbed her sweater and purse and opened the door.

Okay, so she was the one knocked on her ass. Bash was wearing a crisp black suit, a white shirt, and a very fashionable tie.

"Did someone die?"

He frowned. "No. Why?"

"Because you're wearing a suit."

"I can wear a suit."

"Yeah. When someone gets married or dies. So nobody died. Are we going to a wedding?"

"You're funny. Also, you're a knockout."

She smiled. "Thank you. But seriously, Bash. A suit?"

He looked down at himself, then back at her. "You don't like it."

"I love it. I'm just . . . surprised."

"It's on your list. I thought I'd show you I could be list-appropriate."

Her lips curved. "You are definitely list-appropriate in that suit."

He held his arm out for her. "Let's go, gorgeous."

She shut the door and slid her hand in his arm. He led her out to his car. "No truck tonight?"

"You don't want to climb into my truck when you're wearing a dress, though I'd enjoy the view."

She slid into the passenger side. "I'm sure you would."

He took the freeway and headed toward Tulsa.

"You aren't going to tell me where we're going?"

He glanced her way for a few seconds. "And ruin the surprise?"

"We're not going to shoot paintball or do laser tag or anything, are we? Or go to Chuck E. Cheese's?"

He laughed. "I'd never wear a suit for those activities. And you obviously don't trust me."

"Obviously."

She stared out the window for a while, enjoying the bright colors. They'd gotten a significant amount of rain the past few days and everything was greening up. Weather was warming, people were spending time outside, and school was almost over. Summer was approaching, and it was Chelsea's favorite time of year.

"How about I promise to never make you wear a dress when we go play laser tag?" Bash asked.

She shifted to face him. "How about you never take me to play laser tag?"

"I can't make that promise. Laser tag is way too much fun."

She shook her head. "You're a child."

"Life's too short to be a grown-up all the time, Chelsea. Sometimes you gotta let loose and have some fun."

"I have plenty of fun."

"I mean kid fun."

"I'm too old for kid fun."

He leveled a serious look on her. "I'm going to take that as a challenge. And you're never too old for kid fun."

She was about to argue the point, but he exited the freeway, and she was curious about where they were headed. She'd come into Tulsa frequently to eat. She knew where everything was. Not that she'd eaten at every restaurant, but she knew where all the burger joints and franchise steakhouses were.

So when he bypassed the one she'd guessed he was taking her to, she was surprised, and even more shocked when he pulled into the parking lot housing Bodean Seafood Restaurant.

"I haven't eaten here in years."

He turned off the engine and turned to her. "It's one of my favorite seafood places."

Hers, too, though she didn't frequent it. It was pricey, but the food was fantastic.

And also the last place she figured he'd bring her.

He opened her door and held out his hand to help her out of the car. Then he held her hand as they walked inside.

"Reservation for Palmer," he said.

He'd made reservations, too?

"Right this way, Mr. Palmer," the hostess said, showing them to their table.

"The last time I ate here, the place was a lot smaller. And across the highway," she said as they took their seats.

The restaurant had expanded to a new building several years ago. There was a lot more space now. Where before, tables were crowded together and you could overhear conversations on both sides of where you were sitting, this new restaurant was laid out beautifully, with plenty of room for booths and tables and a gorgeous slate fireplace in the eating area. It was modern, yet warm, inviting, and completely luxurious.

She ran her fingertips over the white tablecloth, then looked up and smiled as their waiter approached.

His name was Sean and he presented their menu and wine list. Someone else brought water.

Bash picked up the wine list.

"Do you need me to help you make a selection?" she asked.

He gave her a look over the top of the list that told her he didn't want or need her assistance. Okay, then.

"Is there a particular wine you prefer?" he asked.

She was interested in what he'd order. "No. Go ahead."

When the waiter came back, Bash ordered a very nice bottle of pinot grigio.

She was impressed. It was one she'd have ordered for a special occasion.

"Nice call. And I'm surprised."

"You think it's because I only know beer and hard liquor. You forget that liquor is my business. All kinds of liquor, including wine."

"I highly doubt you serve that particular brand of wine at the bar."

"No, but it's my job to know what's good."

The waiter presented the bottle, opened it, and poured the glass for Bash. He swirled the liquid around the glass, sniffed it, then swallowed and nodded to the waiter, who then poured a glass for Chelsea and filled Bash's glass.

The wine was smooth and delicious. "It's very good," she said.

"I thought you might like it. I know you have a refined palate for wine."

Her lips curved. "I do enjoy a good wine."

"So do I . . . on occasion."

"Like tonight?"

"Like tonight. With great food you have to have a special wine."

There were layers to Bash she hadn't yet uncovered. That made her like him even more. Especially since there were no burgers on this menu.

He ordered oysters for his appetizer, and she had the lobster bisque, which was fantastic. For dinner, Bash had the trout, and she had the scallops.

"Can I taste the trout?" she asked.

He scooped up a forkful and passed it over to her. When she would have taken the fork from him, he held on to it. He wanted to feed her.

Of course. That was so Bash. She took the bite from his fork.

"Mmm," she said after she swallowed. "Good."

He'd been watching her mouth, and she caught that look in his eyes, the one that was becoming all too familiar to her.

Desire.

It made her clench in a way that was also becoming familiar when she was around him. She filed that away for later.

"Would you like a bite of my scallops?" she asked.

"I would."

She sliced off a section and put it on her fork, and like he'd done for her, she fed it to him. There was something so sensual about having someone eat from your fork. Such a simple thing, and yet she found herself watching his lips curve around her fork, saw the flick of his tongue as he captured the scallop and took it into his mouth.

Then again, how could any woman not be fascinated by Bash's mouth? It was a dangerous thing. She could still feel every kiss he'd ever laid on her, and all the other delicious places his mouth had been.

Her nipples puckering in this fancy restaurant was so not appropriate. Nor was her focusing on his mouth.

And the way he smiled at her told her he knew exactly what she was thinking.

She picked up her wineglass and emptied it. Bash refilled it, that enigmatic look on his face ever present.

She was in serious trouble with this man. So instead, she focused on her dinner, which she finished. Along with way too much of their fantastic bread. She was going to regret that during her next workout.

When the waiter brought the dessert menu by, it was all she could do not to groan.

"Dessert?" Bash asked.

She shook her head. "I'm so full I feel like I could burst."

"How about coffee?"

Again, she said no. "I need to get up and move around before I curl up and fall asleep in this booth."

He laughed. "We can't have that." Bash signaled the waiter, then asked for the check.

"Thank you for dinner," she said. "I don't know why it's taken me this long to eat here again. The food was incredible."

He handed the waiter his credit card. "Yeah, it's really good. I don't come here very often, either. Then again, I don't often have the opportunity to bring an amazing woman out to dinner."

He was saying all the right things. If this were their first date—which, she supposed, it technically was—she'd think he was perfect. Suit and tie, great manners, excellent selection in wine, and the choice of restaurant was spot-on.

But she also knew that Bash didn't tick off a lot of the items on her list.

Did that matter?

Not tonight, it didn't.

He signed the credit card slip the waiter brought by, then stood and came over to her side of the booth, holding her hand while she slid out. They walked to the front door and realized it was raining outside. And not just a little rain, either. It was pouring.

"Stay here," he said. "I'll bring the car to the door."

"Okay."

She walked outside, staying underneath the overhang to watch Bash dash through the parking lot. The rain was coming harder now, the wind slashing like sheets so hard her feet and legs were getting wet. She'd long ago lost sight of Bash, but she finally saw headlights as he pulled up in front of the restaurant. She was about to make a run for the car when he got out and she saw he had an open umbrella. He hurried toward her.

He was so wet, the poor guy, but he gathered her against him. And he was smiling down at her. "Ready?"

She pulled off her shoes and held them in her hand, then nodded. "Yes."

They ran toward the car. Bash handed her the umbrella and opened her door. She got inside and he shut the door, then hurried around to the other side, got in, and slammed the door shut.

His hair was plastered to his head, and water ran in rivulets down his face.

"Well, that was wet," he said.

Even though he'd parked the car at the curb, she was soaked, and her dress stuck to her skin. She couldn't even imagine how drenched Bash must be.

"I had no idea it was going to rain tonight."

He shrugged. "Spring in Oklahoma, ya know." He put the car in gear, turned the heater on to full blast, and headed out.

The rain continued the entire way back to Hope, with a

little lightning and thunder thrown in for good measure. Bash drove slowly on the freeway because visibility wasn't good. They finally exited the freeway and headed several miles into Hope, and to his house. The rain hadn't let up, either, which meant when he let Lou out of her crate he was going to have to take her outside in the rain.

He shrugged out of his suit coat and shoes, leading Lou to the back door.

"I'm going to strip and take a hot shower while you do that," she said.

He nodded and led Lou to the back door, while she headed toward the bathroom. She was chilled and freezing. After turning the water on in the shower, she started peeling her clothes off, letting them drop to the floor. As soon as the shower was heated up, she climbed inside and let the steamy water pour over her head. Her skin was so cold, but the hot water was definitely helping. She grabbed the washcloth she'd brought in with her and scrubbed her makeup off.

In a few minutes, the door opened and a naked Bash stepped inside with her.

"Christ, it's cold and wet outside."

She moved aside to let him have the hot water.

"No," he said, pulling her against him. "Stay here."

His body was cold, but not for long. She wrapped her arms around him and lent him some of her own heat, laying her head against his chest.

"I'm sorry about the storm. I was going to take you dancing after dinner tonight."

She tilted her head back. "You were?"

"Yeah. Plans got spoiled after we got soaked."

She started swaying back and forth with him. "We can dance in the shower. It's warmer here."

He smiled. "Kind of hard to dance in here. Slippery."

"We'll take it slow."

"No music." .

She cocked her head to the side, exasperated. "Use your imagination, Bash."

"I have a pretty good imagination, though there's usually no music involved."

She laughed.

He slid his arm around her waist and got into the dance, though she wasn't sure if what he was doing could be considered dancing—unless it was dirty dancing, because he slid his thigh between her legs and she suddenly forgot all about dancing or the music in her head. And when he backed her against the wall and kissed her, she also forgot about being cold.

In an instant, he'd heated her from the inside out, his body pressing into hers, all his good parts touching all of her good parts. She raised her leg and wrapped it around his hip, undulating against him.

He pulled his head away to look at her. "Keep doing that and we're going to have a problem."

Her lips quirked. "A problem?"

"Yeah. No condoms in the shower."

She scraped a nail down the side of his arm. "Hmmm . . . that is a problem, isn't it? I'm already plenty warm."

"Me, too."

He turned the shower off and they got out. Bash handed her a towel. She hurriedly fluffed her hair dry, ran the towel over her body, and then draped it on the counter to dry. Before she could head for the bedroom, Bash backed her against the counter, her butt resting against the towel. He spread her legs and put his mouth on her sex, making her gasp.

The bathroom was hot and steamy, and her temperature rose even more as Bash took her to great heights of pleasure with his mouth. She was primed and ready to go off and came in a lightning-quick jolt, reaching down to slide her fingers through his hair as she shivered with post-orgasmic delight.

He licked her thighs, kissed her hip, and trailed a map of hot, wet kisses up her stomach and breasts, lingering at her nipples until she was on fire all over again. His cock lay heavy against her belly as he finished off at her mouth with a long, deep kiss that made her whimper against his lips.

He led her to the bed, put on a condom, and spread her legs, entering her with a quick thrust that made her moan in deep pleasure. He took her mouth as he drove against her. It was a quick, passionate coupling that she craved as much as he did. Neither of them needed to say anything. Their eyes said it all as they looked at each other while they moved together.

And when she felt the quivers, knew she was close, she raked her nails down his arms, then lifted against him. She saw the furrow of his brow, the intensity in his eyes, and felt the way he ground against her, which shattered her. He kissed her, a deep, soulful kiss she felt through every part of her as he took the ride with her, both of them clinging to each other as they rode out the waves of pleasure that never seemed to end.

Afterward, he brushed her still-damp hair away from her face and kissed her temple. She laid her hand on his chest and felt his heart pump as it went from mad fast to normal again.

She was certain she looked like Medusa. She hadn't combed out her hair, and she wasn't sure all her makeup had washed off.

She didn't care, which was a first for her. She always presented an impeccable appearance, especially around men she was . . .

Dating. She supposed they really were trying out this dating thing.

The funny thing was, she was so comfortable around Bash, she didn't care that she looked like hell right now. Then again, they had been friends for so long, he'd seen her at her worst, and also her best.

That was a first for her.

He looked over at her. "You're staying tonight, right?"

No mention of her raccoon makeup, her crazy, wild hair. No laughing at her. He'd just asked her to stay with him.

Warmth surrounded her.

"Yes. I'm staying."

He gathered her close, and Chelsea was certain she was in way over her head.

She had to keep reminding herself their relationship was just a temporary thing. He still wasn't the perfect man for her.

But for right now? This was really good.

Chapter 27

BASH TOOK HIS car into Carter's shop for some repairs. He'd noticed when driving it the last few times that it was making a grinding noise. He knew it was going to need new brakes soon, but *soon* had become *now*. Especially after being out in that rainstorm with Chelsea in his car. Bad brakes and a rainstorm didn't go together well at all.

Normally he drove the truck and let his car sit. He was considering selling it, but it was an older model Honda and he was going to have to get some work done to it anyway to get it ready to sell.

Today was a good day to get that work started.

He sat in Carter's office while Carter prepared the paperwork.

"This is normally the shop manager's job, ya know," Carter said as he and Bash went over the list of everything Bash wanted done to the Honda.

"But then you'd miss spending time with me. What a loss that would be for you."

Carter shook his head. "Yeah. Right. So, besides the brake work, you want an oil and filter change, and a check on the A/C unit. Then you want some bodywork done as well?"

"Yeah. I got hit a year or so ago on the back quarter panel while I was parked at the grocery store and I never bothered to get it fixed. I'd like that smoothed out and repainted."

Carter nodded, writing it all down. "Drive it around the back and I'll have Brady take a look at it, then we'll figure up an estimate."

Bash drove the car around to the back where the bays were located and parked. By then Carter had walked out with Brady, who'd started working several months ago as his auto body specialist.

"Hey, Brady," Bash said.

Brady nodded. "How's it goin'?"

"Good."

"Carter tells me you want to do some bodywork on the Honda?" Brady was already walking around the car.

"Yeah. I'd like to sell her. The smaller dings are okay, but I want the major dents fixed."

Brady crouched in front of the damaged panel. "This looks like the worst of it. Some grocery cart get violent with you?"

Bash laughed. "More like an errant teenager with a new driver's license. A bash-and-run at the grocery store."

"Even worse." Brady stood. "Should be an easy enough fix."

Brady jotted down some notes on the clipboard Carter had handed him. He gave it back to Carter, and Carter took it inside, saying he'd have a total for him shortly. Bash decided to hang around the shop where Brady was working. Brady had popped into the bar a few times since he'd been back in town, though he tended to drink his beer and keep to himself.

He'd known about Brady's brother, Kurt. Bash and Kurt had been the same age, had gone to high school together. It had been a bad deal for Kurt, and he knew what happened must have devastated Brady, though Brady didn't talk about it.

Not to Bash, anyway.

"How's the job going?" Bash asked as he watched Brady put a finishing polish to a now-shiny, restored Grand Prix.

"Good. There's a lot more bodywork here than I thought there'd be when I first took the job. Both custom work and fixing dinged-up cars—like yours." Brady quirked a grin in his direction.

"Glad to help keep you in business. Carter said word's gotten out that you're here, so you're getting a lot of restoration pieces."

"Yeah. Those take longer, but those and the custom motorcycle jobs are the ones I enjoy the most. I work on them in my off-hours so they don't interfere with regular business."

"That's what you want to do eventually, isn't it? Open up your own shop and just do the bike repair and painting?"

"Yeah. Eventually."

"You're still staying above the shop?"

Brady nodded, then grabbed a rag and wiped his hands. "It's a good spot, and I can easily do night and weekend work on the bikes. It's convenient."

"How are your parents?" He knew it was a personal question, but he liked Brady, and it was an indirect way of asking how he was doing without actually asking.

Brady finally made eye contact. "They're doing okay. It's hard for them, you know? They haven't really been able to grasp that Kurt's gone. And they keep blaming themselves, even though I've tried to explain to them that it wasn't their fault." He paused for a few seconds, then added, "Wasn't anyone's fault, really."

"Not in that situation, no. Not much anyone could have done."

Brady dragged in a breath. "Nope."

Bash felt the pain radiating off Brady and wished there was something he could do or say to take that pain away, but he knew there was nothing. "I'm sorry, man."

Brady shrugged. "It is what it is, ya know?"

"Yeah."

"I need to get back to work." And just like that, his smile returned. "I'll get your Honda shiny and new so you can find a buyer for her."

"I'm sure you will." He shook Brady's hand. "Thanks."

Bash wandered back into the office. Carter handed him the estimate. Bash went over it and nodded. "This looks fine. Since I'm leaving the car here with you while it's being worked on, maybe you can give me a ride home?"

"Sure."

They slid into Carter's Mustang and headed out.

"Where's Molly today?"

"She's doing a training at one of the other shops."

"Ah, okay."

Bash always enjoyed a ride in Rhonda, Carter's '67 Shelby Mustang. It was a gorgeous restored classic, and just to feel her engine rumble was a joy that every man needed to experience once in his lifetime.

Someday, he was going to have to buy a classic car. In his spare time. With all that spare money he never seemed to have.

"I talked to Brady about Kurt," Bash said as they took a slow ride along Hope's main street.

"Yeah? How did that go?"

"About like you'd expect. I mainly asked about his parents, but I thought maybe he'd open up about his brother."

Carter shook his head. "He doesn't talk about it. To me, or to anyone, as far as I know. He's a lot more animated now than he was when I hired him, but Kurt's death really hit him hard."

"It hit all of us hard. I think about him a lot, wishing there was something I could have done. I can't even imagine what goes through Brady's head."

"Yeah, me, too. It has to be tough on him. I just wish he'd talk to somebody about it."

"How do you know he hasn't? He's got friends, right?"

Carter shrugged. "He used to, but as far as I know, no one comes around the shop, and he mostly hangs out there, working or doing bike jobs at night and on the weekends."

Bash nodded. "I've seen him at the bar a few times. Alone. I've tried to engage him, but I haven't gotten very far. He needs friends. Someone to talk to."

"He'll talk to someone. When he's ready. He's obviously not ready yet."

Bash hoped so. Holding that kind of shit inside of you only made it worse.

"So how are things going with Chelsea?" Carter asked, obviously needing a change of topic as much as Bash did.

"Good. I think. I don't really know."

Carter laughed. "That was a vague non-answer."

"I guess it was. I don't know what to think about her. She's got some definite ideas about what she wants in a guy, and I'm not it."

Carter turned the corner, giving Rhonda some gas. "Yet she seems to spend all her time with you."

Carter had a point. "She does."

"So maybe she likes being with you."

"Well, yeah. Who wouldn't?"

Carter laughed. "That's what I've always liked about you, Bash. You're so humble."

"Right?"

"But seriously, about Chelsea, what do you think?"

"I don't know. We're just taking it day by day. Or at least I am. I don't want to get in too deep with a woman who has a perfect-man list when I don't meet the criteria."

Carter pulled up in front of Bash's house, then turned off the engine and turned to him. "Look, I'm not the best at giving advice, and if anyone could fuck up a relationship in the worst way, it's me. But here's the thing. The brain and the heart are two different organs. What one thinks it wants may not have anything to do with how the other feels. Molly and I spent a lot of years apart figuring that out."

Bash nodded. "Yeah, I get that."

"So if you've got feelings for her, then start working on her heart, and maybe her head will eventually fall in line."

Bash got out of the car and shut the door, then leaned in and smiled. "Sometimes you surprise me with how smart you are."

Carter frowned. "I'm going to have to think about whether that was an insult or a compliment."

Bash laughed. "Thanks for the ride, buddy."

"Anytime."

By the time Bash drove to work that day, he was in a pensive mood. Fortunately, he had a goofy dog to help take his mind off whatever plagued him. A couple of the waitresses played ball with Lou before they opened, so she got to burn off some of her excess energy, which was good, since he wouldn't have much time to play with her later. He was running a couple of drink specials tonight, and there were a few baseball games being played that were likely to bring in a big crowd.

Summer filled the air, it was Saturday night, and he hadn't seen Chelsea in a week. She'd been busy with finals and graduation, so she told him she wouldn't be available. They'd talked on the phone a few times, but he'd given her space. He knew what it was like to be busy, and he didn't want to get in the middle of her schedule.

But it was still interesting how she filled the spaces in his head even when she wasn't around. It was probably dangerous to let that happen, considering her state of mind about their relationship.

He shook off thoughts of Chelsea and dove into work. It got crowded early and stayed that way for the majority of the night. The baseball games, plus the drink specials, brought in a lot of people. Bash tried to glance at the game scores while he made drinks. His favorite team was ahead, so that made the night even better.

As usual, Lou wandered around, making friends at all the tables. She'd become a staple at the bar, especially drawing in the women, which made his male regulars damn happy. In turn, it made him damn happy, too. More women coming to the bar meant more guys buying drinks for them.

Lou was good for business. Maybe he should put her picture on one of the front windows. The thought of that made him laugh.

He had his hands full with making six fruity drinks for a table of women when a soft, sexy voice hit him.

"You look busy."

He turned around to see Chelsea had taken a spot on one of the barstools.

He grinned, always gut-punched whenever he saw her. Tonight she wore a sexy, formfitting silver top.

"Hey. What are you doing here?"

"Megan, Sam, and I went to the movies earlier tonight, then over to Megan's place for board games. I didn't want to go home after, so I thought I'd stop here and check you out."

He didn't want to admit to himself how glad he was to see her, but he was. "Checking me out, huh?"

"Yes, you know, to make sure the bar wasn't going to fold due to lack of business." She looked around at the packed house, then gave him a crooked smile.

He laughed. "No fear of that tonight." He finished filling the drink order so his waitress could take it to the table.

"No kidding. Are you giving drinks away tonight?"

"Not exactly. Good baseball games, and I'm running a drink special."

"Obviously it worked well."

"Can I get you something to drink?"

She studied the alcohol behind the bar for a few seconds. "A vodka cranberry sounds good."

"Coming right up."

He made her drink, then handed it to her, sliding his fingers over her hand. "I'm glad you're here, Chelsea."

Her lips curved. "Me, too. I've actually got a surprise for you."

His brows rose. "You do?"

"Yes. For after work."

"Now I'm intrigued."

"You should be."

She sipped her drink while he worked, though he periodically checked back with her. This being Hope, she knew a lot of people, so she mingled. He knew he didn't have to worry about her. For a while, she had Lou on her lap. His dog happily snoozed while Chelsea sat at a table with several couples that had stopped in. Bash recognized one of the guys as a Hope teacher, so he assumed that's how Chelsea knew the group. He was glad she was in good hands.

He didn't see her again until about an hour later, when she came back to the bar, still holding Lou.

"Your girl seems wiped. Mind if I take her home?"

He leaned over the bar. "And by home, I assume you mean my place?"

Her lips tilted. "Of course."

"Sure. You know the code to the garage door."

"I do. I'll see you there in a little while."

"Hang on a second." He hollered to the other bartender that he'd be back in a minute, then grabbed Lou's crate and came out from behind the bar.

Chelsea gave him a quizzical look.

"Walking my girls to the car."

She smiled. "Okay."

Chelsea waved goodbye to her friends. He noticed there were two couples there, and a guy by himself. The guy was definitely giving Chelsea interested looks.

Huh.

He knew one of the teachers, Joe Bretano, was married, so he waved to Joe and his wife.

"Were all of those people teachers?"

"Oh, the group I was sitting with? Yes."

"I know Joe and his wife, Elaine."

Chelsea nodded. "Yes. There was also Terri Frontman and her husband, Rick. Terri teaches English."

They stopped at her car and Bash put Lou's crate in the backseat.

"Who was the other guy? The one by himself?" he asked.

"Oh, he's the new football coach, Zach Powers. He was just hired at the end of the school year, since Red Davis retired."

"I heard Red retired. I didn't know they hired his replacement."

She nodded. "Zach will be teaching history."

"He was giving you looks."

She paused as she was about to slip Lou into her crate, straightening to give him a shocked look. "What? He was not."

"Yeah, he was."

She shook her head and put Lou into her crate. "I think you're imagining things."

"I'm a guy, Chelsea. I know when another guy is giving a woman a once-over. More than once, as a matter of fact."

She leaned against the side of the car and crossed her arms, an amused smile on her face. "You're jealous."

"No, I'm not. I'm just telling you what I saw."

"You are jealous. That's so sweet, Bash." She pushed off the car, shut the back door, then wrapped her arms around him and kissed him, the kind of kiss that told him she was into him, not Zach the new football coach.

When she pulled back, there was definite desire—and promise—in her eyes.

"Don't forget, I have a surprise for you at home. I'll see you later."

She climbed into her car, and he waited until she drove off.

He was not jealous. But as he walked inside, he stopped at the table to say hello to Joe and Elaine, who introduced him to Terri and her husband. And to Zach.

"I hear you're the new football coach at Hope High," he said to Zach.

Zach was tall and well-muscled. He looked like he'd played some football himself in the past.

Zach offered an easy smile. "I am. I'm looking forward to it."

"Welcome to Hope, Zach."

"Thanks, Bash. You have a great bar here. I hope to spend some time hanging out. I'm a big sports fan."

They spent a few minutes talking about tonight's games as well as Hope High's football team's chances for next season. Then Bash had to get back to the bar.

Dammit. Zach was a nice guy. He'd gone to school in Tulsa, had attended college in Texas, and had played football there. He'd gotten drafted by Detroit, but a knee injury had forced an early end to his career. He'd ended up teaching in Detroit, but he wanted to come back home. When Coach Davis announced his retirement, Zach said he applied for the job and got it, so he moved to Hope to be closer to his family.

He wasn't an asshole, and hell, who could blame him for being attracted to Chelsea? Too bad Bash wasn't able to work into the conversation that he was kinda sorta dating Chelsea.

But was he, really?

Then again, she'd showed up at the bar tonight to hang out with him, so he'd take that as a definite . . .

Maybe.

He should just accept whatever was going on between them for what it was. They were hanging out and having fun together.

And she was waiting for him at his house, so right now, he couldn't wait to get finished with work so he could see her.

He pulled his phone out of his pocket and checked the time. Not too long now.

Chapter 28

CHELSEA HAD PREPARED everything in advance—actually, before she'd gone to the bar to see Bash. It was handy having the code to his garage door.

The guy worked long hours and ate too much junk food, and she'd wanted to surprise him tonight, which was why she'd gone to the bar. Getting to bring Lou back here with her had been a bonus. She'd actually had an opportunity to take a little nap. She curled up on the sofa with Lou, turned the TV on, and conked out for about an hour and a half. There was something about a warm dog curled up against you that made you sleepy. Then again, it was late.

She had no idea how Bash kept the hours he did. Of course, he started his day a lot later than she did.

She got up and prepped everything, figuring Bash would be home soon. By the time she had the table set, she heard the sound of his truck pulling into the driveway. Lou heard it, too, because she barked.

"Bash's home, isn't he?" she asked Lou, who responded by barking again, wiggling her butt, and running to the door leading to the garage.

So cute.

He opened the door. "Hey, Lou." He scooped the dog up and cradled her under his arm to pet her.

"And hey to you, too. Sorry I'm late."

She came over to him and brushed a kiss across his lips. "You're not late."

He set the dog down, then looked over at the table. "What's this?"

She smiled. "I made dinner for you."

"You did?"

"Yes. I thought you might be hungry."

"I'm starving. I was going to ask if you wanted to go out to one of the all-night breakfast places and get something to eat."

"Now you don't have to."

"I need a quick shower. I smell like a bar."

"Go ahead. I have to finish dinner anyway."

"Okay." He started to walk away, then stopped. He wrapped his arm around her and kissed her deeply. "Thanks for this. It's . . . really thoughtful of you."

She warmed from the inside out, glad her idea had been a good one. "You're welcome. Now go."

While Bash wandered into the bathroom, she warmed the chicken tenderloins she'd grilled earlier and sliced them into small pieces. Then she mixed the chicken in with the salad she'd made and put out bread and dressing.

By then, Bash had come back.

"Grilled chicken salad? And bread? This looks amazing."

She enjoyed his enthusiasm. And his hunger. "It's not a big deal."

He squeezed her hand. "It is to me."

If she got any warmer from his compliments, she'd start blushing. "Let's eat."

They sat, and he told her about his night at the bar, then asked her what movie she had seen with Megan and Sam. She told her about the movie, a romantic comedy.

"I'm sure you're not interested in those."

He leaned back in the chair. "Why would you say that?"

She shrugged. "I don't know. You seem the action adventure or bloody horror movie type."

"I definitely like those, but I can handle a romantic comedy, too."

"In other words, you'd tolerate that type of movie in order to get a woman in bed."

He waved his fork at her. "You don't think much of the male species, do you, Chelsea? Or maybe it's just me."

Clearly, she'd insulted him. "I'm sorry. I guess I just don't see you sitting through the kind of movie that's chock-full of romance and love scenes."

"Hey. I've seen my share of romantic movies. There were several I liked."

"Name one."

"*When Harry Met Sally.*"

She cocked a brow. "Tell me the plotline."

He did. She was impressed. "Name one you didn't like."

"*The Notebook.*"

She gasped and put her hand to her heart. He laughed.

"Sorry. Too cheesy. Plus, the ending sucked. If I'm going to see a romance movie, I want a definite happily ever after."

Her heart squeezed. "You like the happily ever after."

"Doesn't everyone?"

"I suppose so."

"You pick out some romantic movie you want to see, and we'll watch it together."

She pondered the thought of her and Bash watching a romantic movie together. Sharing popcorn. Holding hands. Her in tears at the ending. Would he comfort her or laugh at her?

She already knew the answer. Bash wasn't that kind of guy. He was sweet and comforting.

"Okay. We'll do that."

"I want you to know, though, that I'm just in it for the popcorn."

She laughed and tossed a hunk of bread at him.

She wondered if this was what it was like for couples who shared their lives together. Talking over dinner, laughing together, sharing their days and their likes and dislikes. This was what she'd been missing all these years, what she craved.

What she wanted so much she ached with yearning for it.

And now, as she sat with Bash in the wee hours of the morning, she realized she'd never felt quite so . . . content.

But he didn't fit the parameters of her list. So this had to be wrong.

Right?

She'd never been more confused.

After they ate they watched TV for a while. Bash actually found an old romantic comedy and they argued over its relative merits. She thought it was funny and over-the-top romantic. Bash thought it was unrealistic, so Chelsea made the point that it was fictional, not realistic. In the end, they agreed to disagree, though Bash liked the happily ever after at the end. Apparently that was a big thing to him.

She smiled about that and laid her head on his shoulder. He wrapped his arm around her.

They fell asleep that way. Bash woke her up later and they wandered off to bed. He made love to her softly, quietly, in a way that made her breath catch and her body ache for him. Afterward, he pulled her against him and she fell asleep with her head on his chest.

It was a pretty perfect night.

Chapter 29

FOR THE PAST few weeks, he and Chelsea had gone to the movies, out to dinner a few more times, and even to see a musical, which hadn't been too damn bad, actually. He'd even gone to brunch with Chelsea and the whole gang one Sunday morning, which had been fun. He rarely hung out with everyone on Sundays because he was typically dead asleep when they were all out for brunch.

They were all surprised and called him a vampire, but they were as glad to see him as he was to see them.

He needed to start taking more weekends off. He owned the damn business, and he'd been grooming Hall for a while now. It was time Bash started living his life instead of giving it all to the bar.

Which brought him back around to thoughts of taking a vacation. And he wanted to take Chelsea with him. Now that it was summer, and she was off school, it was the perfect time. She'd ended up not having to teach summer school, which was great. And he'd talked to Hall about taking over more responsibility at the bar so Bash could take some time off. Hall said he was wondering if Bash was married to the bar, or if he was ever going to trust him to run it in his absence. Bash felt kind of bad about that, but he'd invested everything he had in No Hope at All. If anything went wrong, he'd lose it all.

Hall assured him he and the staff would handle his baby just fine while he was gone.

Now he just had to talk to Chelsea.

He'd texted her this morning. She said she was doing laundry, but other than that, she was available. When he asked if he could come over to talk, she didn't respond right away. In fact, it took her like a half hour. Finally, she replied yes.

So he headed over there and knocked on her door.

She had her hair pulled up in a high ponytail, and she was wearing a sleeveless top and capris.

He gave her a quick kiss. "You look cute."

"I'm not sure what that means," she said, standing aside to let him in.

"It means you look pretty."

"I'm doing laundry and cleaning my kitchen. No one looks pretty when they do that."

"You do." She always looked pretty, even today, with her casual clothes and no makeup on.

She laughed. "Thanks. What brings you by?"

"I wanted to talk to you."

"It sounds serious. And kind of ominous."

"It's neither. It's fun stuff."

"That sounds a lot better. Come on in and sit down. Would you like some iced tea?"

"Sure."

"Have a seat and I'll be right back."

Her place smelled like lemons. It was a small apartment, with a tiny kitchen that overlooked an equally tight living room, but everything was orderly. She had the blinds open, and sun poured in. For an apartment, it wasn't bad.

"Checking out my place?" she asked, handing him his glass of tea.

"Yeah. It's nice. I like the light in here."

"Thanks."

"But I can still see you in a house of your own. So you can get that dog you want."

She sat next to him on the sofa. "You're right that I need to do something about that. I've lived in apartments since I graduated college. I'm so tired of it, especially with the laundry being downstairs. I've saved plenty of money and I can definitely afford the down payment." She shrugged.

"But . . ."

"I guess in my head I was waiting to buy that house with Mr. Perfect."

"Ah." He took a sip of tea and laid the glass down on the table. For some reason, his head immediately filled with images of him and Chelsea buying a place together. Or of her moving into his house.

Until just this moment, he hadn't realized how far into this relationship he'd come. And she obviously wasn't there at all. At least not that she'd said to him.

He shook off the thoughts and got down to business.

"So I wanted to talk to you about a vacation."

She frowned. "You're going on vacation? I thought you never took that much time off."

"Typically I don't, but I've been training Hall for a while now, and I think he's ready to take over for me and run the bar while I'm gone."

"That's great. Where are you going? Camping, I assume?"

His lips quirked. "That's a thought. But I wanted to take you on vacation."

She gave him a look of surprise. "You do?"

"Yeah. And you know, your list and all, I thought we might head to the beach."

Chelsea's heart squeezed. It had been doing that a lot around Bash lately. He wanted to take her on vacation with him, and, mindful of her list, he'd thought of the beach. "Do you even like the beach?"

"Sure. What do you think of South Padre Island?"

"I think it sounds . . . perfect."

"Good. I thought we'd mix up a little of what you like with some of what I like. You can ride the dunes there on ATVs."

She supposed she could give what he liked a chance as well, especially since he was giving up camping to do something she wanted to do. "That sounds fun."

He laughed. "I'm sure you're not the least bit interested in riding ATVs."

She came over and climbed into his lap. "I don't think it would be fair of me to only want to do what I like, would it?"

She leaned forward and kissed him, tangling her fingers in the lush thickness of his hair. Their conversation was put on hold as passion ignited. Bash grasped her hips and squeezed, rocking her back and forth against his quickly hardening cock.

It had always been like this between them. A rapid burst of flaming desire, a need she felt for him that couldn't be denied. He scooped his hands under her thighs and stood. She wrapped her legs around him while he carried her to her bedroom.

She was glad she'd gotten the sheets done early this morning and made her bed. He laid her down on top of the quilt, then followed, covering her body with his, kissing her, his body surging against hers until all she wanted was both of them naked and Bash inside of her.

She framed his face with her hands, breaking the kiss. "Bash."

He lifted. "Yeah?"

"I need a shower. I've been working all morning and I'm sweaty."

"That sounds fun."

He hopped off the bed and took her hand, hauling her upright. He followed her into her bathroom, shedding his shirt and undoing his jeans. It was such a delicious sight to watch him undress. She did the same, turning the water on after she pulled off her shirt.

Bash helped her draw down her capris and underwear, then pushed her against the bathroom counter and kissed her, a long, deep kiss that made her forget what room she was in.

He opened the shower door and stepped in first, adjusted the temperature, then made room for her, pulling her under the spray.

She let the water pour over her, wetting her hair. When she opened her eyes, Bash had a handful of shampoo.

"Turn around and I'll wash your hair."

"Seriously?"

"Yeah. What—no guy has washed your hair for you before?"

"No."

"Good. Turn around."

Well, this was a first. She pivoted and closed her eyes. Bash let the shampoo drizzle over her scalp, then dug his fingers in.

This was nice. He knew just the right amount of pressure to provide, and she had to admit, it felt really good. The only time someone else washed her hair was at the salon when she had it trimmed. And they did it fast. This was slow, sensual, his fingers gliding into her scalp and neck, massaging. It was a tender assault on her senses, his fingers doing an intimate dance on her head.

Who knew shampooing could be so sexy?

"Dip your head under the water," he said.

With a sigh, she turned around and rinsed her hair, then quickly conditioned it and rinsed again.

When she opened her eyes, he had her body wash in his hands.

"Time for the fun part," he said with a sexy smile.

He lathered his hands, then smoothed the wash over her body—all over her body. Her skin had never felt more alive, or ached more for his touch. He soaped her shoulders and down her arms, lingering at each finger and in between before moving to her shoulders, her collarbone, and over her breasts, where he teased her nipples until she wanted to die.

He went lower, over her rib cage and down her stomach, then dropped down to do her thighs, deliberately avoiding her sex, which by now was throbbing with need.

Then he turned her around and soaped his way up her calves and the backs of her thighs, washing her buttocks and back, and lingering at her shoulders, where he massaged with deep, moan-inducing rubs.

"Rinse."

She did, and when she turned around again, he kissed her, pressing her into the wall of the shower. He slid his hand between her legs, cupping her sex. She whimpered against his mouth, her legs parting to give him access as he caressed her.

And when he dropped down to his knees and put his mouth on her, the heat and wetness of his mouth made her cry out, his name spilling from her lips.

"Bash."

She was lost in the whirlwind of mind-numbing need, water pummeling her as sensation catapulted her right over the edge of oblivion. She wanted to hold on, wanted to live in this moment of pure bliss for an eternity, but she couldn't. She orgasmed with a wild cry, her body shaking all over as she let go. Bash held on to her hips, giving her more than she could have ever asked for.

He stood and held her as she continued to quiver, then kissed her. She wrapped her arms around him, needing that lifeline of support as she came down from the incredible high.

"Well now," he said, kissing her ear. "That was one hell of a shower."

She laid her hands on his chest and pinned him against the shower wall. "Shower's not over yet."

She wanted to give him some of what he'd given her. She grasped his cock, sliding her hand over the slippery hardness of his steely erection. She slid down his body, keeping a firm grasp of his shaft in her hand.

He groaned, looking down at her with such fierce desire she could feel every ounce of it deep inside of her. And when she took his cock in her mouth, sliding the soft head between her lips, she shivered, the salty taste of him exciting her beyond measure. She wanted to give him pleasure, to give him that out-of-body experience he'd just given her.

There was such power yet such softness in the way he thrust into her mouth, the way he gently laid his hand on her head. He gave her all he had, slamming his hand against the wall, groaning to tell her he thoroughly enjoyed what she was doing.

"Chelsea. Goddamn. You're killing me."

She knew that feeling, that total loss of control when the pleasure was so great you knew you were going to explode with it. She drove him right to the brink, then over, taking all of him, feeling his body tremble with the effort as he came in a thundering burst that left her as shaky as it had Bash.

He grasped her hands and lifted her, taking her mouth in a blistering kiss that made her glad the water in the shower was cooling, because her body was heated all over.

He turned off the shower and they climbed out and dried off. She combed out her hair and grabbed some clean clothes from her bedroom while Bash put his on.

Then she went into the kitchen and refreshed their iced tea.

"Nice shower," he said, coming up behind her to press a kiss to her shoulder.

She turned around and laced her fingers together around his neck. "I found it extremely refreshing."

He kissed her, then took his glass of iced tea, downing several gulps. "For some reason, my throat is very dry."

She laughed. "Come on, let's sit down and talk about that vacation you mentioned."

They took a seat in the living room. "Oh, right. Vacation. I don't know how we got off topic."

"Hmm, me either. But anyway, when were you thinking of going?"

"My friend has a condo at South Padre and he says it's available next week. Is that too soon for you?"

"Not at all. What about Lou?"

"I already asked Emma. She said she and Luke will take care of her. Lou will have a blast with Daisy and Annie."

"I'm sure she will."

"Oh, and there's one more thing I didn't get to talk to you about before we were—uh—distracted."

She smiled. "What's that?"

"I was talking to Carter about the trip and he said he was thinking about taking Molly on vacation. I invited him to come along."

"That sounds awesome. I'd love to have them with us. I think we'll all have a great time."

"I think so too. We'll leave Wednesday and come back Sunday."

She leaned back against the sofa. "Thanks again for asking me. And for taking me to the beach. It sounds fun."

"I think it will be. It's been a while since I've taken some time off to just go hang out somewhere and relax."

"Are you sure you know how to relax?"

He pulled her against him. "If you're with me? I think we can find ways to relax."

She couldn't wait.

Chapter 30

THEY GOT AN early start on Wednesday and arrived around seven that night. Bash had been to his friend's condo before, so he didn't need any directions.

Rather than trying to cram everyone in one vehicle, they convoyed down, with Carter driving his truck and Bash his. Since it was about a twelve-hour drive, they had to make several stops.

Apparently women had to pee a lot more often than men, something Bash had learned in the past twelve hours. Otherwise, he and Chelsea had a good rapport. Instead of curling up into a ball and falling back asleep since they'd left way early, she'd stayed up and chatted with him. They talked about their jobs, about high school, about former relationships they'd had and what had worked and what hadn't. They even talked about music, and he discovered Chelsea liked switching radio channels—a lot, whereas he was content to pick one and listen to it for the duration of the trip. They had fun arguing that point for at least an hour.

He'd gained a lot of insight into Chelsea during the past twelve hours. Though he'd known her for a lot of years, he was always learning something new. He probably talked to her more than he'd ever talked to any of the previous women he'd dated.

He saw that as a promising sign.

When they finally arrived Bash marveled at the perfect weather—hot with a nice breeze coming in off the water.

"This condo is fabulous," Chelsea said after they had set their bags down inside the front door.

It was a decent-sized place, but nothing stellar. Two bedrooms, a kitchen, and a living area. What made it spectacular was the view, since it overlooked the water.

"And it has a balcony, too." Molly made her way outside, so they all followed.

Chelsea looked out over the railing. "This view is incredible, Bash. You didn't tell me it had a view of the gulf. Wow."

They were on the fourth floor of the condo building, high enough above the trees to have a great view, yet low enough to hear the waves crashing.

"Yeah, it's decent."

She pulled her attention from the water and onto him. "It's more than decent. It's spectacular. I could sit out here the entire week and be perfectly content."

He laughed. "I'm glad you like it. Want to see the rest of the place?"

"Sure."

They went inside and he grabbed their bags, leading her down the hall. "Both the bedrooms face the water. Want to flip for it?" he asked Carter, who was coming down the hall behind him.

"Hey, you invited us to come along. We're happy no matter where we stay. Take your pick of bedrooms."

He nodded at Carter and pushed into the bedroom on the left.

Chelsea walked in and immediately went to the sliding glass door. "There's a balcony here as well?"

"Yes."

"Amazing." She opened that door and stepped outside while he laid their bags on the bed. Then he walked outside with her.

"You like it, huh?" he asked.

"I'm telling you, Bash. I'm never going to be inside. Except maybe to take a shower."

"So, no sleeping these next few days?"

She eyed the cushioned chairs on the balcony. "These will do."

He put his arms around her and pulled her against his chest. "And you said you didn't like camping."

She laughed. "This *is* my idea of camping."

"I can see how rough it's going to be for you this week." He pressed a kiss to the side of her neck.

She relaxed against him and sighed. "I'm willing to make that sacrifice to spend the week with you."

"You're such a trouper, Chelsea."

She laughed, then they went into the bedroom and unpacked. When he saw the hot blue bikini she pulled out of her suitcase, he grinned.

"I definitely want to see you in that."

She dangled the bottom by its strings. "What you're trying to tell me is that you're ready for the beach?"

"Hell yes."

"You'll see me in the bikini tomorrow. Right now I'm hungry, and it's too late for the beach anyway."

They finished unpacking and changed clothes. Chelsea put on a sundress, after she apparently consulted with Molly about what they were going to wear for dinner.

Bash chose shorts and a T-shirt, which was pretty much what he was going to wear all week. He didn't consult with Carter about what to wear, because guys didn't give a shit.

Chelsea looked like a knockout as always, with a flowered sundress and sandals.

"No killer heels?" he asked.

"No. We might end up on the beach, and my heels are not beach ready."

"Yes, we had to modify her shoe attire for this vacation," Molly said, equally gorgeous in a red sundress. "Though I'm certain she's got heels secreted away in there somewhere."

Chelsea shrugged. "Of course I do. I don't go anywhere without them."

Bash laughed, then slid his arm around her waist. "You wouldn't be you without those heels, babe."

Chelsea slanted a smug grin in Molly's direction. "See?"

Molly shook her head.

Bash held Chelsea's hand as they rode down in the elevator, not letting go of it as they walked out onto the street.

They found a little bar and bistro on the beach that served an eclectic mix of food, so they agreed to stop in there. Bash gave his name to the hostess, who told them there'd be a wait, so they headed to the bar.

"It's crowded in here," Molly said.

"Not a problem." Carter pointed out a table outside where a group of four was just getting up. They hustled over there and grabbed the table, which had a perfect view of the water.

"This is a breathtaking view," Chelsea said, turning her chair to face the gulf.

"Isn't it?" Molly pulled her chair next to Chelsea's. "I'm so glad we're here with you and Bash."

"Me, too. This is going to be fun."

Their waitress came by, cleaned up the remnants from the previous table occupants, and took their drink order.

The guys were talking car stuff, so she turned her attention to Molly.

"Tell me how things are going with you and Carter."

"Good. Busy with work stuff, but I'm having a great time. He gives me free rein to work the sales and marketing angle, which is a lot of fun. And then we get to go home together at night. What's not to love about that?"

"I'm glad the two of you reconnected after so many years apart."

"So am I."

Their waitress brought their drinks. Chelsea sipped her wine, already feeling herself relax into vacation mode.

"How is the wedding planning going?"

Molly sighed. "It's intense. I can't believe it's only a few

short months away. I'm so glad Carter suggested we take a
few days off. Who knew planning a wedding would be so
stressful?"

"It is a lot of work, isn't it?"

"Oh my God, Chelsea. The guest list and the venue, and
then catering, cake, flowers, bridesmaids, groomsmen. His
family and my family and . . . ugh." She waved her hands in
the air. "I'm over it. We should have eloped."

Chelsea laughed.

"Seriously. Sometimes I think we planned this too soon,
you know? But then we figured we were apart for so long, we
wanted to just be married, so why wait? But now, as everything is coming to a head, I've realized I could use another
year just to plan."

"You have Emma to help you."

"Emma just barely got through her own wedding."

Chelsea waved her hand. "Emma's fully recovered. The
only one of us currently unavailable is Des, because she's out
of the country filming. You have all of us. Me, Jane, Emma,
Megan, Sam. You do realize you can call any of us for help.
That's what we're here for, Molly."

Molly reached over and squeezed her hand. "I know. I'm
a compulsive do-it-yourselfer. Carter said it's one of my worst
flaws. One of my many flaws, actually." She laughed.

"You're going to have to stop thinking you have to do it
all yourself. I have the entire summer off. I can jump in and
help you in so many ways. You just have to tell me what you
need."

"You're a lifesaver, Chelsea. Thank you. And I'm going to
take you up on that offer."

Bash grasped her hand and leaned over to whisper in
her ear.

"Did I tell you that you look gorgeous tonight?"

A shiver skittered down her spine. "Thank you."

He leaned back. "So what had you and Molly talking so
animatedly?"

"Wedding stuff."

He arched a brow. "What? You're planning to propose to

me tonight? Damn, Chelsea, this is so sudden. I wish you had warned me. I would have dressed better."

Carter chuckled. Molly outright laughed. Chelsea rolled her eyes. "Not happening."

"It's because I'm not wearing a suit, isn't it?"

"Absolutely. My perfect man would wear a suit to the beach."

"I knew it. I'm doomed. I'll just drown my sorrows in this beer." He raised his bottle and took a couple of long swallows.

"He's amazing, you know," Molly whispered.

Chelsea stared at Bash and felt a flutter in the vicinity of her heart. "Yes. I know he is."

They finally called Bash's name, so they headed inside to have dinner. Chelsea had seafood pasta, which was amazing. It was fun to sit back and relax with her friends without having to worry about work or anything else.

Teaching definitely had its stresses, but having summers off was the best perk of the job.

After they ate, they went back outside and hung out to drink and watch the sun set. It was a perfect day. Since they'd gotten up early, they walked back to the hotel, stopping at the store along the way for a few supplies. Important things, like beer, wine, and soda. And, of course, coffee.

They carried their bags up to the condo, put everything away, then congregated outside, chatting for another hour or so before Molly yawned and said she was ready for bed. Carter went with her, leaving Chelsea and Bash alone on the balcony.

"Pretty perfect here," she said, sipping from her bottle of water.

Bash didn't say anything for a minute or so, just took a couple of swallows of beer. Then, finally, "I'm glad you're here with me."

She smiled. "Me, too."

"Are you tired?"

"A little."

"Let's go to bed. We have a big day tomorrow."

She stood. "We do?"

"Yeah. Lots of sun, sand, eating, drinking . . ."

She laughed. "Sounds intense. I'll have to go input all of that in my calendar so I don't forget it."

He put his arm around her. "You definitely should. You don't want to be late and miss it."

They headed toward the bedroom. Chelsea washed her face and brushed her teeth, then undressed and climbed into bed. Bash was waiting there for her and pulled her close.

"First night of vacation. You should probably ravage me before I pass out from exhaustion."

She rolled over and climbed on top of him. "Try to hold out on that passing out thing. I've got plans for you."

He gripped her hips. "See? Another good reason to come with me."

"And another good reason to not vacation in a tent."

He rocked against her, his erection evident. "We can have sex in a tent, too, ya know."

"Oh, but there's so much more room to roll around on a bed."

He did just that, rolling her onto her back. "You have a point. And no rocks on your back."

"Or bugs."

"Still, there's a lot to be said for being able to get up before dawn to go fishing."

"Needing a flashlight to use the bathroom in the middle of the night."

He framed her face with his hand. "I'm going to take you camping sometime, Chelsea. Trust me, you'll enjoy it."

"I highly doubt it. But you're welcome to try."

He kissed her, and she lost herself in the feel of his lips on hers. The debate about camping ended for the night, because she had much more pleasurable things to think about.

Chapter 31

WHILE CHELSEA AND Molly soaked up the sun the next morning, Bash and Carter went searching out ATV rentals and other activities.

They ended up renting Jet Skis for the day and calling the adventure park to rent ATVs for the following day.

"Do you really think you're going to get Chelsea on an ATV?" Carter asked as they made their way back to the women.

"Of course. She's a lot more adventurous than you think."

Carter gave him a skeptical look. "Uh-huh."

"Okay, she's more adventurous than *she* thinks."

Carter laughed, then slapped him on the back. "Good luck with that."

They found Chelsea and Molly by the pool. Chelsea's bikini clung to her curves, and she'd braided her hair today. She looked damn gorgeous, and all he could think about was getting her naked—dangerous thoughts he shouldn't be thinking in public. So he focused on the subject of the Jet Skis.

"You all up to some Jet Ski fun in the water?"

"Sounds great to me," Molly said. "I'm baking here in this heat."

"I'm up for it as well," Chelsea said. "When are we going?"

Carter pulled out his phone. "We have a one o'clock rental. Which means plenty of time to grab an early lunch."

"Perfect." Chelsea got up and took Bash's hand. "Which means we can go get in the water together."

"Pool or ocean?" he asked.

"Either."

The pool was crowded, so he walked her down the sand and into the water. She had no objections, flinging herself onto his back and squealing about how cold the water was.

"I thought you wanted to cool down."

"I did. I'll get used to it in a minute."

Carter and Molly had come with them, so they all swam around, then got out to grab a snack and drinks before wandering down the beach to the Jet Ski rental place.

They put on their life vests, then Bash climbed aboard the Jet Ski, holding his hand out for Chelsea to climb aboard behind him.

She wrapped her thighs snug against him and put her arms around him, and then they were off. He started slow, until he got past the *No Wake* sign.

"Hang on," he said.

He goosed the throttle and they went flying across the water. Carter came up beside him, and they headed out at a pretty fast pace. It was exhilarating, taking the Jet Ski up in the air and slamming down into the water.

"You okay?" he asked Chelsea.

"Fine. Just keep going."

He grinned and gunned it harder, he and Carter racing around the waves, cutting corners and hitting it faster. He kept hearing Chelsea's laugh, and the sound made him smile.

Their time went by all too damn fast. They made their way back and parked the Jet Ski. He held on to Chelsea's hand as she slid off and into the water.

"That was so much fun," she said, grabbing on to him to plant a wet, salty kiss on his lips.

He kissed her back, surprised as hell that she'd had so much fun. He'd expected her to hang on, but not say much. She'd full-on shrieked with laughter, yelling across the waves at Molly. She'd talked to him the entire time as well.

"So, you enjoyed it?"

"Ycs. It was fantastic. I haven't been on a Jet Ski in years. I'd forgotten how much fun that was. We should do it again."

He looked at her.

"What?" she asked.

"You surprise me."

"In what way?"

"I don't know. You seem like . . . fancy clothes and high heels and makeup. Not wild hair and Jet Skis and water in your face."

She laughed. "You have a lot to learn about me, Bash. Just because I said I don't like camping doesn't mean I don't love the water—and everything having to do with the water. And just because I wear makeup and high heels doesn't mean I can't let loose and have fun."

Apparently he had Chelsea all wrong. He had a lot of things wrong.

His stomach tightened at the realization that she was everything he'd been looking for in a woman. Or maybe he hadn't been looking for her at all, yct here she was, a part of his life, despite his best efforts to avoid a relationship all these years.

"You're right. You're definitely a lot of fun."

She grinned and squeezed his arm. "Of course I am. Haven't you been paying attention?"

As she wandered off to catch up to Molly, he stared at her and realized two things.

One, he was in love with her. And two, he was in deep, deep trouble.

Chapter 32

_____

THEY ATE DINNER at an amazing seafood restaurant overlooking the bay. Chelsea had decided she was going to get her fill of fresh seafood while she was here. Tonight she had amazing Chilean sea bass, cooked to perfection, along with the most delicious grilled vegetables she'd ever tasted. The restaurant also served knock-you-on-your-butt margaritas, and she'd had two of those.

"I think I want to live down here—forever."

Molly slanted her a smile. "I'm sad this isn't one of the places I ever chose to live and work. How could I have missed it?"

"I don't know," Carter said, "considering you've lived almost everywhere else."

Molly stuck her tongue out at Carter.

Bash laughed. "It is pretty idyllic. There's so much to do here. But all vacation spots are like that. Very little to do with reality, right? I mean, eventually we all have to go back to reality."

"Shh," Chelsea said, holding her hand palm out toward Bash. "You're ruining my fantasy future, where I live on a boat, catch fish all day, cook and eat it, and don't have to work for a living."

"Sounds ideal to me," Carter said. "Let's make it happen."

"I'm with you two."

"Sure," Bash said. "I'll call your assistant manager and let him know he can take over all your stores. And their profits."

Carter shot Bash a glare. "Buzzkill."

Chelsea took another swallow of her margarita, then slanted a slightly cross-eyed look over at Bash. "Really. Where's your sense of adventure?"

"My sense of adventure doesn't pay the bills."

"*Pfft*. Who needs to pay bills?"

Bash looked over at her margarita. "How many of those have you had?"

She shrugged. "I dunno. Nine."

He laughed. "You haven't had nine."

"They're very strong. It feels like nine." She had a good buzz going and was having a great time. Which was all that mattered.

"Tomorrow we'll be bouncing around on ATVs. Not sure you want to be doing that with a hangover."

She waved her hand at him. "I'm totally fine. And I'm a pro with ATVs."

He arched a brow. "Really. I didn't know that."

"Trust me. You'll be eating my dust tomorrow."

"You mean sand?"

"Sure."

He leaned forward. "I can't wait."

She'd never been on an ATV in her entire life. But she wasn't about to tell Bash that. He could just think that maybe she'd been riding a time or two.

How hard could it be?

Chapter 33

HER HEAD HURT. And she was dizzy.

Damn those margaritas. But she was dressed in her shorts, tank top, and tennis shoes and standing—or trying not to weave, anyway—while the instructor went over the operation of the ATV and the safety rules. She was glad she'd opted for several cups of coffee, followed by a few glasses of water to hydrate.

"Are you doing all right?" Molly asked.

She nodded. She was fine. Just . . . fine. After the instructor finished his safety speech, she looked over at Bash. "It's really hot out here already."

"Are you sure you want to do this? It's fine if you sit this one out."

She lifted her chin. "No way. I'm pumped."

He slanted her a look. "I don't think you're pumped. You look a little tired. Maybe hungover?"

"I am not hungover. I'm very excited about riding."

He grabbed her hand. "Seriously, Chelsea. You have nothing to prove. You don't have to ride."

She put on her helmet. "Let's do this."

He shook his head. "Okay. But if you want to stop, signal me and we'll come back, okay?"

She wasn't listening. She headed over to her machine and stared at it for a few minutes, trying to remember all the things the instructor had said about safety and operation. Finally, she climbed aboard, familiarized herself with the gears, and started her engine.

She'd show Bash she was just as equipped to run this beast as he was.

Though she waited for the others to get started. They weren't the only ones in the group—there were several other people going on this ride today as well. Maybe she'd just hang back. Like . . . way back.

Except Bash roared over to her, stopping his ATV next to hers.

"Ready?" he asked.

Obviously there'd be no hanging back for her.

"Sure."

"Good. You know what you're doing, or do you need me to help you?"

"I've got it." She pushed the throttle, her heart leaping into her throat as the ATV jumped forward.

"Easy," Bash said. "Just give it a little. It might take you a while to get the feel of it."

No kidding. She was fine in a car. This machine, however, was something totally different. She did as Bash suggested, and the ATV lurched forward.

Nausea bubbled around in her stomach. She was not going to enjoy this.

"I'll take the lead. You follow. But don't worry. I'll keep checking on you, okay?"

She nodded and moved forward. Slowly. Feeling totally out of her element and utterly out of control. But she was at least making progress. Slow as hell progress, but she had left the parking area, so there was that.

It took a while, but she finally made her way to the dunes.

It was crazy there, with sand flying in the air and machines leaping over the dunes.

No way she was going to do that. Then again, there were teenagers on some of the ATVs. If they could do it, so could she, right?

Bash made a spinning turn and slid his way to her side. "Are you doing okay?"

"I'm fine. You go ahead."

"No. I'll stay here with you."

"Bash. I'm really getting the hang of this. Besides, our guide dude is behind me. I'm okay."

Bash looked over at the guide, then back at her. "Are you sure?"

"Positive. Go have some fun."

He smiled. "No, I'm going to hang here with you."

This could possibly be the most boring day of his life. But he'd made his decision. She plodded along at a very slow pace, Bash beside her, the guide following her.

They were both so patient, Bash telling her she was doing well. Their guide was so bored back here with her he probably had a whiskey flask tucked in his pocket and would likely be dead drunk before they got back.

She felt like an idiot. A terrified idiot. And she was certain the guide cringed every time she hit the brakes, which was a lot.

"You're doing great, Chelsea," Bash said.

She didn't believe him, but she appreciated the pep talk.

When she came to one of the dunes, she almost slammed on the brakes, but she remembered the guide telling them to ride over them and not to hit the brakes sharply, so she gritted her teeth and rode over the dune. Her butt came off the seat and she held tight to the grips, certain she was going to fly right over the handlebars and die a flaming, painful death in the sand.

She didn't. In fact, it was kind of . . . exhilarating. She looked over at Bash and grinned.

"See? You're doing it."

She was doing it. She increased her speed a little more. Not too much more, but a little more. She rode over several dunes, finally convincing Bash that instead of riding beside her, he could go ahead, and she'd follow him. Which she did—more or less. He got ahead of her because he rode a lot faster, but the poor guy had to have at least a little fun before their time was up, and poking along with her wasn't going to cut it.

Finally, she waved him off, and she throttled back to watch him.

He was . . . amazing. There was something inherently sexy about a man in charge of a machine like that. The way he flew across the dunes, sand spraying in all directions, the roar of the engine deafening her.

Bash's sex appeal had been off the charts before. Now, though, seeing him standing as he rode across a precariously high dune, she wasn't sure she'd ever seen anything hotter. She should have brought a video camera, though these images of him would be burned in her mind for a very long time. He was as lean as the machine, and when he popped a wheelie and the guide chastised him, he turned and grinned at her, making her laugh.

Bash might just be showing off a little, just for her.

And she might just have appreciated that. More than a little.

She could have sat on her vehicle and watched him ride for hours. Because on a machine where she was decidedly uncomfortable, Bash looked as if he were a natural extension of his.

In fact, she enjoyed watching the rest of them speeding along, sailing across the tops of the dunes, sand flying in their wake. It looked amazing. But she already knew that wasn't for her. Not today, anyway. She stayed mostly to the smaller crests, and when she mastered those, she felt victorious.

Bash finally made his way back to her. "You're getting good at this. Ready for a higher dune?"

"Maybe."

She was just starting to get comfortable enough to think about venturing out to the bigger dunes when the guide hailed them that their time was coming to a close.

She actually felt disappointed. She smiled at Bash. "Next time, for sure."

He grinned, then followed her in toward the parking area. She made it much faster, and this time she stayed with the group. She put on the brake, turned off the engine, then climbed off and took off her helmet.

"That was so much fun," Molly said. "We have to do that again sometime."

"We can ride ATVs in Oklahoma," Bash said. "I do it a lot when I go camping."

"Whenever you go, count us in," Carter said, putting his arm around Molly. "We had a blast."

"How about you, Chelsea?" Bash asked.

"I had a great time. I was just warming up when it was over. I'd do it again."

He put his arm around her and kissed the side of her head. "That's my girl."

She'd done it. Maybe she'd had to prove to herself that she could, but she'd done it. And surprisingly, she'd had fun with it.

They all went back to the hotel, changed into swim stuff, and stopped at a restaurant near the beach for lunch.

"Who knew all that riding would work up such an appetite?" she asked as she dug into the best burger she'd ever eaten.

"You're normally not a burger lover," Bash said. "I think you have a hangover."

"I do not." But she was exceptionally thirsty today. And hungry. For carbs. The fries were delicious. Maybe she was hungover. Not that she'd admit it.

"They are great burgers," Molly said. "Though I didn't have as many margaritas as Chelsea had last night. I just like burgers."

Chelsea shot Molly a look. "Hey. You're supposed to be on my side."

"We're taking sides? There's an argument? Did I miss something?"

Chelsea sighed. "I need a nap."

Bash laughed. "No arguments. You did great today. I'm really proud of you for even getting on the ATV. You rode it like a pro."

"Ha. I did not. But I rode it. And had more fun than I thought I would."

"So, next up, camping."

She tilted her head to meet his teasing gaze. "That's not going to happen."

"We'll see. I'll bet I could entice you."

"You could always go glamping," Molly suggested.

"What the hell is glamping?" Carter asked, frowning.

"It's luxury camping. Beyond tents and porta-potties," Chelsea said.

Bash leaned back in his chair, picking up his iced tea. "Oh, you have to explain this. I can't wait to hear about it."

"Say you want to camp with a tent," Chelsea said. "There are resorts that provide the tent—a more glamorous version of the kind you throw in the back of your truck, of course. Maybe nestled in a mountain hideaway, with full bathroom amenities and food provided."

Bash shook his head. "Might as well stay at a hotel."

Chelsea shrugged. "It's still camping."

"Not the way I camp."

She lifted her chin. "It would be considered a compromise, though."

He arched a brow.

"Seriously, look." She pulled out her phone and typed in the search engine, pulling up a site, then handed her phone to Bash. "Check this out."

He looked it over, then laughed and handed her phone to Carter. "Did you see the prices for this? You might as well book a room at the Four Seasons."

Carter scrolled through the site. "Holy shit."

Chelsea sighed, then looked over at Molly. "Clearly they don't appreciate glamping."

"Clearly," Molly said. "Maybe you and I will take a separate vacation sometime. The guys can go rustic camping. We'll go glamping."

"Yeah, I can see the two of you 'roughing it' in some spa-like conditions out there in the 'wilderness,'" Bash said, accentuating *roughing it* and *wilderness* with air quotes.

"Okay, fine, so maybe we don't see eye to eye on camping. I rode the damn ATV, didn't I?"

He laughed, then put his arm around her. "Yes, you did. And without heels on, too."

She shrugged off his arm. "You're being a dick, Bash."

"No, I'm not. I appreciate you doing those things you're not comfortable doing. Seriously."

She was being cranky and she knew it. But he was being unreasonable about the whole camping thing. This was why she had her list. She and Bash were incompatible in so many ways.

Or, maybe she just needed perspective. And a nap.

After they finished eating they went down to the water and rented a couple of cabanas, and she stretched out in the shade.

"Do you want to get in the water?" Bash asked.

"Not right now. My head's still pounding. I think I'll close my eyes for a few minutes."

"Okay."

He left her alone after that and disappeared. She took a couple aspirin and guzzled a lot of water, then settled in under the shady cabana and promptly fell asleep. When she woke up a while later, she was sweaty and disoriented. Neither Bash nor Carter and Molly were anywhere around, so she walked down to the water and cooled herself off. It refreshed her and cleared her head. She stood in the water for a bit, searching up and down the sandy beach for Bash or her friends, but didn't see them, so she headed back to the cabana, grabbed her things and went back to the room. She sent Bash a text message letting him know where she was.

She took a shower, combed out her hair, and slipped on a sundress. She felt a lot better, too. By then she heard the door open. Bash came into the room.

"Did you get my message?" she asked.

"Yes. Thanks. You were really out cold after we swam, and I didn't want to wake you. Molly wanted some ice cream, so we took a walk down the beach."

She smiled as she ran the towel through her hair. "Sorry I slept through the ice cream."

"It was pretty good. I'm going to grab a shower."

She dried her hair while he showered, then left the bathroom, grabbing them some iced tea. She brought them back to the bedroom with her, closing the door behind her.

He came out of the bathroom and over to her, putting his arms around her.

"How's your headache?"

She smiled. "Better."

"I'm glad. Though I was wondering if you wanted me to rub your head. Or . . . any other parts of you that might need rubbing."

"Oh. In that case, every part of my body hurts."

He laughed. "You know I'm always happy to put my hands on you. Wherever you want me to."

"I know. That's one of the things I like best about you."

"My hands?"

"Definitely. Along with other parts of you."

He bent his head to brush his lips over hers. She drew in the fresh scent of him, the taste of him, the way he could melt her with just a simple kiss. She leaned against him and went with the kiss, letting herself slide easily into the passion he always brought out of her.

He moved her to the bed, raising the back of her dress with his hand, smoothing his hands over her butt, driving up her desire to a frenzy by slipping his fingers inside her panties.

He laid her on the bed and followed her there, covering her body with his, deepening the kiss, his tongue swiping over hers and drawing her deeper into that hazy, passionate web where she so often lost herself whenever she was with him.

He pulled up, sliding his hand around the back of her neck to rub the muscles there. There was something about Bash's touch that was both soothing and unnerving, in the best possible way. She wrapped her fingers around his wrist and drew his hand down, past her neck and over her breasts.

"So these need rubbing?" he asked.

"Most definitely."

She drew the straps down on her dress, baring her breasts for him. He rubbed, teased, and sweetly tortured her nipples until she arched her back, begging for his lips, mouth, and tongue to do the same. When he had her a moaning wreck, he pulled the dress over her hips, taking her panties as well.

He scooted up beside her, kissed her, and at the same time cupped her sex. She moaned against his lips, tangling her fingers in his hair and tugging, letting him know how very much she enjoyed his touch.

He made her breath catch as he expertly stroked her right to climax. She fell into that blissful, splintering state with abandon, letting go and holding tight to him as she trembled with each delicious sensation.

He left her only long enough to grab a condom, shuck his clothes, and climb back on the bed. He grabbed her leg and lifted it over his hip, then slid into her, his gaze firmly planted on hers as he moved within her.

Everything inside of her quivered. When he brushed his thumb across her bottom lip, she sucked it inside her mouth.

"Christ," he said, thrusting into her. "Do you know what you do to me, Chelsea?"

She knew what he did to her, what he'd been doing to her for months. And the way he looked at her, like he was baring his soul to her while they were connected in the most intimate of ways, shattered her.

She was his. She wanted him to be hers, and the agony of it was almost too much to bear. So instead, she kissed him, drawing him down to her, letting passion overtake her, swamping her as he rolled her onto her back and took her over and over again until she called out his name and the two of them climaxed together, leaving her in a state of oblivion. He held her hand as they shook through their orgasms.

She'd never fallen so hard, or so perfectly, before.

They laid like that, still entwined, for a while, just settling, stroking each other's skin and kissing each other.

It was perfect.

Finally, they got up and went into the bathroom to clean up, and then got dressed.

"I'm going to go freshen up our iced tea," she said.

Bash nodded.

She thought Carter and Molly might be in the living room or kitchen, but they weren't. She didn't see them on the balcony, either, but on her way back down the hall she saw their bedroom door was closed. Maybe they were taking a nap.

Or something. She smiled and went back in the bedroom. Bash had taken a seat out on the balcony. She went out there and laid their glasses on the table.

He had put on a pair of shorts and wore no shirt. She couldn't help but take a few seconds to admire his chiseled abs and tanned torso.

"I'm sorry about earlier," she said.

He frowned. "What about earlier?"

"Earlier today, at lunch. I was a bitch. A cranky bitch with a hangover and a headache, and I took it out on you. I apologize."

"You have nothing to apologize for. I was baiting you about camping. I'm sorry for that."

She reached out for him and he took her hand. "Thank you. Maybe camping isn't ever going to be my thing. Would that be a problem for you?"

He looked over at her. "No. Why should it?"

She directed her attention over the water. "I don't know. Just . . . thinking."

"Thinking about what?"

"This and that. Nothing important really."

That was a lie. She'd been thinking about a lot of things. Like how much fun she'd had with Bash over the past few months. How few of the items he'd ticked off on her list. And how little her list meant to her now.

Bash had started to mean everything to her.

She dragged her gaze from the water, putting it on him.

He was fun, passionate, ridiculously good-looking, and sexy as hell, and he'd been there for her every step of the way over the past few months, never asking for more than she was willing to give.

She was head over heels in love with him.

She wanted to tell him. She wanted to tell him right now. The words hovered on her lips, ready to spill, but something held her back.

Just say it, Chelsea.

She'd always been fearless, had always spoken her mind. Now shouldn't be any different.

But it was. This was love. This was her heart. It was a big deal.

"Chelsea."

She focused on Bash. "Yes?"

"Something on your mind?"

Say it.

She tried, but it just wasn't the right time. Or something.

"No. Other than thank you again for bringing me here. I've had a great time."

He grinned. "Me, too."

She'd talk to him later. Maybe tonight or after they got back home.

She'd tell him.

Soon.

Chapter 34

THEIR IDYLLIC VACATION had come to an end. Bash had enjoyed the hell out of it, and he hated saying goodbye to South Padre Island. He could have easily spent a week here, but he was glad to have been able to spend at least a few days on the beach.

They packed up and headed back, convoying again with Carter and Molly, at least until they reached Hope, where they honked and waved goodbye.

Bash drove to Chelsea's apartment so she could drop off her bags, but for some reason he wasn't ready to say goodbye to her yet.

He wondered if he'd ever be ready to say goodbye to her. He liked the way things were going with them. He enjoyed spending time with her, liked having her in his life.

Hell, he loved her. He just didn't know what to do with these feelings. Being in love was something he'd done once, and he'd done it badly. He needed time to sort out his feelings. Make sure of where he stood, where things were going with them. He'd fucked up his relationship—his marriage—with Cathy. He knew better than to do that again. He had to take things slow, be sure he knew what the hell he was doing this time.

Did he even know what love was? Could he ever be certain of anything regarding his feelings?

He wasn't sure.

Things with Chelsea and him were good right now. That's all he did know for certain. It was best not to upset the balance by introducing love into the equation.

Love changed everything.

Right now, he wanted to hang on to the vacation a little bit longer. He wanted to hang on to her a while longer, too, before work and reality came crashing in.

"I know you probably have laundry and unpacking to do, but I was wondering if you wanted to come with me to pick up Lou. We could grab something to eat."

She nodded. "I'd love to. Besides, I'm hungry and I don't have any food here, and I'm sure not ready to do any grocery shopping."

His lips curved. "Good."

They went over to Emma and Luke's place. Lou was beside herself with excitement, wriggling and barking when he picked her up and cradled her against him.

"How did she do?" he asked.

"She was perfect," Emma said. "She got along great with Annie and Daisy, running around like crazy in the yard. Though she might think she's a big dog now."

He laughed. "She always thinks she's a big dog."

He thanked Emma and Luke, then they piled in the truck with Lou and her stuff, stopped off at a pizza place to pick up the order Chelsea had called in along the way, and headed to his house.

Lou had to sniff every corner of the house again to make sure nothing had changed while she was gone. Chelsea set out plates for their pizza, and Bash fixed drinks for them. They settled on the couch and watched some television while they ate.

"Tired?" he asked her.

"A little. It's a long drive. But I had a great time. I wish we could have stayed longer."

He brushed his fingers along her arm. "I do, too. But you're already pretty tan, for a redhead."

She laughed. "Even with a lot of sunscreen I tan well. That old adage of redheads having fair skin doesn't really apply to me."

"So I noticed. Looks good on you." He leaned over and brushed his lips against hers. "Mmm, you taste spicy."

"Like pepperoni?"

He laughed. "Yes, like that."

"It's like an aphrodisiac for men. Women like sweet things, like cherries or vanilla. Men? If we tasted like beer or pizza, you'd fall in love with us."

"I don't know about that. You always taste sweet." He was about to say that he'd fallen in love with her because she tasted sweet, but he checked himself.

He wasn't ready yet. He wasn't sure when he would be—or if he'd *ever* be ready to make that commitment.

He loved Chelsea. Knowing it was one thing. Saying the words was another.

"Do you have to go back to work tomorrow?"

He nodded.

"And did you miss your baby?"

He cocked his head to the side. "Huh?"

"Your bar."

He laughed. "Oh. Kind of. I'm anxious to see how Hall handled things."

"Did he call or text you while you were gone?"

"No."

"Then chances are, the place hasn't burned down."

"Bite your tongue."

She shoved against him. "I like how dedicated you are, how much you love that place."

He appreciated that she didn't mind how much he loved the bar. He'd lost a lot of girlfriends because of the bar. But Chelsea understood.

They watched a movie after dinner, then Chelsea stood and stretched her back. "I should go."

"You don't want to stay?"

"Do you want me to stay?"

He slid his arms around her, tugged her against him, and gave her ponytail a little tug. "Yeah. I want you to stay. If you can live without your laundry until tomorrow."

"It'll be tough, but I'll make an attempt to get through the night."

He tipped her chin up and brushed his lips against hers. "I'll try to give you something to take your mind off of your dirty clothes."

"Something dirtier, I hope."

He smiled against her lips. "I like the way you think."

He ran Lou outside, and when he came in, the lights were off except in the bedroom. He came in to find Chelsea had pulled the comforter down. She was naked and sitting cross-legged on his bed. He went hard instantly.

"Now there's something I'd like to find in my bed every night."

She leaned back against the pillows. "Is that an invitation?"

"Might be. If you intend to show up naked in my bed."

"I'll think about it." She patted the pillow next to her.

He slipped out of his clothes and joined her on the bed, facing her, sliding his legs on either side of her. He gathered her onto his lap and she wrapped her legs around him, her sex sliding over his cock.

"What now?" he asked, cupping her butt.

"I suppose we could meditate."

"We could, but it's not quite what I had in mind." She reached under the pillow and handed him a condom.

"Already?"

"Yes. I want you."

He put the condom on, then lifted her and slid her onto his cock. She tightened her legs around him, then began to move.

It was the most excruciating pleasure he'd ever felt. Chelsea kissed him, her body undulating against him, her nipples brushing his chest as she rocked his fucking world. He held on to her and drew her back, then pulled her in, thrusting deeply into her until he thought he was going to burst listening to the sounds of pleasure she made.

She kissed her way along his jaw, letting her tongue slide

down his neck, then sinking her teeth into that spot between his neck and shoulder. And when her movements sharpened along with her breathing, he knew she was close. She tightened around him, cried out, and climaxed. He was right there with her seconds later, groaning as he came.

He held her like that, gathering his bearings and enjoying the feel of her kissing his neck, when she whispered in his ear.

"I love you, Bash."

He stilled, not quite sure if he'd actually heard those words. He pulled back.

"What did you say?"

She smiled, her eyes bright. "I said I love you."

And then his world crashed around him.

Chapter 35

CHELSEA KNEW AS soon as she said the words that it was the wrong time. Or the wrong thing to say.

She smoothed her hands over his shoulders. "Bash."

"Yes."

"Is something wrong?"

"No. No, Chelsea. I mean, that's great."

Wow. Talk about the wrong response. She climbed off of him and he went into the bathroom for a few seconds, but he didn't come back to bed. Instead, he leaned against the bathroom door, gloriously, beautifully naked.

Whereas she wanted to be fully clothed and preferably out the door. She grabbed the pillow and put it in front of her, needing it as a shield.

"So, you obviously didn't want me to say those words to you."

"It's not that." He finally pushed off the wall and came over to sit on the side of the bed.

Not on the bed with her. As if she had some communicable disease. God, this was awful. She tossed the pillow aside and scrambled to find her clothes, climbing into them in a hurry.

Bash got dressed, too.

But this wasn't over. She needed answers, so she sat on the side of the bed next to him while he put on his tennis shoes.

"Bash, what is it? You obviously don't love me back, and that's okay. I didn't expect you to reply."

"No. I do love you."

He'd said the words so softly she barely heard him. "You don't have to say that, Bash. You're not obligated."

"Of course I'm not. It's just . . . Christ, this isn't going to come out right. I do love you, Chelsea. I was just thinking the other day that I had fallen in love with you."

He'd realized it the other day. As if it was a bad thing? "But you didn't say it to me then."

"I wasn't ready. I'm not ready. I don't know, I might never be ready." He dragged his fingers through his hair. He looked as miserable as she felt.

He couldn't be as miserable as she felt.

"I don't understand."

"I'm sorry." He wasn't looking at her. He was staring at the sheet.

Something was terribly, terribly wrong. She wanted to find out what it was.

"Tell me what's wrong, Bash."

The silence was unnerving when he didn't respond.

Finally, he did.

"You know, someday you're going to find that perfect guy, Chelsea. And when you do, he's going to love to do everything you love to do, and you're going to love everything about him."

He finally looked at her. "But that guy can't be me."

The blow to her chest crushed her.

She stood. "Take me home."

He cocked his head to the side. "Chelsea . . ."

"Take me home, Bash. Now."

He hesitated, then finally nodded, grabbing his keys. She walked out of the bedroom and grabbed her purse, not even pausing to look at Lou, who'd perked up when she walked by. If she stopped to pet Lou, she was going to break down and cry.

She refused to do that. He didn't deserve to see her tears.

The short ride to her apartment was excruciating. There were so many questions she wanted to ask, so many awful things she wanted to say to Bash. But what was the point?

They were done. She'd told him she loved him, and he'd told her that someday she'd find some other guy who'd love her back.

She was finished with him.

When he pulled up in front of her apartment, he put his truck in park, then turned to her.

"Chelsea . . ."

She turned her head sharply in his direction.

"You did everything you could to make me fall in love with you, Bash. You pursued me. You teased me. You were sexy and seductive and you wanted this as much as I did. So don't pretend I was the one who pushed for this, when we both know that's not how it was. You were there with me—we were in this together—every step of the way. Well, it worked. I fell in love with you."

Her voice trembled as the tears fell down her cheeks, and she couldn't stop them. "And now you're walking away. I've always considered you warm and considerate, a man with true heart. But this is the most heartless thing you've ever done."

She opened the door, grabbed her purse, shut the door, and walked off without looking back. She wouldn't look back.

She didn't hear his truck pull away until long after she'd gone inside her apartment and locked the door. She didn't turn the lights on, just waited until she heard him pull away. Then she went into her bathroom, turned on her shower, climbed inside, and let the water spray over her.

Then she let the tears fall in earnest, and they didn't stop.

Chapter 36

BASH WIPED DOWN the bar until it gleamed—or as much as the beat-up bar could gleam, anyway.

The problem was, he'd already cleaned it four times, along with the rest of the bar. It was still three hours until opening, he was alone, and he needed to stay busy.

Lou sat up on his foot, looking at him with a mournful expression.

Even his dog judged him. Not that he could blame her. It had been six days since he'd let Chelsea walk out of his life. Six days since he'd acted like an utter jackass.

It felt like six days since he'd last slept.

Megan wouldn't make eye contact with him when he went into her bakery for coffee and baked goods. He'd passed Samantha on the street the other day, and if looks could kill, he'd be a dead man.

Obviously, Chelsea had talked to her friends. And he hadn't come out of it looking good. Of course he hadn't, because he'd broken her heart.

He didn't know what was wrong with him. He knew he was in love with her, but her saying the words to him first had caused a knee-jerk reaction of fear and flight. Knowing you're in love with someone and actually saying the words out loud were obviously two different things.

He'd reacted badly. More than badly. He'd hurt her, and that's the last goddamn thing he'd ever wanted to do to Chelsea.

This was why he never got involved. He wasn't good with relationships. Hadn't he learned that with Cathy?

He should have kept his distance from Chelsea, should have kept dating the same women he'd dated before. Kept it light and easy, with no commitments.

He'd known all along that Chelsea was a relationship and commitment type of woman, and he'd still walked into a relationship with her. He had no one to blame but himself for how this had all turned out.

He heard a knock on the door of the bar and lifted his head, saw Logan standing there, and smiled.

Great. Something to get his mind off of what a dick he was. He went and unlocked the door.

"Sorry, dude. Bar's not open yet. You'll have to get your beer at the liquor store."

"Funny," Logan said, sliding inside so Bash could shut and lock the door again.

Logan bent to pet Lou. Once she was satisfied, she wandered off.

"Damn, that dog is cute."

"I know, right? She's a bar favorite."

"I imagine she is. Draws in women, too, doesn't she?"

"She's half my marketing right now."

Logan laughed.

"What are you doing in town?"

"Des is flying in tonight for a visit. She's got a short break from filming, so I'm going to the airport to pick her up."

Bash grinned. "That's great. I know you miss her."

"Like crazy."

"You want a beer?"

"I wouldn't say no to one."

Bash went behind the bar and grabbed two beers, popped

the tops off the bottles, and came around to where Logan had pulled out a seat at one of the tables. He handed Logan's beer to him.

"Thanks." Logan pulled out one of the other chairs and propped his booted feet on them.

"I just wiped down those chairs," Bash said.

"You can do it again."

Bash shook his head. "What did you, Luke, and Reid decide about the mercantile?"

"We put in an offer to the city to buy it, so we're waiting to hear back."

"I think that's a good choice. Reid could do something great with that place."

"We'll see." He took a swig of the beer, then rested it in his lap. "How's the bar?"

"Really busy. Business is picking up, and I'm looking forward to the expansion."

"Reid told me about that. It's a good idea."

"Thanks."

"How's Chelsea?"

He was hoping Logan wouldn't bring her up. "Not good."

Logan frowned. "Is she sick or something?"

"No, it's not that." He stared at the bottle of beer. "It's . . . We kind of broke up."

"Kind of?"

"She told me she loved me. I told her someday she'd find some other guy who'd make her really happy."

"Ouch. So you don't love her back."

Bash stared at the label on his beer. "Well, that's the problem. I do love her."

"Okay. So I don't understand."

He sucked in a breath and let it out. "You know my past, Logan, what I went through with Cathy."

Logan gave him a look. "Chelsea isn't Cathy."

"I know that. Logically, I know that. But as soon as she said the words, I froze. I pushed her away. And hurt her badly."

Logan took a couple of swallows of beer and didn't say anything for a while.

"Look, Bash, relationships are hard. And sometimes we don't do them right. Your first marriage was a mistake. I think you realized that. But is Chelsea a mistake, too?"

Bash shook his head.

"So I guess the question is, are you really willing to let her go?"

"No." He realized right then that he hadn't even hesitated when he answered. "I don't want to lose her."

"Then do whatever you have to do to fix what you broke."

"I don't think she's going to give me a second chance."

Logan laughed at him. "You've never been the type to be afraid of hard work. So suck it up and grovel your ass off, but make Chelsea understand that you love her."

Bash was afraid it might already be too late.

But Logan was right. He wanted her, he'd made a huge mistake, and he needed to rectify that right now.

The problem was, he didn't know how he was going to make that happen.

CHELSEA FOLDED AND put away laundry, then cleaned her kitchen with a fury. When she was done, she picked up a book to read, but after reading the same page four times, she gave up in disgust and texted Megan. Then she took a shower, got dressed, and drove over to Megan's. It was Saturday afternoon and she knew Megan would be baking.

Megan was always baking.

Megan opened her door and the scent of something wonderful greeted Chelsea.

"You're just in time," Megan said. "I just pulled muffins out of the oven."

"I don't know how you bake all the time and still look so damn good."

Megan chuckled. "I only taste a little. And I'm always on the run. It burns a lot of calories."

"Witch." Chelsea walked in and headed straight for Megan's kitchen. She had a small place, but it had a dream kitchen, with a double oven, tons of counter space, and the

most gorgeous stove Chelsea had ever seen. It was charming
and retro and mint green and Chelsea coveted it in her dreams.

"Would you like a latte or a cappuccino?"

Megan also had an espresso machine. It was a wonder
people weren't lingering outside her door, considering the
awesome smells that emanated from her house.

"A latte sounds fantastic."

Megan fixed drinks while Chelsea made herself at home
putting two muffins on the plate.

"None for me. I already tasted."

"You're going to sit down and have a muffin and a latte
with me. And I'm going to whine."

"Oh. Okay."

They sat together at the island. The muffins were cranberry
orange, and, of course, delicious.

"These muffins are fantastic, Megan."

"Thank you. I'm trying out a new recipe."

Chelsea shook her head. "Is there anything you make that
isn't good?"

Megan laughed. "Plenty. You don't think I'd let my friends
taste my disastrous mistakes, do you?"

"Good point. Then I'm glad to be your friend so all I get
to taste are your successes."

Megan lifted her cup, took a sip, and said, "Amen to that.
Now start whining."

Chelsea took another bite of fabulous muffin and washed
it down with the amazing latte. "I'm moping about Bash."

"I'm sorry. I still can't believe he hurt you like that. What
an ass. I should send him some of my disastrous, lumpy,
burned, horrible pound cake where I used too much salt and
not enough sugar."

Chelsea fought back a laugh. To Megan, baked goods gone
wrong were the kiss of death. "Yes. That'll show him."

Megan nodded. "Indeed it would. Hurting one of my
friends like that. It's unforgivable. So what now?"

"What do you mean, what now? We're over."

"Are you sure? You love him, Chelsea. I don't think those
feelings end overnight."

"It hasn't been overnight. It's been a week."

Megan cocked her head to the side. "A whole week. You're probably ready to marry someone else by now."

"Okay, fine. I'm not over him by any stretch of the imagination. But I'm going to *get* over him. I have to."

Her phone buzzed and she glanced down at it. It was a text message.

From Bash. It was the first time she'd heard from him since that night she slammed his car door and walked away. Since that night he'd crushed her.

I'd really like to see you. I want to talk.

So few words. And yet her heart started to pump faster and her eyes welled with tears.

Damn him.

"It's from Bash, isn't it?" Megan asked.

She looked up at Megan and nodded.

"What does it say?"

"That he wants to see me. To talk."

"Okay. So?"

She shrugged. "So what? He said enough already, didn't he?"

"Maybe he's sorry about that night."

"Tough."

"Chelsea."

"I don't care if he's sorry, Megan. I told him I loved him and he ripped my heart out. He doesn't get a second chance."

She wouldn't allow him to hurt her again. She couldn't go through it twice.

She didn't care what he had to say.

She wasn't about to listen.

Chapter 37

BASH KNEW THIS wasn't going to be easy. Chelsea wasn't easy. And he'd made it even harder by slamming the door on their relationship, by throwing her "I love you" back in her face.

He'd texted her multiple times. He'd called her even more. He'd even gone by her apartment, but she hadn't answered.

The only thing left was to involve her friends, and they'd circled her like protective wagons against him—the bad guy.

But he had no other choice. He needed to give it every effort, and he wasn't about to give up.

He tried Emma, but she said she was swamped all the time and would talk to him next week—a blow-off if he ever heard one. Jane told him she was busy with the kids. Sam cut off his phone calls, saying she was doing flowers for a wedding so she couldn't give him the time.

These women were damn experts at being evasive.

He finally cornered Megan one afternoon just as she was putting the *Closed* sign out on the bakery.

"I'm just closing, Bash. Sorry," she said, just about to shut the door in his face.

"Five minutes, Megan. Please."

She hesitated. Chewed on her lower lip and scanned up and down the street as if she were contemplating inviting the devil himself into her shop.

"Five minutes. Hurry up and get inside before someone sees you."

There was nothing worse than losing a woman, and then losing all her friends, who used to be your friends, too.

This sucked.

She pulled the shades, then stood there in the semidarkness with her arms folded. "Five minutes."

This felt like a test he took one time at the front of history class. His mind suddenly went blank and he felt sweat start to pool at his back.

But he also knew this was his last chance, so he had to make it work.

"I love her, Megan. I panicked when she said it first. It was a stupid thing to do and I need to make it right. But in order to do that, I have to be able to see her."

Megan didn't budge for a few seconds, then she sighed. "Let me talk to the others. We'll see what we can do."

"Thanks."

It took Megan a few days to get back to him. For a while, Bash thought she was going to ignore him, that she'd said whatever she could to get him out of her shop. But she finally called him and told him the plan.

There was going to be a party Saturday night for Emma's birthday. Everyone was going to be at Emma and Luke's house for barbecue, drinks, and cake. Megan made sure to mention she made a cake for the event. He smiled at that part.

If he wanted to talk to Chelsea, they all agreed that was the place to do it.

He made sure to ask if it was okay with Emma if he showed up. Megan told him Emma said it was fine.

Which meant he was going to have to face her in front of all of his friends. All of *her* friends.

He could do this. He had to, because it was the only way he was going to be able to talk to her.

He arranged for Hall to cover the bar Saturday night. Megan

told him the party was going to start at seven, so he made sure to wait until about eight before he headed over. He wanted everyone to already be there, especially Chelsea.

He pulled up to Luke and Emma's house. Seeing all the cars parked outside the house, he was certain he'd never been more nervous in his entire life.

He saw Chelsea's car parked at the end of their driveway as he walked up and rang the doorbell.

He had no idea what he was going to say, but he knew damn well that he wasn't going to let her run away from him. And he wasn't going to walk away this time.

Whatever she had to say to him, he was going to stand and take it, because he deserved her anger.

He just wanted her to actually speak to him.

He wanted her back.

CHELSEA HELD HER drink in her hand, trying her best to enjoy the festivities surrounding Emma's birthday party.

She was surrounded by all of her friends, and the atmosphere was fun and chaotic. She was happy for something to do on a Saturday night. She didn't know what she would have done without her friends the past couple of weeks. It was bad enough that it was summer vacation from school, so her days were free. Now she wished she were teaching summer school, because the days were endless.

The nights, however, were brutal. She hadn't been sleeping well, instead tossing and turning, her thoughts filled with Bash and everything they'd done together.

She'd lain there night after night, replaying every moment in her head.

How could she have gotten it so wrong? His sweetness, his humor, the way he'd touched her, looked at her, the things he'd said.

Had it all been an act? For what purpose? So he could dump her as soon as she said, "I love you"? That made no sense. That wasn't Bash. He wasn't that kind of guy.

Though right now, she had no idea if she knew anything

about men. She'd made a list, and she'd dated men who fit the
list. That hadn't worked out so well.

Then she'd dated Bash, who hadn't met any of the criteria
on her list.

That hadn't worked out, either. But it had, hadn't it? They'd
gotten along and the chemistry between them had been powerful. They laughed together and had fun together, and the feelings
she had were real. She had felt they were reciprocated by Bash.

She'd been so wrong.

She'd been in love before, but never like this. She'd never
fallen so hard and so fast. Or so deep.

And she'd never been so hurt.

Over the past couple of weeks she tried to convince herself
that she should have stuck to her list, but she'd come to the
realization that her list had been complete and utter . . .

Crap.

She'd never find a man based upon a list.

She leaned against the kitchen counter, watching her
friends talking and laughing. Emma with Luke. Carter with
Molly. Will with Jane. So damn happy. They'd had no list.
For them, it had just . . . happened.

She and Bash had just happened, too.

So what had gone wrong?

The doorbell rang and she saw Emma go to the door. She
couldn't see who was on the other side, but Emma stood there
for a few seconds talking to whomever was there.

Then Emma stepped aside and turned and made eye contact with her, almost as if in apology.

And then Bash walked in.

Her legs started shaking. Everything on her started shaking as her pulse went haywire. She laid her wineglass down
on the kitchen counter, her hand trembling.

Everything inside of her screamed no. She shook her head.

"No," she heard herself whisper as she backed away,
toward the back door. Bash advanced into the room, smiling
and saying hello to everyone.

He hadn't seen her yet. Maybe he didn't know she was here.

But he had to know. Emma knew. She'd given her a look.

Did Emma invite Bash? Why would she do that?

Her body heated, and a sudden need to escape overwhelmed her.

Until a cool hand circled her wrist. She turned to see Megan next to her.

"You need to talk to him, Chelsea."

She shook her head. "No, I don't."

"Yes, you do. If for no other reason than to get some answers and closure."

"Closure is overrated."

Megan smiled, then pulled her close and hugged her, though Chelsea wasn't sure if that was actual affection or Megan trying to keep her from running like hell out the back door.

Either way, it was too late, because suddenly Bash was there in front of her looking taller than she remembered. He had on a pair of dark jeans and a tight black T-shirt that fit him better than any shirt had the right to fit a man. Even his hair looked good, and he smelled great, and why did she even care? He wasn't hers anymore.

"I'll let you two talk," Megan said, slipping away.

"Thanks, Megan," Bash said, never taking his eyes off Chelsea.

"Can I talk to you?"

She shook her head. "No."

"Chelsea."

He reached for her, but she stepped away. "Don't."

She turned around and slipped out through the back door, knowing he was going to follow her. But she couldn't have all her friends bear witness to this.

She wrapped her arms around herself and stood on the patio, staring out at the moonless night. The stars were everywhere. She wished the blackness of the night would swallow her up and take her anywhere but here.

"I never meant to hurt you."

She let out a short laugh. "Such an insincere statement, spoken by every guy who ever dumped a woman."

"I didn't dump you." He came around and stood in front of her, forcing her to meet his gaze. "I never meant for us to end."

"Really. You telling me that someday I'd find some perfect guy—a guy who wasn't you—wasn't an end to us?"

He dragged his fingers through his hair. "You're right. It was a stupid thing to say. When you told me you loved me, it scared the shit out of me."

"I'm so glad to hear that. It's what every woman wants to hear when she declares her love."

"Dammit, Chelsea. Please let me try and explain."

She took a seat in the nearby chair. "Go ahead."

He pulled up a chair right across from her, their knees a fraction of an inch from touching. She wanted nothing more than to fall into his lap and beg him to love her. But she wasn't going to get that, was she? So she'd settle at least for an explanation. That closure thing that Megan mentioned. She didn't think it would help, but maybe he'd leave after that and she could start healing.

"What I did was unforgivable. The really sad, awful thing was I had already realized I loved you. You were the brave one, though. You said the words when I couldn't."

"Why couldn't you?"

"I don't know. My past relationship, I guess. My first marriage. God, that was such a disaster. Cathy had this idea of what I was supposed to be, and I . . . wasn't. No matter what I did, it wasn't good enough. Not the right job. I didn't make enough money. She wanted a house and we couldn't afford one. She wanted a new car and we could only afford used cars. It's like no matter what I did or how hard I tried, I could never be the man she wanted me to be."

Despite her discomfort, she felt that pain coming from him. "Bash, that's on her, not on you. You have to know that."

"Logically, I know that. But there's your list. And all those things on your list that I'm not. I couldn't live with myself if I disappointed another woman. Especially you."

Tears pricked her eyes. "And that's on me. You have to know by now that I never expected you to be anything other than who you are. I long ago gave up on that list. Maybe I should have told you that."

He shrugged. "It's really not about the list, but more about who I am. Or maybe who I can never be."

She sighed, realizing her part in what had happened to mess things up for them. "We've both made mistakes. I tried to develop this image of a perfect man, when there is no such thing. I'm sorry if by doing that I set you up—I set us up—for failure. But Bash, when I told you I loved you, I meant I loved *you*. The you that you are now, not some other you. I would never try to change you."

He grasped her hand. "I know that now. And God, Chelsea. I'm so damn sorry I hurt you. You're the very last person I ever want to hurt. I love you. I love you more than I've ever loved another woman. I haven't slept since that night. You're in my head every waking moment, because you're in my heart. It's where you've been for the past few months, and that's where you're going to stay, no matter how things end up between us. But I hope you can forgive me for hurting you and tell me you'll give me another chance to show you I deserve your love."

She hesitated, trying to push away the hurt, the things he'd said to her, because she knew now where they'd come from. She looked into his eyes and saw only clear love.

She had to take the chance, because Bash was worth it. And looking at him, and seeing the way he looked at her, the genuine caring in his eyes, and the deep pain she saw there, she knew.

He was it for her. He was the one.

She pushed off the chair and climbed into his lap. "I love you, too. I could never stop loving you."

He kissed her, tunneling his fingers into her hair as they poured out passion, desire, and love in their kiss. She grabbed hold of his shirt, needing that lifeline, smoothing her hands over his chest to feel the beat of his heart, to know that this was real.

It was perfect.

Until she heard whoops and hollers from inside and realized they had an audience.

She looked up to see everyone looking out at them, wide grins on their faces.

Chelsea laughed. "Okay, so maybe we need a more private venue for this reconciliation."

Bash leaned his forehead against hers. "Yeah, I think so."

They went inside.

"So, everything's okay now?" Emma asked.

Chelsea nodded. "Yes. Everything's great."

"Best birthday present ever." Emma grinned.

They hung out for a while, then left early, Chelsea following Bash to his house. They barely made it inside the front door before he shut the door, locked it, then pushed her against the door and kissed her.

She felt every bit of his love for her in that kiss—a powerful passion that told her exactly how much he loved her.

They shed their clothes on the way to the bedroom and told each other without too many words how much they'd missed each other. She couldn't take her eyes off of him, this perfect man who was now hers, and always would be.

Afterward, he held tight to her.

"Would you move in with me?"

She rolled to her side and faced him. "Are you sure you don't want to think about that?"

"Actually, it's all I've thought about since we've been apart. Even before that, actually. I envisioned you here, wanted you here. And after we broke up, I missed having you here, sleeping in my bed. I've missed waking up with you next to me. That's what I want. If that's what you want."

She loved hearing him say the words, loved knowing he wanted her in his life. "Yes. I'd like that."

He smiled, swept his hand over her face. "And at some point I figured we'd sell this place and you and I could pick out a new house together."

"You have thought about this a lot."

"Like I told you, I haven't done much sleeping. But I have done a lot of thinking about you. And me. And our future together."

She shuddered in a breath. Bash might not be a perfect man, but he was *the* perfect man—for her.

Epilogue

THE PAST FEW weeks had been a whirlwind. Chelsea had given notice at her apartment and had been packing up and moving into Bash's house. In addition, she'd kept busy helping Molly with wedding planning.

She and Bash were also talking about things they were looking for in their next house. It wasn't coming up in the near future, but it was their next step.

"So I have a list," Bash said that night as they climbed into bed together.

She assumed he'd made a list about their future house. They'd been debating whether to build a new house or look for an existing build, so they'd talked a lot of pros and cons. She told him to make a list.

"Is this about the house?"

"Not exactly."

She frowned and looked over at his notepad. "Then what kind of list did you make?"

"It's my list for the perfect woman."

She laughed. "I see. I can't wait to hear all about it."

He scanned the list. "This is important. You have to follow this closely."

She turned to face him, her legs crossed over each other. "You have my full attention."

"Must like divorced men, because a guy has to learn from his mistakes before he can find the right woman for him."

Her lips quirked.

"Must like a guy who has crazy ex-girlfriends, because a certain crazy ex-girlfriend will bring him the perfect dog."

Since Chelsea had Lou on the bed with her, she ran her hands over their dog. "Yes, we can't thank Gertrude—"

"Gerri."

"Whatever. We can't thank Gerri enough, because Lou is everything I could have wanted in a dog."

Bash reached over and scratched Lou behind the ears. "That she is."

"Okay, continue with your list."

"Must like a guy who works at a bar, because you can do a lot of fun things on top of a bar."

Chelsea felt herself blush. "Bash."

He grinned. "It's true, isn't it?"

"Well . . . yes."

"Okay, then. Continuing on. She has to be a redhead. I have a thing for redheads. No blondes or brunettes or raven-haired women need apply. A redhead is it for me."

She took a deep breath, then sighed. "This is a very intriguing list."

He looked over at her and nodded. "Right?"

"What's next?"

"Must be willing to tolerate sports. And all my friends."

She shrugged. "That one's easy. I actually like sports."

He cocked a brow. "You do?"

"Of course."

"Then why did you have 'must hate sports' on your list?"

She shrugged. "Because I figured guys who were all into sports would be focused on just that, and not on me."

Bash shook his head. "That's ridiculous."

"And you haven't dated the kinds of men I did."

"Obviously not."

"Anyway, and I love all your friends because they're all my friends."

"That's true. But back to you actually liking sports . . ."

"It's not my fault you're not paying attention to the fact that I like baseball and football."

"I'm going to test your baseball knowledge during the game tomorrow." He waved a finger at her.

"You do that."

"Okay, moving on. Must like burgers and fries and the occasional onion ring love fest."

"I like burgers and fries just fine. Just not every day."

"I can live with that."

She leaned against him. "Just how long is this list?"

"Almost done. Must like a guy who wears jeans and T-shirts."

She laid her hand on his chest. "It's quite obvious you made the cut."

He grinned down at her. "I'm willing to pull out a suit on occasion, though, mainly because you look sexy as hell when you're all dressed up."

"Deal."

"Must like kids. I'd like a couple."

She tapped her fingers on his notebook. "You know, that was on my list as well."

He gave her a heated look. "Can we start right now?"

She laughed. "Maybe not just yet. We have to get a house. And we should probably talk marriage at some point."

"Oh, we're going to do that. Very soon."

Her heart swelled.

"Now this is a deal breaker. Must like getting dirty in the mud now and then."

She lifted her gaze to his and gave him a very sexy smile. "I like dirty."

He stared at her. "You're making my dick hard."

"You should focus on your list."

He tossed the notebook aside and gathered her close.

"Bottom line. I'm not looking for the perfect woman, just the woman who'll love and accept me for who I am."

She kissed him, deeply, then looked at him with all the love she had for him.

"I already do," she said.

He gazed down at her, and she'd never felt more loved. "Then you're perfect for me."

She smiled up at him. "I know."

TURN THE PAGE FOR A SNEAK PEEK AT
THE NEXT TWO JACI BURTON NOVELS

All Wound Up

A PLAY-BY-PLAY NOVEL
AVAILABLE AUGUST 2015 FROM BERKLEY BOOKS

AND

Make Me Stay

A HOPE NOVEL
AVAILABLE DECEMBER 2015 FROM JOVE BOOKS

All Wound Up

IT WAS COOL, dark, and, most importantly, private in Clyde Ross's wine cellar, which was why Tucker Cassidy had brought Laura, his girlfriend, down here.

She'd had a lot to drink today, and when she drank, she got loud.

She was also pissed at him at the moment.

Laura pissed off, drunk, and loud? Not a good combination at the house of the owner of the St. Louis Rivers. Clyde Ross was his boss, and the last thing he needed was his girlfriend making a scene. He had enough of a bad-boy image without Laura making things worse by screaming at him in the middle of Clyde's very nice backyard garden.

"I'm not going to tell you again, Tucker. We're moving in together."

Yeah, that so wasn't happening. "We can talk about this when I take you home tonight, Laura."

He'd brought her to the wine cellar in the hopes of cooling her down. Plus, they were alone here and no one could hear them. Okay, mainly Laura, who had a tendency to get on a roll once she had a topic in mind she wanted to discuss.

"We've been dating two whole months, Tucker. Don't you think it's time we make it official?"

It had been the most awful *two whole months* of his entire life. Okay, maybe not at the beginning. Laura was a knockout. Tall, with long dark hair and curves that just didn't quit and the best ass he'd ever seen. She was a cocktail waitress and they'd met one night when he'd been having drinks in the bar where she worked. They hit it off right away and had gone out, had a night of hot sex, and had started dating. She'd been fun, adventurous, great in the sack, and they had a lot in common.

Plus, she liked baseball, and he played for the Rivers. Not that it was a deal breaker if a woman he dated wasn't a baseball fan, but it didn't hurt. She'd come to his games and she actually knew the game, as opposed to other women he'd dated who claimed to know the game but in fact didn't know balls from strikes or a curve from a fastball. In his mind, that was a goddamned crime.

But as the weeks progressed, he'd noticed she didn't hold her liquor well, and when she drank, she was not a fun drunk. She was loud and obnoxious, and she insulted his friends. She'd also grown more demanding of his time. Whenever they weren't together, she wanted to know where he was and how soon he was coming over. He didn't need a mother—he had a pretty great one already.

And now the past few times they'd been together, she'd thrown down hints about the two of them moving in together. He was so not ready for that.

So now he had to redirect her and calm her down before things got out of hand.

"How about we check out Clyde's awesome wine collection?"

She pushed at his chest. "I don't give a shit about Clyde or his wine. I want you to make a commitment to me."

He sighed and raked his fingers through his hair. He didn't want to do this here, but she hadn't left him much of a choice. "That's not gonna happen. We've only been dating two months and I'm not ready to live together."

She poked at his chest. "You know what? You're a sonofabitch. I thought we were heading somewhere. You led me to believe—"

He was going to have to stop her there. "I never made promises to you, Laura."

And now the tears. He'd seen a lot of those lately, too. Especially when she'd been drinking.

"I thought we were in love."

"I never said that, either."

She broke down then and sobbed.

Well, shit. He walked over to her and pulled her into his arms. "I'm sorry."

He didn't know how a woman could be so drunk, yet so accurate, but her knee hit his crotch at just the right angle, and he went down like a fighter getting a perfect punch.

Lights out. Only instead of a hit to his jaw, she'd KO'd him right in the balls.

"You're an asshole. We're done, Tucker. I'm out of here. I'll call a taxi to take me home."

He heard the click of her heels on the stone floor as she walked away.

He couldn't even breathe, let alone care that she'd just fucking left him on the ground.

Jesus Christ, that had hurt. His balls throbbed like someone had—

Well, someone *had* shoved a knee into them.

He lay there for what seemed like hours, but he knew it was only minutes before he managed to stagger to his knees. He found the wall, still struggling to catch his breath.

In a minute. He'd be able to stand in just a minute.

"Oh, my God. Are you okay?"

He heard a female voice.

Great. Just what he needed. A witness to his humiliation.

Then cool, soft hands swept across his forehead.

"Are you hurt? Did you fall?"

He shook his head. "I'm fine."

"You are not fine. You're practically hyperventilating. Tell me what happened?"

His eyes were still closed and he was concentrating all his effort on trying to determine if his balls were still attached to his body. He did not want some female being nice to him.

Actually, he wanted nothing to do with any female. Possibly ever again.

He finally managed to stand—with the woman's help, unfortunately.

"Tell me where you're hurt," she said.

He shook his head. "I'm not hurt. Just go away."

"I am not going to go away. I'm a doctor and I can help you."

Awesome. This night was getting worse by the second. "I don't need a doctor."

"How about you let me be the judge of that?"

He finally managed to open his eyes and look over at his unwanted savior.

She was, of course, gorgeous. Which made her immediately untrustworthy, since he'd just vowed to never again fall for a beautiful woman.

She was average height, with short blond hair and the most intense blue eyes he'd ever seen. She also had the most perfect mouth—

Not that he was ever going to think about a woman in a sexual way again. Thoughts like that only led to trouble, and crushed testicles.

He leaned against the cool wall and closed his eyes. She slipped her fingers around his wrist.

"What are you doing?" he asked.

"Shhh."

Fine with him. Maybe if he didn't say anything, or look at her, she'd disappear.

But she didn't. She kept holding on to him.

"Your pulse rate is a little high."

He opened his eyes and looked down at her. "Not surprising since I just got kicked in the balls."

She pursed her lips as she met his gaze. "Literally or figuratively?"

"Literally."

"Ouch. I can't speak from experience, of course, but that must have been painful. What did you do to deserve that?"

Figures she'd think he was deserving of a knee to the groin. "Nothing. I had a drunk girlfriend who had it in her head we were supposed to move in together. When I tried to let her down easily, that was her response."

"Ouch again. Sorry."

He shrugged. "Not your fault."

She rubbed her hands together. "I should examine you."

He let out a laugh. "Honey, no offense, but the last thing I want is any woman near my balls tonight. Or possibly ever again."

Her lips curved. "You say that now. You'll change your mind once they feel better. And you need to let me take a look and feel them to make sure your girlfriend—"

"Ex-girlfriend."

"Okay. To make sure your ex-girlfriend didn't seriously injure you."

"Uh, no. I'm okay."

She put her hands on her hips. She had nice hips, show-cased in a white, lacy sundress, which showcased one very cute figure. Not that he was into noticing that kind of thing at the moment. Or ever again.

"Who's the doctor here? Me or you?"

"You. Or so you say. This could be some conspiracy. You could be a friend of Laura's setting me up for round two of let's-destroy-Tucker-Cassidy's-manhood night."

Now it was her turn to laugh. "I can assure you I have no idea who your girlfriend—"

"Ex-girlfriend."

"Right. I can assure you I am not in league with your nefarious ex-girlfriend."

"I like that." He finally had something to smile about.

"Like what?"

"Nefarious. It fits her. But you're still not getting in my pants."

"Playing hard to get, Tucker?"

"I'll show you mine if you show me yours."

"I see you're starting to feel better. That's a very good sign. But no, I'm not showing you mine. I am going to look at yours, though. And in your weakened condition, I'm pretty sure I can get into your pants."

His balls still throbbed. What if Laura had broken them? What if he was unable to have kids? Not that he wanted any—right now. But someday . . .

"Okay. Fine. You're really a doctor?"

"I really am. So drop 'em and let's take a look at the goods."

He reached for the zipper of his pants. "If I had a dollar for every time a woman said that to me . . ."

She snickered and came over, and he caught a light citrusy scent. He breathed it in, the best thing he'd smelled all night. It smelled like renewal, like starting over.

Which was ridiculous because he didn't even know the doctor's name. But if she fixed him, she'd be his savior.

She cradled his ball sac in her hand, then examined his dick. There was something about having a woman so close to his goods that should be exciting as hell. But he wasn't getting hard. He hurt too damn bad.

"A little red and swollen, but she didn't break your penis."

"Well, hallelujah."

She tilted her head to the side and gave him a wry smile. "Right? She hit you pretty hard, though. Your testicles are swollen and red."

She took a step back. "You can pull your pants up now. You're going to be sore for a couple of days. But I think you're going to be fine."

"Thanks."

"You're welcome."

He zipped up. "I hope your husband or boyfriend doesn't mind you inspecting my stuff down here in the wine cellar."

"No husband. No boyfriend. I'm a resident at Washington University here in St. Louis and way too busy for that."

"I see. So who are you here with?"

"Oh, my father is Clyde Ross." She held out her hand. "I'm Aubry."

Shit. Shit, shit, shit. The boss's daughter. This night couldn't get any worse.

"Oh. I didn't know that. I mean, I knew he had a daughter

in medical school or something. I don't know why I didn't make the connection."

"No reason for you to. Nice to meet you, Tucker. I've seen you pitch. You're pretty damn good."

"So are you, Doc. Thanks for the once-over."

"You're welcome. I actually came down here to grab a bottle of wine for my dad." She wandered off as if she knew exactly where she was going, plucking a bottle from the rack before turning to face him. "Got it. Shall we go upstairs, or do you need more time to reflect on your evening?"

"No, I think I've spent enough time down here."

He followed her toward the stairs, hoping like hell Aubry was discreet enough not to tell her father what had happened to him.

But there was something he needed to know, so he stopped and turned to face her. "One question."

"Sure."

"Did you make me drop trou because it was medically necessary, or because you wanted to get a good look at my dick?"

One side of her mouth curved up in a sexy-as-hell smile. "Tucker. I'm surprised you'd ask that question. I am a doctor, after all."

She turned and headed up the stairs.

Which wasn't an answer at all.

The night was starting to look up.

But his balls still hurt like hell, and after the debacle with Laura, and the fact that the doc was Clyde's daughter, he should definitely avoid Aubry Ross.

Or . . . maybe not.

Make Me Stay

REID MCCORMACK STUDIED the blueprints for the old mercantile he'd agreed to renovate in downtown Hope. He still had no idea what he was doing back in his hometown, or why he'd agreed to this job.

It was a big project, and he had plenty of projects with his company in Boston. Shifting responsibilities over had been a giant pain in the ass, as was taking a leave of absence and putting his company—his baby—in the hands of his associates. He'd sweated blood and risked a hell of a lot of money to get his architectural firm up and running, and with numerous late nights and damn good work, he'd made a success of McCormack Architectural Designs.

It made him nervous not to be in Boston overseeing the business. But, he'd had to admit, when he'd come to town for his brother Logan's wedding in the spring and they'd taken a look at this old place, it had been childhood memories, plus the challenge of restoring the mercantile to its former glory, that had been too much to resist.

He had ideas for the mercantile. A lot of them. And now that he and his brothers had bought the old building back from the town, it was their responsibility to do right by it. Although, Logan and Luke's contributions were limited to providing their part of the capital. As the architect in charge of the project, Reid was going to be the one to put the actual work into it. He intended to do it justice.

And then he'd head back to Boston, where he belonged.

Because while Hope would always be home to him, it wasn't his home anymore.

So now he stood in the middle of a pile of crap covering the main floor, his boots kicking around years' worth of dust and debris. He might be the youngest McCormack brother, but he had great memories of this old place.

His lips ticked up as he remembered the building in its former glory. Dad walking them past, trying to corral three rambunctious boys on their way to the ice cream store. Reid was always the best behaved, so he'd stayed by Dad's side while Logan and Luke ran off ahead, getting into one thing or another. But he and Dad had stopped to look inside. At the time, there had been offices, with busy people doing their jobs. Even at age five, Reid had been fascinated by the old brick building. Dad had been, too. He could still remember the people inside stopping to smile and wave at him. And he'd waved back.

Mom hadn't been with them that day. She often wasn't. Raising kids hadn't been her favorite thing. Ever.

He heard a knock on the front door, dissipating the cloud of memories.

Figuring it was the general contractor he'd hired—or maybe his brothers, who were also supposed to meet him there today—he went to the door and pulled it open.

It wasn't the contractor or his brothers. It was Samantha Reasor, the owner of the flower shop around the corner. Sam was the one who'd pushed hard for them to take on this project. Or rather, for him to take it on. She was as passionate about the mercantile as anyone in Hope.

Today she wore dark skinny jeans that showcased her slender frame. Her blond hair was pulled high on top of her head, and she had on a short-sleeved polo shirt that bore the name

Reasor's Flower Shop. And she had the prettiest damn smile he'd ever seen, with full lips painted a kissable shade of pink.

Not that he was thinking about kissing her or anything. He was back in Hope to work.

"Hi, Reid. I heard you were in town and getting ready to start the project. I couldn't wait to get inside here again."

"Hey, Sam. Come on in. Though the place is still as dusty as it was when we did the walk-through in the spring. Are you sure you want to get dirty?"

She waved her hand as she stepped in. "I don't mind. I've been snipping and arranging flower baskets all day for an event. There are probably leaves in my hair."

As she walked by, he inhaled the fresh scent of—what was that? Freesia? Roses? Hell if he knew, since he didn't know jack about flowers. He only knew that Sam smelled damn good. And there were no leaves in her hair.

She turned in a circle, surveying both up and down the main room. "It's amazing, isn't it?"

He laughed. "Right now it's a dump."

Her gaze settled on him. "Oh, come on. Surely you can see beyond the trash and the layers of dust to what it can be." She spied the rolled-up documents in his hand. "Do you have blueprints?"

"Yeah."

"Care to share? I'd love to see the plans you've worked up."

"Actually, the general contractor is due to show up here shortly, along with Luke and Logan. You're welcome to hang out while we go over them."

She pulled her phone out of her back pocket. "Unfortunately, I can't. I have a delivery to make in about thirty minutes. But I'd really like to see the blueprints. Are you busy for dinner tonight?"

"Uh, dinner?"

"Sure. Why don't you come over to my place? I make a mean plate of spaghetti. If you're not busy with your family. I know you'd like to get reacquainted with them, so I don't want to step all over that."

"No, it's not that. I've been here a couple days already, so we've done the reacquainted stuff." He didn't know what the hell was going on. Was she asking him out, or was she just interested in seeing the blueprints?

"Perfect. Give me your phone and I'll put my address and cell number in it."

He handed his phone over and Sam typed in her info. "Is seven okay? That'll give me time to close up the shop and get things going."

"Sure."

"Great." She grasped his arm. "I'm so glad you're here, Reid. I'll see you later."

She breezed out the door and he found himself staring at the closed door, wondering what the hell had just happened.

Sam probably just wanted to get a good look at the blueprints when they'd have more time. She was interested in the old building. Not in him.

And he wasn't interested in her. Or any woman. He was in town to refurbish the mercantile, and nothing more.

But at least he'd get to enjoy her company and a home-cooked meal tonight.

SAM WENT BACK to the shop, wishing she'd had more time to check out Reid—check out the blueprints. Not that Reid wasn't some awesome eye candy. Today he'd worn loose jeans, boots, and a short-sleeved T-shirt that showed off his tanned, well-muscled arms.

It had taken everything in her to walk out of the mercantile. Fortunately, she had a job and a timeline, and that always came first. She loaded up the flowers that Georgia Burnett, the mayor, had ordered for the Chamber of Commerce luncheon today, put them in her van, and drove them over to the offices. Georgia, who'd had a terrible fall last year and had spent several months laid up, was back to her old cheery, mobile self again. And since she was the mother of two of Sam's friends, Emma and Molly, Georgia was like a mother to Sam as well. Which was so nice since the only family Sam had left was her Grammy Claire.

And family was a big deal to Sam.

"Hello, Georgia, how are you?"

"Doing wonderfully, Samantha. And you?"

"Great." She pressed a kiss to Georgia's cheek while simultaneously juggling two baskets of flowers.

"The baskets are gorgeous, honey," Georgia said. "The tables are already set up inside, so you can place them in the center of each one."

"Will do."

Sam went about her business, and once she finished, she said goodbye to Georgia and headed back to the shop. She had several individual flower orders to prepare and deliver, which took up the remainder of her day.

Which suited her just fine. Busy was good for business, and business had been great lately. She had two weddings coming up, including that of Georgia's daughter Molly in a few weeks.

When her phone buzzed, she smiled. Speaking of the bride-to-be . . .

"Hey, Molly," she said, putting her phone on speaker so she could continue to work.

"Are you sure the peach roses are going to come in on time?" Molly asked.

"Yup."

"And how about the lilies? Oh, and the corsages for my mom and for Martha?"

"All under control, honey."

Molly paused. "I'm being a neurotic mess, aren't I?"

"Nope. You're being a bride. This is normal."

"I have a checklist of items, and then I came across flowers and I know we've gone over this a hundred times, but you know, I just had to check."

Sam was used to this. Brides called her all the time, even if everything was perfect. "Of course you had to check. Call anytime. But Molly? I've got this. Trust me."

"Okay. Thanks, Sam."

"You're welcome. I'll talk to you soon." She hung up, figuring Molly would call her again tomorrow.

Which didn't bother her at all, because as a florist, your job was to keep your customers happy. And when one of your customers was also one of your closest friends, that counted double.

She delivered the afternoon flowers, then came back to clean up the shop and prep things for tomorrow morning. By then it was closing time, and she made a quick grocery list so she could dash in and get what she needed for dinner tonight.

She had no idea why she'd invited Reid over for dinner. An impulse suggestion, because she really wanted to see the blueprints. But was that the only reason? When he'd been in town in the spring, she'd felt a tug of . . . something. She'd ignored it then, figuring it was nothing more than mutual interest in the mercantile. But seeing him today, that tug had been something entirely different, and totally biological.

She chewed on her bottom lip and decided to call her best friend, Megan, for some advice. She punched in Megan's number on her phone.

"What's up, Sam?" Megan asked when she answered.

"Reid McCormack is back in town."

"Oh, great. So he's going to start work on the mercantile."

"Yes. I popped over there today when I saw him go in. And then I invited him to dinner."

Megan paused. "That's interesting. Why?"

Sam pulled up the stool behind the counter and took a seat. "I don't know. Impulse."

"Always go with your impulses, Sam. You're obviously attracted to him. Did he say yes?"

"He did. And why do you think I'm attracted to him?"

"Everyone saw the way the two of you hung out at the mercantile in the spring."

Sam frowned. "What do you mean, everyone saw? What did they see?"

"Oh, you know. Heads together, wandering around, checking the place out. And when you climbed up the ladder to look at the tin ceiling? He checked out your butt."

Sam leaned her arms on the counter. "He did not. He did? Really?"

"He did. Chelsea and I were watching. And he was not looking at the ceiling. He was looking at your butt."

"Now that *is* interesting."

"I know. So enjoy dinner. And see what happens for dessert."

"I will. But you know, I didn't invite him for dinner to have . . . dessert with him."

Megan laughed. "Sure you didn't."

"Megan, I'm serious. I just wanted to see his blueprints."

"Is that what we're calling it now?"

Sam rolled her eyes. "You're so funny."

"I know I am. Call me tomorrow with all the details."

"Okay."

She hung up, grabbed her purse, and locked up the shop, then headed out to her car. She got in, and looked at her phone to double-check her grocery list.

She was going to cook a spaghetti dinner for Reid McCormack tonight, and then she was going to look over his blueprints. And by blueprints, she really meant actual blueprints. Nothing involving "dessert."

But if he checked out her butt again, dessert might be back on the menu. And she wasn't talking sweets.

From *New York Times* Bestselling Author
JACI BURTON

Hope Burns

Molly Burnett dreads returning to her hometown of Hope for her sister's wedding, especially knowing she'll have to endure a weekend with Carter Richards, the *one* man she never wants to see again. Despite bitter memories, she still can't forget what they once meant to each other.

But when Molly is forced to extend her stay, Carter sees this as his second chance to do things right. And this time, he isn't going to let Molly run away from him and a future as bright as the flame that still burns hot between them…

PRAISE FOR JACI BURTON AND HER NOVELS

"Jaci Burton's books are always sexy, romantic, and charming!"
—Jill Shalvis, *New York Times* bestselling author

"Jaci Burton's stories are full of heat and heart."
—Maya Banks, *New York Times* bestselling author

jaciburton.com
facebook.com/AuthorJaciBurton
facebook.com/LoveAlwaysBooks
penguin.com